MC HUTSON

A Slow Drip With A Latte Drama

French Pressed Love

MC Press

ISBN: 9781738253845
French Pressed Love
Copyright© 2024 M.C. Hutson

All rights reserved. No part of this book may be used or reproduced in any manner whatsoever without written permission except in the case of brief quotations embodied in critical articles and reviews.

This is a work of fiction. Names, characters, places, and incidents are either the product of the author's imagination or are used fictitiously. Any resemblances to actual persons, living or dead, businesses, companies, events of locales is entirely coincidental.

Cover Design: Cath Grace Designs

Character Art: Masha Grimm

Shoutout to Toronto, where the lesbian scene is mad drama.
Nyeah Eh!

Note For Readers

- This book is written in Canadian English
- In Canada, Thanksgiving is held on the second Monday in October
- This book contains profanity, homophobia, mentions of drug use and abuse, explicit sex scenes, and reference to sexual assault (off the page)
- There's nothing clean and easy about making French pressed coffee. It's messy. It takes work. It takes so goddamn long to brew, and at the end you're left with sludge to clean up. The process isn't for everyone.
- Sign up for my newsletter for an extra chapter of French Pressed Love. You can sign up by visiting: **mchutson.com**

Toronto Slang

Toronto slang can be linked back to the widespread migration from the Caribbean, East Africa and the Middle East to Canada from the 1960s to the 1990s. Many words come from Jamaican patois, but Somali and Arabic are also huge influences. Toronto slang (Toronto accent) has been the butt of jokes lately, but it's a source of great pride for many who live in the city and grew up speaking it. Some common words and definitions:

- "Bashment" (party)
- "Bare" (many)
- "Boydem" (police)
- "Cheesed" (upset)
- "Chop" (selling drugs)
- "Cut" (leave)
- "Cyattie" (obnoxious female)
- "Fam" (friend or family)
- "Fuckery" (bullshit)
- "Headtop" (mental state)
- "Jam" (party)
- "Likkle" (small amount)
- "Live" (amazing)
- "Mans" (I, we, me, us, them)
- "Marved" (hungry)
- "Mashup" or "Moshop" (messed up)
- "Mission" (journey)
- "Nyeah eh" (sure, usually sarcastic)
- "Proper" (done right)
- "Quick times" (done fast)
- "Say less" (I agree)
- "Snake" (untrustworthy person)
- "Soft" (weak)
- "Styll" (truth)
- "Ting" (hot chick)
- "Two-twos" (quickly)
- "Vexxed" (pissed off)
- "Wagwan" (what's up)
- "Waste" (not good or waste of time)
- "Waste mans" (loser)
- "What are you saying?" (what are you up to?)
- "Zeen" (got it)

Playlist

- Myself (Nav)
- Know Yourself (Drake)
- Fall Back (Lithe. Ft Nav)
- Wus good (Partynextdoor)
- If Only I (Loud Luxury, Two Friends)
- Selecta (Skrillex and Beam)
- Leave Me Alone (Flipp Dinero)
- Try Honesty (Billy Talent)
- Pattycake (Jordie)
- Je T'adore (Kim Petras)
- Love Nwanti remix (Véyah)
- 365 (Charli XCX)
- After Hours (Kehlani)
- Fever (Vybez Kartel)
- Tempted to touch (Beres Hammond)
- Talk Talk (Charli XCX ft. Troye Sivan)
- Morphine (Lights)
- Tibet (Artbat, Argy & Zafir)
- Give it a Chance (Sanchez)

MC HUTSON

A Slow Drip With A Latte Drama

French Pressed Love

MC Press

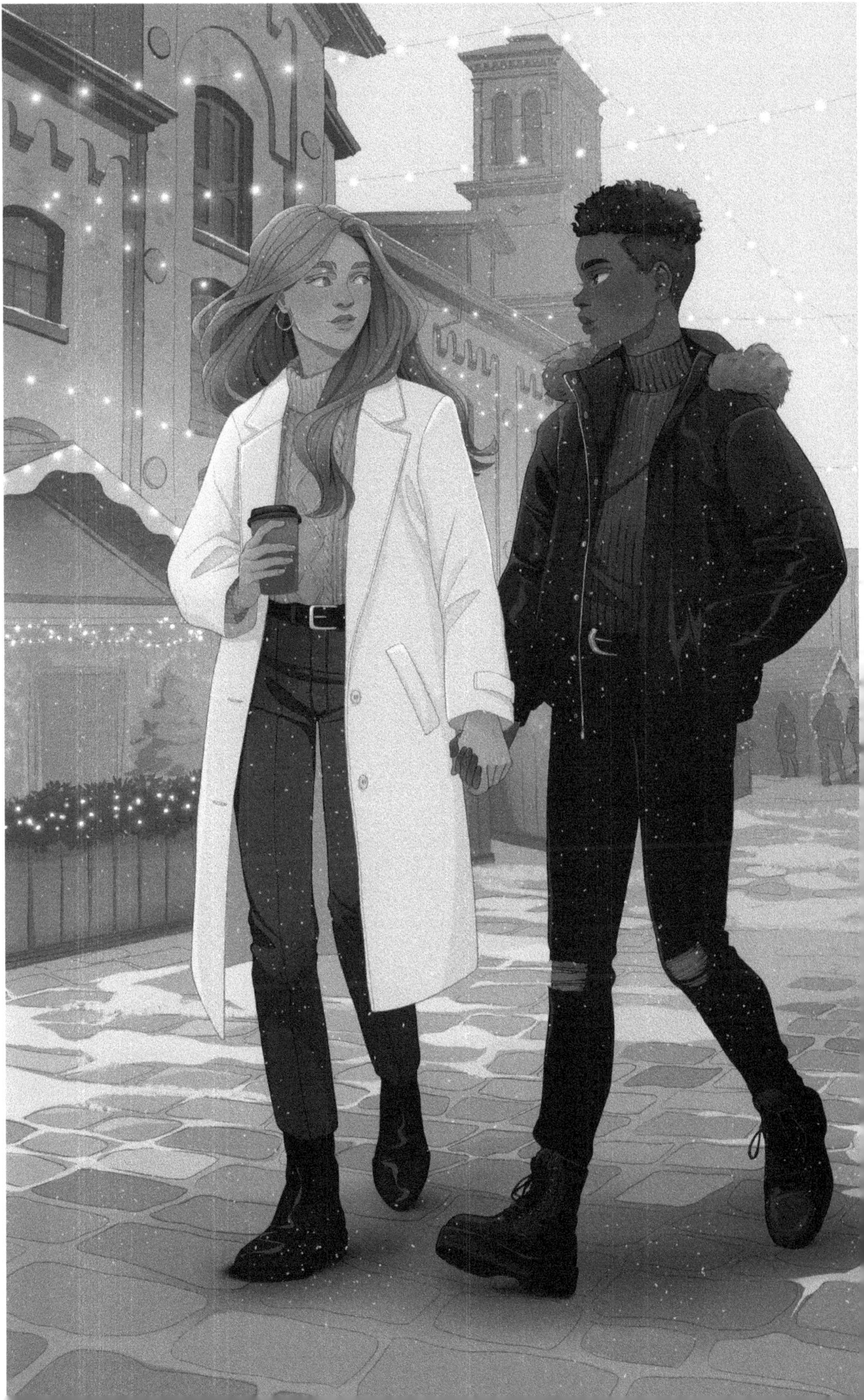

Chapter 1

The whines and hisses screaming from the espresso machine drill a hole through my skull, adding to the headache I woke up with. The steady hum of background music and chatter from the morning rush isn't helping much either. And the wafting aroma of freshly ground coffee beans makes my stomach swim.

Above me, a screen beeps, ringing in yet another order. I don't look up. I don't want confirmation of just how far behind we are.

For a moment, the world spins. I grip the cool metal counter with my free hand and close my eyes for a second. Then another.

You're in the weeds—quit standing around like an idiot, I tell myself as I open my eyes. *You have only yourself to blame for being hungover.*

I blink rapidly when I hear another beep.

In my periphery, I spot a flash of orange and a severely slicked backed ponytail. I glitch. Lagging, I forget what I'm doing and set down the milk jug a little too hard. Frothed milk lurches from the stainless-steel vessel, splashing on the counter and on my hand.

"Shit," I say, scrambling for the towel slung over my shoulder and mopping up the mess. Lucky for me, I don't need to start the drink over. Not too much spilled. There's enough milk left to complete the order—thank God.

"Colleen," I call, slapping a lid onto a vibrant purple cup and setting it down at the pickup counter.

Within a blink, the cup is snatched by a smartly dressed man whose eyes are glued to his phone. He takes a sip and scowls. "Hey, sir, I ordered a flat white—not whatever the hell this is."

A woman in a frilly white blouse and a restrictive pencil skirt steps up to him. "I'm Colleen, and that was my drink," she says, bringing her hands to rest on her hips.

Pinching my forehead, I try and fail at resisting the urge to groan. I'm not even mad about being called sir—again. I don't have the brain space for anger. The shift is dragging and nothing is going right.

Normally, I don't drink heavily on nights before I'm scheduled to clock in. At thirty-two, I need a full day's rest after drinking myself under a table. But my best friend Sarah's confession and subsequent announcement drove me to the bar.

Stress is my kryptonite, and I probably self-medicate too much. It's a weakness, and I like to think that I'm working on it. But my bad habits like to resurrect the moment I feel the teensiest bit of pressure. Maybe it isn't that bad that I reach for a bottle or a spliff or a woman when things get a little tough. But I do worry sometimes. My father is—was an addict. I don't want to be like him.

There's another beep. I flinch.

Breathing out like a bull, I force out thoughts of my father and of Sarah.

Ugh … the man and Colleen are still at it. Can't they shut up already? Their raised voices bang against my eardrums, exacerbating my headache.

The screen beeps again. The tail of the snaking line of customers keeps growing. It feels like there are a million eyes on me. There's nothing worse than suffering the judging stare of a waiting customer. And I know *she's* one of them, watching from the horde.

Businessman and Colleen are now full-blown shouting at each other. They're all up in each other's airspace, chests almost touching. On any other day, I might find the spat over something so trivial funny.

But today, I'm not laughing. Today, I'm just annoyed.

These rich professionals, who buy eight-dollar lattes every day, don't have any real problems, so they go hunting for them.

Fuck, I need a cigarette.

For what's got to be the hundredth time, I blame Marquess for putting me in this mess. Me being hungover is only part of the reason we are drowning. If I wasn't down a barista, we'd be somewhat afloat. It's the second time in the last few weeks that Marquess has flaked on a shift last minute. He's got one strike left. If he fails to show up one more time, he's gone. I don't care how much he begs.

I am rubbing my temples when I hear a familiar voice behind me say, "Jay, you okay?"

Wayne Carson, my assistant manager, comes to my side. His perfectly shaped brows furrow with concern.

Wayne and I have the most seniority at Grind That Bean. We both started when the coffee shop opened its doors five years ago. The first year or so, we hadn't gotten along. But in our third year of working together, I began to find Wayne's penchant for gossip a great source of entertainment during the slow hours, and Wayne seems to live vicariously through me. He claims my love life is as dramatic as a telenovela, which I think is a stretch.

"Yeah, I'm good," I say. "But could you handle this for me?" I gesture towards the quarrelling customers.

Wayne winks at me. "On it."

I trust he will find a way to diffuse the situation. Wayne's like the customer whisperer.

Letting out a deep breath, I finally look up at the screen. I wince—and not just because there are ten flashing orders queued. The next order is *hers*, which shouldn't come as a surprise to me since I spotted her moments ago. But still …

Unable to stop myself, my gaze wanders past the cash register. My skin prickles and my stomach twists when I see her—Noémie St. Pierre. I hate the way she affects me.

Having been with my share of gorgeous women, usually it takes more than a pretty face to hold my interest. But Noémie is like a cyst—she's under my skin in the worst way and growing. I'm not sure how to extract her, and I'm probably just a little obsessed with her. Looking at her hurts—like what I imagine staring at an eclipse without protective sunglasses feels like. But I can't stop myself. My eyes drink in the sight of the vexing woman.

The Poutine Princess—so dubbed by Wayne—looks out of place amongst the throng of stiff-backed financial district professionals. As expected, she's decked in her signature colour. Orange is not a colour most can pull off. I certainly can't. One of the few times I swapped my usual black tee for an orange sweatshirt, a giant street cone stared back at me in the mirror. But Noémie always sports a pop of the retina-searing hue, and she makes it look good. Sometimes it's just a bag, or a pair of heels or jewellery. More often than not, the colour is a staple stitching her outfit together.

This morning, she wears an oversized tangerine blazer with the sleeves cuffed at her elbows. Underneath it, she's got on a ribbed white crop top that exposes her sun-kissed midriff. Dark jeans hug her hips. Impractical stilettos give her inches over most patrons in the coffee shop.

My heart blips when our eyes meet. Hers are steely grey with a hint of blue—they are as striking as their owner is irritating.

I don't like the Poutine Princess. She's spoiled, standoffish, and rude. She's also probably a homophobic conservative just like her prick of a father. But, fuck, she's beautiful.

Trying to get back on track, I wipe my sweaty palms on my apron and grab an empty cup to start Noémie's order. It's a nuisance to put together. Grind That Bean's most exasperating customer insists on having a large double shot latte with an equal blend of whole milk and almond milk, followed by exactly half a pump of vanilla syrup and half a pump of hazelnut syrup. The steamed milk needs to be micro-foamed to perfection. If it isn't, she complains. If her drink is too bitter, she complains. Too watery? Another complaint. On average, Noémie makes a fuss twice a week. She never seems to be fully happy with our service. For some unknown reason, she keeps coming back.

Not in the mood to deal with Noémie's antics, I take great care to ensure the drink will pass scrutiny. I'm confident when I set down the completed order for pick up and call out her name. My confidence dissolves like sugar when the Poutine Princess takes a sip and wrinkles her nose.

"Excuse me, you got my order wrong," she says.

Despite the pleasantness of her voice—soft and feminine—the muscles in my back tense at her words.

She leans over on the counter and waves at me. She's so fucking annoying.

I don't get paid enough to deal with her shit. And, fuck, my head hurts—I am dying for a fucking cigarette.

"What's wrong with it?" I say, marching towards the pickup area and folding my arms over my chest.

Noémie pushes the large purple cup towards me. "It's way too sweet," she answers. "I find your tone abrasive. There's no reason for you to get defensive." She smiles sweetly. Her grey eyes sparkle with a challenge, as if daring me to argue with her.

My hands drop and clench at my sides. Heat creeps up the back of my neck and burns my ears. My brain pounds against my skull.

It's not the first time she's said something like this to me. She's also called out other Grind That Bean staff for being rude when she's the one who isn't reasonable. Sometimes, I think she only comes to the coffee shop to stir up shit—to add zest to her life. There's a part of me that wants her to never come back. Another part of me dreads the day she stops coming.

I look at the large purple cup. It crosses my mind that I could accidentally knock it over, making its contents splash onto Noémie's expensive clothing and handbag. Boy, wouldn't that be funny? But a good chuckle isn't worth the aftermath. The Poutine Princess would definitely throw a fit if even a drop got on her. I also wouldn't put it past her to slander us all over social media.

About six months ago, Wayne uncovered Noémie's Instagram and TikTok accounts. The Poutine Princess has quite the following. Last time I checked, she's got over 150K followers on IG and another 50K on TikTok. She frequently posts about Grind That Bean. Surprisingly, so far all her commentary about our small coffee chain has been positive. However, I can easily see Noémie turning and disparaging us. I get the feeling she's that type of person—a snake.

"I'm so sorry," I say, putting on my best customer service voice. "I'll remake your order right away."

"Merci," she says, flipping her auburn ponytail over a shoulder. I catch a whiff of her shampoo—spicy and citrusy. She smells good, but my hangover makes it hard to enjoy the scent of her. It's too much—too overwhelming. I'm back to feeling dizzy.

Noémie's attention drops to her black purse. She fishes her phone out of it.

I turn and walk back to the espresso machine.

Two minutes later, I set down a new drink for her. Fortunately, she finds no fault with it. Latte in hand and eyes transfixed on her iPhone, she struts out of the shop. When she's gone, I find that I can breathe easier.

It isn't until eleven that the rush dies, and I escape outside for a smoke. Leaning against a brick wall, I light up. The nicotine hit weighs down my body with a sense of calm.

I notice the overcast sky and pray to the heavens that it doesn't rain. When I checked earlier this morning, rain hadn't been on the forecast. But the clouds above me now are dark and billowing. The air is thick with moisture.

In the warmer months, my method of transportation is a 2006 Kawasaki Ninja. It had been my father's bike. It's one of the few things he left me when he died. It, along with his comic book collection, are my most cherished possessions.

Riding a motorcycle in the rain is no fun at best and dangerous at worst. The first and only time I got caught in a downpour, I lost traction coming to stop at a red light and nearly collided with a Jeep in front of me. I'd been so fucking terrified.

Outing my cigarette, I push back into the shop.

Inside is dead, and I welcome the quiet. Corrine, a newer hire, is busy wiping down the stainless-steel counters and the electric purple high-top tables.

Grind That Bean is the antithesis of the conventional coffee shop. It isn't cozy vibes and slow jazz music. It isn't a third place where customers can gather to comfortably connect or sit down to study. Chrome stools without padding provide the only seating. Harsh fluorescent lighting bounces off purple subway tiles that stack the upper half of the walls. Right now, Metallica growls from the speakers.

The aesthetic shouldn't work—especially not in Toronto's financial district. Surprisingly, it does. We are never hurting for customers. But maybe it's because the coffee is better than Starbucks and the pastries are bomb.

Wayne leans against a counter, scrolling through his Instagram feed.

I slide up next to him. "You shouldn't be on your phone."

"Someone's pissy today," he says, tucking the phone into his front apron pocket. "What's eating at you? Is it the reason you're smoking again? I thought you quit?"

A sigh escapes my lips. I'm not ready to tell Wayne about what happened with Sarah. I'm still trying to digest her confession. Also, I don't want to hear him say "I told you so."

"I'm just really hungover," I say, rubbing my eyes with the backs of my hands.

Wayne arches a brow. "Drinking on a work night?"

I know he is expecting me to say something, but I let silence hang between us.

"You're really not gonna to tell me what's up?" He pouts. "Is this about the girl you're fooling around with—the crazy chick bent on wife-ing you up?"

"First of all, Audrina is not a girl, she's a woman—a really great one too. She's got, like, her shit together and a good job. She even has her own place with a mortgage," I reply. "And she's not crazy—just crazy about me."

Wayne rolls his eyes. "I wonder why."

"Because I'm irresistible." I nudge him with my shoulder.

"If she is so great, why won't you settle down with her? It's about time, Jay. You aren't getting younger."

I shrug. "I'm not the settling type," I lie. Truth is, I do want to be in a relationship, but it isn't possible. And while Wayne and I are close, some secrets I won't voice again. Some truths are best left buried.

Audrina might want me now. She might swear to love me now. She might get ridiculously jealous and play clitorference whenever she sees me talking to someone else now. But what happens when she realizes how broken I am?

Wayne's lips pucker. "While I am devastated that you don't want to talk to me about whatever it is that is making you like this," he says, gesturing at me with a flourish, "I will stop my probing—for the time being."

"Thanks." I'm glad he's not pressing. Usually, Wayne doesn't give up until I fold and spill the tea.

"Changing the topic, did you see the purse Poutine Princess was toting today?"

I try to remember. "The black one?"

"Yeah, it's a Birkin," Wayne states. "Costs as much as a car."

My mouth drops. "You're kidding."

"If you cared anything for fashion, you'd know that Birkins are the Hope Diamond of handbags," he says. "One of them went on auction recently and fetched three hundred thousand fucking dollars."

I don't bother correcting Wayne, telling him that I do care for fashion. Sure, maybe I don't dress to impress. And yeah, I probably only know the names of the most popular designers. But at heart, I'm an artist who appreciates all beautiful things. Fashion, like a sketch or a painting, is a form of artistic expression. A lot can be learned about a person from the way that they dress. I'm sure there's always a story to be found amongst the colours, textures, and silhouettes of garments.

I wonder what it says about me that I pretty much only wear black.

When I do speak, I say, "Some people have too much money to know what to do with it." I shake my head. If only I could have three hundred thousand dollars ... Hell, if I could somehow find an extra five hundred dollars a month, that would be enough.

Soon I won't be able afford rent, and I'm freaking out. Meanwhile, the Poutine Princess walks around with a bag that probably costs more than my annual salary. I should have "accidentally" spilled her drink.

The shittiest part about life is the unfairness. Some people are born into money and the ability to follow their dreams while the rest of us scrape by and stay stuck in unfulfilling jobs.

At one point, I really thought I'd be something. I thought I'd be the first one on my mother's side of the family to climb the financial ladder and find success. But the joke was on me. Then again, I should call myself lucky to even be where I am now, working as a shift manager. Having a Bachelor of Fine Arts, I am not very employable. Things could be far worse.

"So how long do you think Corrine will stick around?" Waynes asks, cocking his chin in the direction of the seating area where Corrine is somehow still wiping down tables. A part of me wants to shout at her to hurry up. She was a horrible hire, but she's my boss's best friend's niece. The choice to add her to the roster wasn't up to me.

I shrug. "I don't know … three months."

Corrine trips over a stool. The cruel devil that he is, Wayne chuckles. "I bet she only lasts a month."

Just then, a customer walks in. Wayne takes his place at the register, and I go to the espresso machine. My eyes dart to the clock. In a few hours, my shift will end. I'm looking forward to going home, but I'm dreading facing Sarah.

Chapter 2

When my shift ends, the rain comes down hard like bullets. The persistent clatter drowns out all other sounds. Riding my motorcycle is out of the question, and I don't have enough space on my Visa to get an Uber or Lyft. So I'm stuck taking the trashy transit.

Waving goodbye to Wayne, I step out into the storm and make a mad dash for the subway. By the time I make it to King Station, my clothes are soaked all the way through and stick to my skin. Every step I take is punctuated by a distinct squish.

The train is delayed, and the platform gets more packed by the second. I stand in the middle of the throng of disgruntled and mostly wet commuters.

Ten minutes comes and goes. Finally, the train arrives. Doors ding open, and a few passengers struggle to step out as a mass of people surges forward, eager to board. I manage to be one of the lucky ones, squeezing into the train car just before the doors chime as they close. The car is bursting at the seams. It reeks of wet clothing, stale breath, and body odour.

The janky train sways and screeches on the tracks. I feel my nausea return and grip the metal pole a little tighter. Beside me, a dirty old man with chapped lips and an unkempt beard coughs. He isn't covering his mouth, and I see spittle. Recoiling, I try to sidestep to put some distance between us, but there isn't anywhere for me to go. I'm trapped, and he's still hacking away. Turning my head, I give him my best side-eye. Either he doesn't notice or doesn't care.

"You'd think after Covid, people would learn to cover their damn mouths," I mumble. My words fall on deaf ears.

Nearly an hour and a half later—after enduring a second crammed train, a frustratingly late bus, and another walk in the rain—I finally get home and kick off my sneakers. My socks leave imprints on the wooden treads as I descend the squeaking staircase that leads to the basement apartment I share with Sarah—my best friend and soon to be ex-roommate.

Our space is roomy, but that's pretty much its only good attribute. The dropped ceilings are stained, the cheap vinyl floor tiles are peeling, and the horrendous faux-wood panelling is everywhere—even in the bathroom. No amount of Febreze or Bath and Body Works candles can rid the air of its musty smell, and I've yet to find a bug repellent strong enough to keep the ants out. I hate my living situation, but it beats living with my mom.

Like many large cities, there's a renter's crisis in Toronto. It's probably easier to win the lottery than to find a decent place with a reasonable rate. And soon, even my shitty Scarborough basement apartment won't be affordable.

I want to be mad at Sarah for putting me in this situation—for moving away. But she's moving away because of me.

Last night, Sarah confessed to being in love with me and told me that she is U-Hauling all the way to Vancouver to be with Veronica, who she met like a month ago at a Pride party. Almost immediately after her confession, I bolted to the bar—shutting down the conversation.

I know Sarah has more to say on the subject. I fear what else she might say. She's been my best friend for forever, and while I have love for her, my feelings aren't romantic. What if she tells me we can't be friends anymore? What if her move to Vancouver isn't the worst part?

Usually, I call for Sarah when I get in to see if she's home. Today, I don't. I walk into my bedroom and slam the door shut behind me. Stripping out of my sodden clothes, I hesitate to grab my towel.

According to my grandma Janet, taking a hot shower immediately after coming inside from outdoors is a sure way to get sick. So many of my grandma's Caribbean beliefs are not grounded in science, but I grew up hearing them so much that I kind of believe them myself.

Deciding to take the risk, I wrap my towel around my torso and head for the bathroom to wash off the cold and stink of the day. Post shower, I feel somewhat refreshed.

I'm lotioning my legs when I hear the side door jerk open. Soon after, footsteps drum down the staircase—Sarah's home. My stomach clenches. I reach for a pair of boxers and I am just sliding them up over my ass when the door to my bedroom bursts open. Sarah steps in.

"The fuck—how many fucking times do I have to tell you to knock?" I cover my chest and rush over to my closet to grab a t-shirt.

"Nothing I haven't seen before," Sarah says.

Very true—there's been more than a handful of occasions over the last decade where we've hooked up. Our last hookup had been on St. Patrick's Day. We'd both gotten sloshed. I don't remember much, but I awoke sprawled naked on top of Sarah with my strap still inside her.

Wayne has warned against us having casual sex, saying we're both playing with fire. Sarah and I had laughed him off. Looking back, maybe it had just been me laughing. Not once had I considered the possibility of one of us getting burnt. Not once had it ever crossed my mind that Sarah might want something more than our friendship. She's never so much as hinted at it.

The definition of a "Hey Mama" lesbian—complete with the swag, the undercut, and a long list of women whom she's rendered heartbroken—Sarah fit the role of a detached fuckboi for the entire time I've known her. Her sudden declaration of love flipped my entire world upside down, and I don't know what to feel or think. Like, who even is this person standing in my bedroom? Have I ever really known her? The Sarah I know doesn't get attached. The Sarah I know would never want a relationship to work out so badly that she'd jet all the way across the country. The Sarah I know wouldn't abandon me.

I pull on my shirt and turn to face her. My insides are still all coiled up because I know she wants to talk and I'm not sure I'm ready to finish last night's conversation.

"I come with a peace offering." Sarah smiles and lifts a grease-stained brown paper bag.

I spot the bright blue logo, depicting a plate of piping-hot poutine flanked by angel wings, and frown. "Homophobic poutine is your peace offering?"

Sarah snorts. "Hypocrite. I've seen you forking down Poutine Heaven before. You love it."

"Only because they're open after last call." I've always found it ironic that there's a Poutine Heaven in the heart of Toronto's gay village. "Otherwise, I avoid eating there, and you should too."

"So you don't want it?" She arches a brow.

"I'm not going to let perfectly good food go to waste." I snatch the bag out of Sarah's hand and collapse into my desk chair.

The aroma of oil and salt greets me when I tear into the bag and pop open the container's lid. My mouth waters. It's only now that I'm realizing just how hungry I am.

One of those stupid wooden forks with the too-short prongs sits at the bottom of the bag. I won't be using it. Not only is it useless, but it has the effect of making anything it touches taste like a rancid popsicle stick. I miss plastic straws and plastic utensils in a bad way. I care about the environment, but I also miss the days when I wasn't rushing to finish my pop because my paper straw disintegrates in two minutes.

Ravenous, I pick up a few fries with my fingers. The cheese curds stretch out, becoming a long and unmanageable string. Hot gravy drips onto the hand I have cupped under my chin. The poutine does taste like heaven. I close my eye in bliss as I chew.

Despite being drenched in gravy and transported in a covered container, the fries are still so crisp—a feature unique to Poutine Heaven that sets them apart from competitors. The establishment discovered the secret to preventing fries from turning to mush, and it's the reason why the young chain restaurant is seeing so much success. In some areas of the city, you can now find more Poutine Heavens than Tim Hortons, which is really saying something. Last I heard, they are starting to expand internationally, opening a few stores in the U.S. and a location in Tokyo.

Usually, I'm all for Canadian businesses doing well, but Poutine Heaven's founder—Noémie's father—is a hateful bastard who backs the most despicable political candidates. Every time he opens his mouth, he makes the most ludicrous statements on national news, and he openly donates to anti-2SLGBTQIA+ organizations.

As I shovel a few more fries into my mouth, I start thinking about my least favourite customer. In my mind's eye, I see Noémie's face—her auburn hair down and framing her face. I wonder—not for the first time—if she's anything at all like her father, Hugo St. Pierre.

"You know there's a fork in the bag?" Sarah says.

"It's one of those stupid wooden ones."

Sarah makes a face of disgust and leaves. I hear rattling in the kitchen, and she returns half a minute later with a metal fork. She holds it out to me.

"Thanks." I lick the gravy from my fingers and take it.

"Are you ready to talk now? Or are you going to run again?" Sarah folds her arms over her chest and leans against the doorframe.

I look away from Sarah and stare down at the container of poutine resting on my lap. "Is there even anything else to talk about? I understand why you're leaving. Do I think it's the right decision? No. But I get it, and I …" There's a lump forming in my throat. I try to clear it away, but it's not going anywhere. So I decide to not even bother finishing my thought.

I'm so terrified about the state of our friendship. Is bringing romantic love into a friendship the equivalent of bringing a wrecking ball over to a construction site? I wouldn't know.

It's hard to imagine my life without Sarah. We've been in each other's orbit for so long, and I fear distance will weaken our gravitational pull. Or has that already happened with Sarah's confession? She mentioned needing to move on, but did moving on mean we'd find ourselves in different galaxies.

"Jay, quit doom spiralling."

My eyes snap to Sarah's. Hers are brown and warm, like honey. "I'm not doom spiralling."

She snorts. "Sure, you're not. What's on your mind? Spill it. Let's just get it all out in the open."

I close the lid on my food and set the container down on my desk. "I don't know what any of this means," I say. Bending forward in my chair, I rest my elbows on my thighs and rub my temples. The headache I awoke with this morning is making a reappearance. A cigarette would help. "You say you love me, but what does that mean? You want a relationship with me?"

Sarah snorts again. "Absolutely fucking not."

I blow out a breath of relief, but I'm still so confused. "I don't understand." I pin Sarah with a hard look and sigh.

She moves away from the door and crouches down so that our heads are level. This close, I smell the Irish Spring soap on her skin and the cinnamon gum on her breath. I don't know how Sarah can chew cinnamon gum. It's gross.

"I'm not a bitchy femme pillow princess, so we'd never work out even if you did do relationships." Sarah chuckles, and then she sobers immediately. Her gaze narrows on my face. "That's not a stab at you, Jay. There's nothing wrong with you. Your preferences are your preferences, and Samira's a bitch. She didn't appreciate what she had with you, and that's her loss. But I really wish you'd get over her."

It's my turn to snort. "I am over her."

"Are you though? Are you really? Because it seems to me like you've let her dictate your entire future—"

"Can you stop? I don't want to talk about her." Just the mention of my ex raises my blood pressure, and I'm back to rubbing my temples. My head is pounding.

Sarah doesn't stop. "All I'm saying is that you deserve to be happy, Jay. You deserve to find someone who treats you right," she says. "And while I've dreamed of being that person, I don't think I ever could be. Yes, I love you, but I love our friendship more. And I think some distance will help me get over my stupid feelings. Also, I really want things to work out with Veronica."

Sarah's new girlfriend is beautiful and super nice, but she's also super clingy and jealous. And Sarah's a huge flirt. I can see Veronica never fully trusting Sarah to be faithful. I don't think they are end game. I probably should have told Sarah as much earlier. But now I can't. I've lost the opportunity. If I tell Sarah what I think about her girlfriend, she will likely think I'm inventing shit to try to get her to stay.

"Okay, I think I understand," I say, releasing a breath.

I feel a bit lighter. The coils in my stomach unspool. Some of the tension behind my eyes recedes. I'd been so afraid about what Sarah's confession meant for our friendship, but it seems like nothing will be changing between us. Unless she's lying. Unless the physical distance manifests into actual distance. I bite my bottom lip.

Sarah stands and changes the topic. Now she's the one doom spiralling. She tells me that she's worried about what moving to Vancouver will mean for her financially. "I will have to start all over—all my clients are here."

Sarah runs a personal training business, and while she's great at her job, I've always felt that she undercharges her customers. So maybe Vancouver will be a good change for her. It will be a fresh start, and she can raise her rates without feeling so guilty. I tell her as much, but she's not really listening.

When Sarah finally leaves my bedroom, I feel a lot better about everything. Sarah's acting like nothing's changed. I can try to do the same.

The fries are still somehow crispy when I dive back into the poutine. Despite being lukewarm, it's still fucking delicious. Every bite is bittersweet. Two-thirds through it, I'm stuffed and can't eat anymore. Leaning back in my chair, I pat my stomach.

Above me, the floorboards creak loudly as the tenants on the first floor walk around. I hear their muffled voices and the hum of their TV—I grit my teeth. My neighbours aren't being loud, they're just living. But still, their noise annoys me. I don't think I've ever experienced true silence before. Like most things, it feels like a luxury that is bought and out of reach for someone like me.

From my desk drawer, I remove a pair of noise-cancelling headphones that my father bought me a few years back. While I've treated them with the utmost care, the ear pads are cracked in places, exposing the brownish foam beneath.

Next, I take out my iPad and pencil.

I slip my headphones over my head and start up my playlist. I click on my tablet and stare down at the last panel I'd drawn.

Zara Williams—the main character of the graphic novel I'm working on—takes up most of the rectangular frame. In many ways, she's a replica of me. In many ways, she's an alter ego—someone I'd maybe want to be in another life. Like me, Zara is black with short curly black hair. Her style leans masculine, but her face is too pretty to be mistaken for a boy's. Unlike me, Zara is successful, but not in a good way. What nobody knows is that she lives a double life.

By day Zara's an accountant who fiddles with spreadsheets. By night, Zara paints the streets with blood. Nobody knows that Zara is an assassin, killing villainous men who have more enemies than allies.

I'm currently halfway through completing the third volume of *The Diaries of Zara Williams*, and I think it's my best work yet. Not only are my drawings better, but the story really feels like it's taking shape. The plot is far more immersive and compelling—perhaps because I've finally introduced a bit of romance.

The love interest is Detective Pamela Cross. She's been tasked with finding the culprit behind the gruesome string of murders. The perpetrator, Zara, cozies up to Pamela to find out more about the investigation.

I've reached a point in the story where the cold-hearted Zara is starting to fall for Pamela, and she doesn't know what to do about it—she's never been in love before.

As I pick up my stylus and begin sketching out a new scene, for a flickering moment I wonder again why I even bother. Is art even art if only the artist sees it? Is art even art if I create it just for me?

I'm proud of my work, but I know it isn't a good fit for mainstream publishing—I've been told as much. But even if I think *The Diaries of Zara Williams* is stronger than the first series I pitched, it might not be—I might never be good enough. I've been told that there isn't a market for the stories I want to tell. No one wants a comic with a dyke as the main character.

After I got rejected all those years ago, I'd been so devastated that I gave up drawing for years. My father had been on my back about not giving up. He'd always been my biggest fan, and he'd been the one who fed my love for comics as a kid. After he died, I start drawing again. I got lost in my art to escape my grief, and I think I'm creating something beautiful.

I wish my father could see it. If he was still around and was sober, I'm sure he would have talked me into trying to reach for my dream again. But he's gone, and I'm scared to put myself back out there.

Sighing, I fill in a box with markings that soon render a busy bar, and then I sketch out Zara's androgynous figure. My heroine is pulling out a stool to sit down beside a gorgeous woman who will be depicted to have auburn hair and orange-painted fingernails.

Pamela Cross, the beautiful detective, probably looks a little too much like my least favourite customer. I don't know why I modelled her character after Noémie. Okay, I do know why. But it's kind of embarrassing to admit that I wish there existed a universe where the Poutine Princess saw me as something more than just a barista.

Chapter 3

I awake to a trio of unwelcome companions: a stuffed nose, a sore throat, and a fever. For the first time in over a year, I call in sick.

Sarah runs to the pharmacy to restock the Vicks and Buckley's. She also picks me up some chicken noodle soup from Timmie's.

Slathered in VapoRub and groggy from the cough syrup, I sleep through most of the day and then endure a horrendous night. In the dead hours, I nearly hack up a lung and I am compelled to blow my running nose every other minute. A part of me forgets what it's like to breathe normally.

The hours crawl slowly towards dawn, and when the sun pokes through my tiny basement window, I know that I won't be able to go into work for a second day in a row. It's Friday, and I only work weekdays, which means I'll have the weekend to recover. It's hard to think that I'll ever get better. That's how disgusting I feel.

When Monday rolls around, my nostrils are clear but fiery, and I can finally swallow without it feeling like a cactus is being shoved down my esophagus. I step outside for the first time in four days and allow myself to appreciate the fresh air and the brush of the wind on my face. It's too early for the sun to be up. The sky is grey as I head over to the bus stop.

As I commute into the city, anxiety fists my gut. All weekend I've been worried about my motorcycle. Vehicle thefts are on the rise in the Greater Toronto Area, and I pray that my baby is still there.

Turns out that I worried for nothing—my bright green ninja is exactly where I left her. Feeling relieved, I head for the storefront. I'm right on time for my 6:30 a.m. shift.

Wayne leans against the brick wall near the coffee shop's entrance. He hunches over his phone, frowning down at the screen.

"What's wrong?" I ask.

Startled, Wayne jumps and clutches imaginary pearls. "Fuck, I didn't hear you."

"Seriously, you should pay more attention to what's going on around you," I say, sliding the store key into the lock and turning it over. "I don't get your obsession with those dance videos." I pull open the door and gesture for him to enter first.

"I'm not watching dancing videos," he replies, shuffling inside.

"What's so interesting then?" I bolt over to the alarm to disarm it.

Wayne slaps a switch, and the harsh overhead lighting makes me squint. Twirling towards me, Wayne hops up onto the counter and crosses his legs. He's smirking in a way that tells me he's got tea to spill.

"Oh my God, what happened?" There's a tickle in my throat. I cough into the bend of my elbow.

Wayne makes a face. "You sure you're not still contagious?"

"I'm better. My throat's just dry." I roll my eyes at him. "Spill it. I'm dying for some juicy tea after being cooped up all weekend."

"It's the Poutine Princess—she's gone dark," he says.

At the mere mention of her, my pulse spikes. I'm not quite sure what Wayne means by she's gone dark though. I raise an eyebrow at him.

"She hasn't posted since the incident. Usually she's so active online," he explains.

I hadn't heard of any incident happening with Noémie, but I'm sure Wayne will fill me in. He's good for that. "The way you stalk that girl is not normal," I say.

Wayne snorts. "Says the one who malfunctions whenever she struts her pretty ass in here."

"I don't malfunction."

"Oh yes, you do. I've got receipts." He uncrosses his legs and leans back on his hands. "I wouldn't be surprised if you stalk her more than I do."

My mouth drops open for a second. I consider denying it, but I know Wayne. He will latch on to any protest, and somehow, I'll end up revealing more than I want to.

Truth is, I do occasionally scroll through the Poutine Princess's Instagram—but only for inspiration for my graphic novel. And yes, there was that one time that a video of her and her hottie blond friend popped up on my TikTok FYP. The two women had been dancing to "WAP," and yes, it'd been sexy. And yes, I might have rewatched it. Maybe I rewatched it more than a dozen times. Maybe I favourited it. If that makes me a stalker … Well, I'm not ever going to admit it.

"I'm human and I have eyes—the Poutine Princess is beautiful. But she's also so-so-so not my type."

"I thought you were into bitchy femmes." Wayne pouts.

"Femme is a queer identity. She can't be femme if she's straight," I state. "And you know I can't with straight chicks anymore. I'm too old for their kind of drama. I'm only looking to hook up with women who already know that they're down for women."

Wayne chuckles. "Sure, I'll believe it when I see it."

I begin setting up the stools, pulling them down from the high-top tables. "Are you planning on helping?"

"I am helping. I'm the entertainment."

"I'm not entertained," I say. "Start the coffee."

"Sure thing, boss," he says, hopping down from the counter.

After arranging the seating area, I go to the back office. There, I retrieve cash and coins from the safe. I return out front and stock the register drawer with the money.

The aroma of freshly brewed coffee flavours the air. Wayne's moved on to his next task. He's busy lining a baking tray with a half-dozen frozen croissants.

It occurs to me that he never mentioned the incident with the Poutine Princess. I want to know what happened. Closing the money drawer, I approach him as I tie on my purple apron. "What was the incident with Noémie?"

Excitement flashes in his dark brown eyes. "Oh yes, I was getting to that. But someone told me they weren't entertained."

"You're so petty."

"Yes, don't ever forget that." He pops the tray of croissants into the preheated oven and sets the timer.

"So, what happened?"

Wayne seems to consider my question, but only for a moment. When a smirk breaks across his face, I know he's not going to hold out on telling me. "So get this, Poutine Princess comes waltzing in here last Thursday morning with her Prada bag and Loro Piano loafers—"

"As she does."

"As she does," Wayne repeats, nodding. "And guess what happens?"

"What?"

"Her Visa declines," Wayne says with a squeal, clapping his hands together. "But wait, there's more."

"More?" I'm already so invested in this story. It makes me rather happy to know that Noémie suffered an embarrassing moment. I can just imagine her outrage at seeing the word *declined* on the payment system.

"So she tries to pay with her American Express card, but it also declines," Wayne continues. "And then her phone is buzzing. She looks down at it, and gurrrrrrl, she went whiter than Casper and scrambled out of here like an egg."

I frown. "That's definitely weird."

"Even weirder, she hasn't been back since. And the Poutine Princess is totally M.I.A. She hasn't posted anything since last Wednesday."

"What do you think happened?" I rub my chin as I consider possible scenarios.

"Dunno. Maybe the girl got hacked."

I nod. "That would explain why her cards weren't working. We both know that Poutine Heaven isn't hurting for money, even in this economy."

"True, true," he says.

Everything is all set up for 7:00 a.m. Two of my staff clock-in and don their aprons just as we're opening our doors to customers.

The morning rush is chaotic as ever, but I'm in the right headspace to keep my team on track. All in all, it's a good shift. But Noémie doesn't show, and there's a sorta hollowness to the morning without her appearance.

When she doesn't show up on Tuesday morning, my curiosity about her disappearance peaks, and I find myself scrolling through her socials. I'm searching for a clue, but there's none to find. The Poutine Princess's last post is from almost a week ago.

Chapter 4

A week goes by. And then another. And Noémie doesn't come into the coffee shop.

It's pretty weird to admit, but I feel her absence. It feels like something isn't quite right. Like perhaps the Earth's tilt changed. Everything is just a little off—slightly less vibrant and less interesting.

There are moments when I think I glimpse her. I'll see a flash of an orange vest, bag, or dress, and for a second, it's Noémie. But then I blink, and like a mirage, she's gone.

Wayne's moved on. He no longer seems interested in the mystery surrounding the Poutine Princess. Meanwhile, I think about her often. Too often. Which is stupid.

I know Noémie's gotta be fine. Just the other day, her father was on the news boasting about yet another international location of Poutine Heaven opening in the U.K. If something was wrong with Noémie, Hugo St. Pierre wouldn't be smiling so brightly, right?

Besides, what's the worst thing that could happen to a spoiled rich girl anyways? I imagine that the Poutine Princess is likely vacationing somewhere lavish, like Ibiza. She's probably suntanning on a yacht in the Mediterranean downing negroni after negroni. Personally, I think negronis are vile—they taste like lighter fluid. But every rich girl I've spent time with loves that cocktail. Noémie's probably no different.

Before I know it, the end of the month arrives and Sarah's flying out in a day. I'm in an awful mood about it. I'm not quite sure what I'm more upset about: losing my best friend to Vancouver or the fact that I can't afford rent on my own.

The stress of having to find a new roommate or find a new place gnaws my insides. I probably should have started my search the moment Sarah told me she was leaving, but I kept deferring. And now, there's about sixty days left—that's my window since Sarah is nice enough to cover her portion of rent for two months after she moves out.

I'm so on edge about my renting situation that when Marquess calls in—announcing he can't make his 8:00 a.m. shift—I lose my absolute shit and fire him over the phone.

After slamming down the receiver, I turn to see Wayne watching me all wide-eyed. "Remind me never to piss you off," he says.

I snort and roll my eyes at him.

Down a barista, the shift is hell. After work, my commute is also hell, and I'm sure the rest of my Friday night is going to feel like sucking Satan's giant balls. The last thing I want to do is go out, but I have no choice in the matter. To celebrate Sarah's departure, our friends have planned a night out at one of Toronto's fanciest lounges. We're meeting at 9:30 p.m., which gives me roughly two and a half hours, and I want to take a quick nap before getting ready.

More than a dozen haphazardly stacked cardboard boxes greet me at home. Some of them will be shipped to Sarah's new address in Vancouver, but most are destined to collect dust in her parents' garage.

I manoeuvre around the obstructions blocking the path to my bedroom. Changing into a fresh pair of sweats, I collapse on my shitty spring mattress and close my eyes.

What feels like a second later, my alarm goes off. Yawning, I grab my towel off the hook on my door and do some more manoeuvring to get to the bathroom, where I shower off the smell of bitter coffee and sour milk.

I dress in one of my nicer outfits—a black blazer and a black satin shirt that I opt to leave several of the top buttons undone. I tuck the shirt into the waistband of my pinstripe slacks and slip my feet into a pair of polished Oxford shoes that I got for a great deal on Boxing Day.

Sarah and I slide into the back of an Uber at 8:46 p.m. We're splitting the cost, so the ride won't break the bank for me. But, I'm again reminded that soon I won't be able to make rent on my own. Time is ticking down for me to find a new roommate or place.

The Uber gets to the lounge at 9:32 p.m. We exit the vehicle and thank the driver, who takes off without acknowledging that he heard us.

"Rude," Sarah says.

I nod in agreement.

Tonight, Sarah's wearing an outfit similar to mine. But where I am decked in black, she's in white. She wears her blond hair pulled back into a tight bun, showing off her barber's handiwork—a freshly trimmed undercut with a star pattern.

We join the line to get into the club. After being screened by security, we are let inside. Sarah gives her name to a hostess who guides us through the swanky establishment over to a booth where several of our friends are already seated.

I plaster on a smile a fake smile and greet everyone.

My good friend Kristen stands and shuffles out of the booth to hug me. It doesn't escape my notice that Hailey, Kristen's girlfriend of six months, scrutinizes our embrace. I don't like Hailey. I don't know her well, but I've seen enough to know that Kristen can do better. Both Kristen and Hailey work in law enforcement. Hailey's a cop, and I get the sense that she feels superior to Kristen, who is a correctional officer. I suspect that Hailey thinks she's better than everyone.

I ease into the booth beside Sarah and reach for the drink menu. After a quick look at the prices, I immediately put it down. The way they've marked everything up, I can't even afford a Budweiser. It will be water for me tonight, which really sucks. I'd like a drink or two or five.

Looking around, my unease builds. I'm not used to being in places like this—places that have plush and comfortable seating. Places with fancy light fixtures and sleek tables made from possibly real stone. Even the air smells expensive. It's like the fragrance of jasmine petals is being pumped through the central air system. Or perhaps it's just the candle that my nose is picking up. A large one is lit in the middle of our table.

Coiffed men in breasted suits peacock around the long 360° bar. They chat up women in smart cocktail dresses with their chests all puffed out. A part of me seethes at the display—I'm not sure why.

Over the next hour, the rest of our group arrives. The entire time, I fix a faux smile to my lips and try to engage politely. Usually, I am not such a poor sport, but I'm tired and want the day to end.

By 10:45 p.m., Sarah is four drinks in, and I can tell she's more than just tipsy. She's practically yelling as she recounts how she met Veronica. Having heard the story too many times before, I tune her out and toy with the condensation on my glass of water. My knee bounces under the table as I consider possible excuses to leave early.

Suddenly, I'm itching for a cigarette. I need one badly. I reach into my bag and withdraw a pack of nicotine gum, but when I slide out the plastic cartridge, it's empty. *When the hell had I finished them all?* Annoyed, I flick the empty package onto the table and take a gulp of my water.

"So when are you planning to ditch the single life, Jordan?" Paula asks, taking a sip of an espresso martini that I know costs twenty-eight bucks.

After me, Paula is Sarah's closest friend. We've never gotten along. I've tried to befriend her, but she has a bad habit of giving me stink eye when I get too close. Half the time I don't think she notices that she's doing it—hostility is her visceral reaction to me. I'm pretty sure Paula is in love with Sarah, so maybe that's why she hates me. Maybe she's known all this time about Sarah's romantic feelings for me.

All eyes are on me. Everyone is waiting for my response to Paula's stupid question.

"I don't do relationships," I say, giving my best nonchalant shrug.

Hailey's eyebrows pinch. She takes a long swig from her beer bottle. "And why's that?"

"Does there need to be a reason?" I say.

Hailey burps and leans back in her seat. She slips a possessive arm around Kristen. "It isn't natural to want to be alone."

"Are you calling me unnatural?" There's a tightness in my voice. Even drunk, Sarah notices. She squeezes my knee under the table. But I'm not in the mood to be comforted and shift away from her.

"You're twisting my words," Hailey says.

"No, I don't think I am."

"How about we change the topic?" Corie says. She's a Libra and diplomacy runs in her veins. It's her M.O. to try to deescalate heated conversations. Though we aren't really close, I've always liked her.

Corie is a high femme who used to date Paula ages ago. It hadn't been a messy breakup. In a very adult way, they mutually agreed that they were better off as friends. Hell, they even kept living together for a year after their split and to this day co-parent a Russian Blue cat named Ben.

"Yeah, let's change the topic," Kristen says. "Has anyone watched *Love Lies Bleeding*?"

Hailey rolls her eyes and reaches for her beer. Her expression tells me that she'd much rather continue to debate with me.

"You know what," I say, rising from my seat, "I'm gonna get some fresh air."

"Want me to come with you?" Sarah begins to rise as well.

I wave for her to sit back down. "Nah, I'll be back in a bit."

Leaving the group, I navigate around couples and gaggles of cologne-drenched men until I reach the exit.

Fall is a few weeks away, but I'm still surprised at just how chilly it is outside. Hugging my arms around my torso, I shuffle towards a woman who is sparking a cigarette a couple metres away from the entrance of the lounge. She's nice enough to let me bum one. They aren't the brand I like, but beggars can't be choosers.

As I smoke, I think about Victoria, my first everything—girlfriend, love, and heartbreak. Back when I'd been in high school, there'd been such a stigma around being gay, and teenagers were exceptionally cruel. So when the rumours started going around that Victoria and I were more than just friends, she quickly shut the gossip down by boxing me out of her life and spreading her legs for the starting point guard on the boys' basketball team.

Nine months later, Victoria gave birth to a baby boy while I'd still been working to tape my broken heart back together. I listened to a lot of emo music back then, playing songs by Taking Back Sunday, The Used, and Senses Failed on repeat. It'd been a dark time.

I think about Jessica Moretti, the married professor, who'd strung me along for over a year. Our first few months together, I hadn't known she'd been married. But when I did find out, Jessica began filling my head and my heart with promises about a life together. "I do not love him," she had told me. "I'm going to divorce him," she had said.

I saw how false her words were on the day her husband stumbled in on me eating her out on the kitchen counter. Jessica literally threw herself at his feet. A blubbering mess, she swore to him that I was a mistake and that she loved him—only him.

Finally, I think about Samira, but my thoughts can't linger on her. Even all these years later, my heart aches from the absence of what once was.

I crush the glowing cigarette under my heel and exhale a cloud of smoke.

I'm just about to turn to head back inside when a red Ferrari screeches to a stop at the curb just ahead of me. A gorgeous woman in a strapless orange dress gets out of the flashy sports car and slams the passenger door. She flings back her auburn hair over a shoulder, exposing her profile.

My breath catches—it's Noémie.

The passenger window whirs down, and a man shouts. "Get back in the car."

"No," Noémie snaps. Her skin is red, flushed from anger. Her hands are balled at her sides.

She spins away from the vehicle, angrily strutting in my direction. Our eyes meet, and my stomach soars up into my chest. There's a look of surprise or maybe recognition on the Poutine Princess's face. She falters. The heel of her shoe sinks between a crack in the pavement.

I spring forward, catching her before she falls.

Our contact is brief, but it's electric. A current buzzes through my entire body. The skin of her arms is smoother than I could ever have imagined. Her perfume is spicy with notes of citrus, and I want to bathe in it.

But there's another scent heavy on her—alcohol.

Whoever the man in the car is, he decides not to hang around. The window zips back up, and the Ferrari peels away from the sidewalk with a growl from its engine.

Noémie looks over her shoulder, watching the taillights disappear with distance. She sighs and rubs her temples. Her body sways slightly.

I hover closer—just in case she needs someone to lean on.

"Fight with your boyfriend?" I ask, mostly out of curiosity. It's been weeks since I've last seen her. Weeks since she's posted anything on social media. And maybe it's creepy, but I want a clue as to what she's been up to.

Noémie spears me with a look that tells me that she will not be answering my question—that it's none of my business.

I wonder if she recognizes me. Just a moment ago, it seemed like she had, but I could be wrong. Do people like her even register in their minds the people who serve them on a day to day?

Her gaze drops to the Chanel clutch she holds. She pops open the clasp and removes her phone. The screen is dark, and even as she taps on the glass surface, it remains black. "Tabarnak!" she says, scowling.

I have no idea what that means, but the word sounds like a curse.

It bothers me how easily she dismissed me—as if I am nothing but background noise. "You know, a thank-you would be nice," I say.

Her head snaps up from her phone. Steely grey eyes meet my own, making my pulse quicken.

Like always, her makeup is applied flawlessly. Tonight she wears deep-red lipstick and smoky eyeshadow. The blush on her cheeks has a shimmery element to it that sparkles in the streetlight, giving her face an ethereal glow. Fuck, she's beautiful.

"And what exactly would I be thanking you for?" Her tone is tart, and I hear more of her French accent than usual. It's the kind of tone I might imagine the gentry used with peasants.

"Stopping you from faceplanting," I reply.

Before Noémie can think to answer, a scrum of exuberant young men stagger around the corner. The moment their eyes land on Noémie, the catcalling begins.

My entire body goes stiff, and my protective instinct kicks in. I put myself between Noémie and the drunk boys.

They continue to throw crude comments her way. One of them makes a lewd gesture, acting out giving a blowjob. It's disgusting. It's the kind of behaviour that once sent me into a panic. Now, all I feel is anger. I want to hurl insults at them—attack their manhood and take shots at their mamas. But that's not wise. There's ten of them, and I'm smaller than them all. Luckily, they are gone as fast as they came.

I turn to face Noémie.

She looks visibly upset, and she holds her clutch tightly to her chest. Her body shivers, but that might just be because it's chilly outside.

"Where are you headed?" I ask.

Noémie blinks. "Home."

"Are you going to call a Lyft or Uber? I can wait with you."

"My phone is dead, so no, I won't be calling a Lyft," she says. "But, I don't live far. I can walk."

"I don't think you should walk home alone," I say.

Personally, I don't consider Toronto to be dangerous. For the most part, I am left alone. I became almost invisible to the male gaze the day I chopped off my hair and began dressing more masculine. But, even so, I've learned that it's never a good idea to be a single woman going anywhere alone, especially not at night. And especially not at night while intoxicated.

"It's a good thing I don't need your permission," Noémie mutters. She begins walking away from me, her off-balance strides taking her east along Richmond Street.

Annoyed at being dismissed again, I grit my teeth and start back towards the lounge, then stop at the entrance. I want to put this run-in with the Poutine Princess behind me, but I can't in good conscience go back inside. I need to make sure Noémie gets home safe. And so, I follow after her. If Noémie notices, she gives no indication.

Turns out that the Poutine Princess lied—she does not live close to the lounge. She lives in bloody Yorkville. It takes almost forty-five minutes to reach her semi-detached home. By the time we get there, my feet are crying. I'm not sure how Noémie managed the trek in heels.

Noémie climbs the short staircase up to the front door and then turns to finally acknowledge my presence. She doesn't thank me. She doesn't smile. Frankly, she looks rather unimpressed. When she disappears through the front door, it dawns on me that I've been M.I.A. from Sarah's party for over an hour—fuck.

Perhaps Wayne is right. Perhaps I do malfunction around Noémie. The entire walk, all I thought about was her—how annoyed with her I was, how rude she was, how beautiful she looked in the orange dress. Everything else, I forgot.

My phone is almost always on silent mode. Tonight is no different. When I dig it out of my pocket, I see a slew of messages from Sarah, Paula, Kristen, and Corie. They want to know where I am, and if I'm okay. Shit.

I shoot off a text message to the group chat.

Jordan, 10:55 p.m.

I'm good, but I'm heading home. Sry. Will explain tmrw.

Chapter 5

"You're so fucking selfish, Jay," Sarah shouts. Her face glows hot. Her pupils burn like coals. "You only care about yourself."

"You're drunk. Let's talk in the morning," I say, trying to walk around my friend to get to my bedroom.

Sarah blocks my path.

"Look, any conversation we have right now won't be productive, let's talk tomorrow," I say again.

"No, we'll talk now!" Sarah's voice is slurred. She stumbles forward and jabs my shoulder.

"Fine. I'm sorry, I shouldn't have taken off like that."

Sarah snorts. "You're not sorry. You don't care. You've never cared. Meanwhile, I …" She sniffles and turns her head to look away from me.

Sarah's always been an emotional drunk. Mostly, she's a tight vault, keeping her thoughts and feelings to herself. But when she drinks too much, the vault door creaks open a bit and some of her secrets spill out. Considering how often she gets drunk, it's kind of amazing that she managed to keep her romantic feelings for me to herself for so long.

Sarah's back hits the wall, and she slides down it until she's sitting on the floor. Tears roll down her plump cheeks like raindrops on a car window.

I go to her, crouching down beside her. "I shouldn't have taken off like that. It was wrong of me to leave," I repeat.

"Why did you?" Sarah asks, wiping her eyes.

Something tells me that bringing up Noémie would be a bad idea. "I guess, I'm not taking your leaving well," I say. "I just needed some time to think. And before I knew it, I walked so far away from the lounge that it made no sense walking back." It's not a complete lie, and I think it's what Sarah needs to hear.

"I'm sorry that I'm going," Sarah says, sniffling. "But I need to go. I can't stay here with you. I need things to work with Veronica."

I don't think things will work out with Veronica. I think her moving to Vancouver is a mistake. She shouldn't go. She should stay here. But I can't say that. And space is probably what our friendship needs.

I squeeze my friend's shoulder. "I know. And all I want for you is the best. You deserve it."

"I just want you to be happy too. I know you're miserable," she says. "You've got so much love to give, but you've let Samira trick you into thinking that you'll never be good enough for anyone. I hate her for that."

I want to deny it, but I know that if I do, it will only rile Sarah back up. So I say nothing.

Samira never tricked me. She only pointed out truths about me that I thought were surmountable. She'd been my longest relationship, and for a very long time, she'd been my everything. I thought we'd be together forever. But my ex wanted a type of intimacy I can't give anyone—even her. She broke things off with us because of that. And it sucked, and it hurt—it still hurts so much.

The worst part of it all is knowing that she was right to end things. I'm not normal. I have a mountain of hangups that's too high to climb, and I don't think there's a person out there who'd stick with me knowing they'd never be able to reach the top.

I push thoughts of Samira away. It hurts too much to think about her.

"I want you to find someone, Jay. A part of me wishes it could be me, but I know we'd never be able to make it work. We're better as friends," she whispers, her voice cracking.

A minute ticks by and then Sarah rises to her feet. I stand too.

"I need sleep," she says, shaking her head and wiping her eyes. "Fuck, I'm going to be so hungover."

She ambles towards her room. It's only when the bedroom door clicks shut behind her that I make for my own bed.

The next day, around midday, Sarah's father comes over with his truck. I help Sarah and her father haul boxes up the stairs, and we stack them neatly into the bed of the silver F-150.

Sarah isn't looking too good. A few times, she looks like she's going to toss her cookies. But she doesn't.

We say goodbye with a hug that lasts a lifetime but is also somehow way too short. Then Sarah is waving from the passenger window as her father backs out of the driveway.

As I watch them drive away, I am consumed by the feeling of being left behind. I stay rooted to the asphalt until the truck is completely out of view.

The basement apartment feels less like a home without Sarah. I've always hated the space, and I never imagined that I could hate it more, but I do now.

I am irritable and revert to old bad habits. I chain smoke my way through Saturday and Sunday, not touching my tablet to work on my graphic novel. Instead, I rot in my bed and curse my upstairs neighbours for living and making noise. I watch video after video of some bald guy in Australia cutting rough opal gems because Sarah and I used to enjoy watching his videos together, and I want to recapture those moments with her.

I decide that I fucking hate Vancouver because it's so fucking far away. I mindlessly scroll through Instagram. Flicking through the curated snapshots of my family, friends, and acquaintances deepens my sense of ennui.

Everyone appears so much happier than me.

My peers from high school and university are travelling the world or starting families. A few of them have bought their first house or condo. They brag about new jobs and announce engagements. They smile at Raptors games, plays, or concerts. All of them are moving forward in their lives while I am stuck—doing nothing. I've been left behind.

At some point, I wind up on Noémie's account. The Poutine Princess still hasn't posted anything recently.

After seeing her the other night, I'm even more curious to know why she's gone dark. Does it involve the guy in the Ferrari? Maybe he's her boyfriend? What had they been fighting about?

I get a WhatsApp message. Audrina's name flashes at the top of my screen. I close out of Instagram and open WhatsApp.

Audrina, 4:16 p.m.

How's your day going?

Usually I avoid responding too quickly to Audrina. But seeing her message right now is the highlight of my day. So pathetic.

Jordan, 4:16 p.m.

Sarah's flying out today.

Ngl

feeling a little down :(

Audrina, 4:18 p.m.

Want to come over?

Accepting the invite is a bad idea. I know what Audrina is looking for. She wants a relationship—with me. In my opinion, she deserves to be with someone as amazing as she is. And I'm not amazing—I'm just a pretty face to look at. If Audrina and I ever got serious, she'd realize soon enough that I have nothing to offer and that I'm broken. Then, she'd break up with me just as Samira had.

But I need a distraction. I need to feel something other than this throbbing emptiness that weighs down my bones.

Jordan, 4:21 p.m.

Yeah, sure. Omw

Chapter 6

Around 1:00 p.m. on Monday, the coffee shop is dead, giving me the opportunity to finally sift through the stack of resumés. I'm desperate to fill Marquess's spot on the morning roster, especially now that school is back is session, stealing Kevin and Stacie from me several weekday mornings. And Corrine still isn't pulling her weight.

One of the shop's owners is on location, working out of the back office, so I'm stuck vetting applications out front. I sit at a high-top table in the farthest corner from the register. The chrome stool is hard and uncomfortable, and I just know my ass is going to be crying soon.

I've just finished reviewing the first application when Noémie walks through the front door. My breath catches.

Her presence is unexpected. Not only has it been weeks since she last graced Grind That Bean with her presence, but it's also surprising to see her at this hour. The Poutine Princess only ever came during the morning rush.

My eyes eat her up, and I'm glad she's not looking in my direction. Today, she resembles a model in a photograph more than a person in the flesh. She's decked mostly in black—a shiny leather motorcycle jacket studded with silver hardware, distressed black jeans with the knees torn out, and a pair of chunky heeled boots. A beret rests at an angle atop her head. Beneath it, her auburn hair is pulled up in a tight bun. An orange messenger bag is slung across her body. Thick framed Ray-Bans hide her eyes.

She's absolutely stunning.

Noémie doesn't approach the front counter. Instead, she stands off to the side of the entrance.

Lowering her sunglasses down the bridge of her nose, she surveys the area. Her visual sweep ends the moment she spots me. Our eyes meet, and a strange sensation makes my skin buzz.

She begins walking towards me.

As the distance between us closes, I grip the batch of applications tighter.

"May I sit?" she asks, stopping at the edge of the table. Before I can even think to answer, she's dragging a chrome stool out from under the table.

"Yeah, sure," I mutter, letting go of the resumés. I should be annoyed that she started taking a seat before I could answer. I should be annoyed by her attitude and rudeness, but I'm more curious than anything. And I've always had a thing for bitchy women who take what they want and ask questions later.

Noémie removes her bag, setting it down on the vacant stool beside her. Next, she takes off her sunglasses and hooks them onto a pocket near the lapel of her jacket.

Like on Friday night, her lips are painted red, but the rest of her makeup is applied so lightly that it's not really apparent that she's wearing any.

I can't read the expression on her face, but it seems serious. A storm brews in the depths of her grey eyes. There's the tiniest crease between her brows.

My knee bounces as I wonder what the Poutine Princess could possibly want with me.

I can't quite believe she's here, sitting in front of me. She sought me out, and I assume it's because of what happened on Friday night. I can't quite believe that she recognized me—that I'm not invisible to her.

I urge myself to play the part of being indifferent—like my heart isn't beating a million times per minute. I hope my face isn't giving away my nerves.

A thick silence settles between us as I wait for her to say something.

Leaning over the pickup counter, Wayne observes us with his jaw dropped. Pointing at Noémie's back, he mouths, "What the actual fuck?"

I almost chuckle, but I catch myself. "So …" I say, crossing my arms.

"So … I just wanted to say thank-you for walking me home Friday night." She drums her fingers on the table. Her manicured nails are clipped short. They are painted a vibrant orange that contrasts nicely against the purple tabletop.

"I didn't think you recognized me."

Noémie blinks. A flush creeps up her neck. "I come here all the time, of course, I recognized you," she says forcefully. Her defensiveness takes me aback.

I clear my throat. "Okay. You're welcome."

I don't know what else to say. This conversation is awkward, and I want to abort it while also not wanting it to end. Where she's concerned, I've always had conflicting feelings, and maybe it's because she's someone that I'd love to take to bed but never could.

Where women are concerned, I've never had any troubles finding someone to keep me company at night. But the Poutine Princess is so out of my league, and her nearness makes me anxious the same way parallel parking on a busy city street does.

"If that's all you had to say, I'm kind of busy," I say, nodding at the heap of resumés.

Noémie's grey eyes narrow on the stack. "You're hiring?"

"Yeah."

Her brows furrow. For a moment she goes quiet. Then, she says, "I want to apply."

This time, I can't stop the chuckle from bursting from my lips. "You want to work here?"

"Why is that funny?" Her frown deepens. Her scarlet lips press together in a display of unmistakable exasperation. "Why wouldn't I want to work here? It's not far from where I live, and I'm more than qualified. I've been working in the hospitality industry since before I can even remember. Also, I recently graduated from Le Cordon Bleu in Ottawa, where I received my Grand Diplôme."

"Le Cordon Bleu—I think you're a bit overqualified for a barista job," I say. Frankly, I'm shocked to hear that the Princess has worked a single day in her life. Her family is ridiculously rich. "I don't know much about culinary school, but isn't Le Cordon Bleu a big deal? Wouldn't you rather work in one of those fancy restaurants where they plate food with tweezers?"

Noémie folds her arms over her chest and leans back a bit in her seat. A sigh escapes her lips. "Here's the thing—are you familiar with Poutine Heaven?"

I decide to play dumb. "Yeah, I think so," I say. "It's the fast-food chain with the founder who hates gay people?"

Her jaw visibly clenches. "My father doesn't hate gay people. He just thinks they're confused."

I snort. "And what do you think? Do you think the gays are confused?"

"I … I'm an ally," Noémie replies.

I don't buy her answer. Her faltering words aren't assuring. The look I send her tells her as much.

"I'm an ally," she repeats, sounding a lot surer.

"Okay, so your daddy owns Poutine Heaven. I'm even more confused why you'd want to work here."

Noémie bites her lip. "The plan was that my father would help me open my own restaurant, but a few weeks ago he cut me off," she admits. "So I just need a job to help tie me over until he cools down."

So that's what had happened—that's why Noémie's credit cards declined. I'm nosy and want to pry for more information. But it'd be unprofessional to ask, so I don't.

"The way I see things, it makes no sense to hire you," I say. "I need someone I can depend on, and you're a flight risk. The moment your daddy forgives you, I'm down an employee."

"My father is stubborn. It's unlikely he'll be forgiving me any time soon."

"Your background is in food and restaurants. I think coffee is outside of your niche," I say.

"Coffee is one of my hobbies, and I'm not interested in working in a restaurant that isn't my own," Noémie counters. "Look, if you are looking for someone you can depend on, I'm super dependable. I'll work whatever hours you want. I'm a fast learner. I'm a team player. Just give me a chance and I'll show you." Her grey eyes sparkle with a challenge and a hint of what I can only read as desperation.

I need to hire someone who doesn't suck since Corrine is still fumbling on the cash register and is still shit at operating the espresso machine. And while I know hiring Noémie is risky and that I'm likely to regret it, I'm compelled to.

If Noémie isn't lying—if she really did graduate from culinary school—than making drinks shouldn't be much of a challenge for her.

Picturing Noémie in the Grind That Bean uniform tickles me. A smile almost breaks across my face at the thought of me directing her to clean tables.

Before I fully can unpack all the pros and cons of hiring her, I find myself saying, "Fine, I'll take a chance on you, but I'll need you to fill out an application and your references will need to check out."

I can't quite believe those words came out of my mouth or that the Poutine Princess will be working at my coffee shop and reporting to me. Grind that Bean's most vexing customer is about to be an employee.

"Merci infiniment," she says, and before I can react, she's out of her seat and her arms are wrapping around me.

She's hugging me. Noémie St. Pierre is hugging me, and my insides are turning to goo.

I freeze and try not to focus on how good the warm press of her soft body feels. Christ she smells so good.

She pulls away quickly. "I'm sorry." Red colours her cheeks. "The last few weeks have just been really rough, and I'm just so grateful and excited to start."

A part of me doubts that she's actually excited. How could she be? Barista isn't a glamourous position.

Nodding, I rise from the stool. My ass hurts, and I resist the urge to massage it. I grab the stack of resumés with the intention of returning them to the back office.

"Wait here," I say. "I'm going to grab an application for you."

"Okay." Noémie beams. I don't think I've ever seen her smile like this. Usually, she's so … bitchy. It's uncanny seeing her so pleasant.

I walk away from her towards the counter. Wayne watches me like a hawk.

When I attempt to pass him by, he grabs my arm. "What the fuck did I just witness?"

"It's exactly what it looks like—I've hired the Poutine Princess."

Chapter 7

There's an empty space on the road near the coffee shop, and I back my bright-green motorbike between a mud splattered Nissan Sentra and a shiny Range Rover.

Cutting off the engine, I dismount and remove my clunky black helmet that's got the hideous Bell logo stamped on the front. For the last two years, I've seriously contemplated spray-painting my helmet to match the colour of my Kawasaki Ninja. But I don't think an entire can of spray paint can hide how hideous of a helmet it is. I'd rather just replace the darn thing, but the helmets I lust after are uber expensive. My wallet can't handle the expense.

I cross the street, toting my helmet by its thick chin strap. My steps slow when I catch a glimpse of her. Noémie hovers over Wayne's shoulder. They are staring down at his phone and laughing like best friends. The sight is odd. I never envisioned Wayne getting along so quickly with the Poutine Princess. I don't know how I feel about it.

Wayne took forever to warm towards me. Usually, he's so catty towards new hires, and he tends to stay catty until he uncovers something about them that he likes. Sometimes, there's nothing to like, and he stays cold.

It's also weird seeing Noémie in uniform. The purple t-shirt, with Grind That Bean printed across the chest in big bold white letters, swallows her. The hem of the shirt almost reaches her knees. I'll have to check again to see if there's a smaller size hiding somewhere in the back office. But even dressed down in khakis and an oversize tee, Noémie's allure is undeniable, especially when she's smiling the way she's smiling at the moment.

"Dancing videos?" I ask, coming to a stop near the store front.

They both jump slightly at the sound of my voice. So engrossed by whatever was on Wayne's phone, they hadn't noticed my approach.

"Grindr," Wayne corrected, slipping his phone into a front pocket.

"Only a week ago you were telling me that you were done with that app," I say. "I thought you were looking for something real, something more than just a hookup."

Wayne rolls his eyes. "I've decided to do both: look for something real while also hooking up."

I snort. "You aren't good with casual—you get too attached."

He pouts.

"Morning, Jordan," Noémie says softly, almost shyly. It's strange. I don't think I've ever heard her say my name before. And usually, I prefer to be called by my nickname. But my name rolling off her tongue makes my skin tingle.

I nod curtly to acknowledge her greeting.

When the three of us enter the coffee shop, I dash to disarm the alarm and Wayne flips on the lights.

Looking at Noémie, I cock my head towards the seating section. "You can start by taking down the stools."

Noémie hesitates. She looks like she wants to say something but decides not to. She saunters towards the tables and begins pulling down the chrome stools.

I head for the back office and hang my jean jacket and helmet on the hooks near the stockroom.

I sense Wayne's presence behind me. "I can't believe she's actually working here," he says in a hushed voice.

"I can't believe it either," I say, entering the office and shutting the door behind us so we can talk freely.

I grab a stack of shirts and looked for a small or medium size, but everything's extra-large. Noémie's out of luck.

Squatting, I punch a code for the safe. When the light blinks from red to green, I open the door and remove the money from within.

"She was such an annoying customer—always bitching and complaining—such a Karen." Wayne leans against a filing cabinet. "I wanted to kill you for hiring her. I thought she'd be a total bitch and drive me crazy."

Bills and rolls of coins in hand, I nudge the heavy door shut with my toe. The mechanized pins whirr as the lock reengages. "So you've determined that she's not a bitch?"

I can't help but recall my encounter with Noémie outside of the lounge last Friday night. She'd been pretty bitchy that night, but maybe there'd been a reason for her attitude. Again, I find myself wondering about the man in the Ferrari. The man who she'd been arguing with. Were they dating?

"Oh, she most certainly is, but there's a good reason for it—she's a Gemini," Wayne states. "She's got a personality to match every season."

"That doesn't sound promising."

"Maybe not for you since you're a moody Cancer, but I'm a fire sign, so the Poutine Princess gives me life," he says. "And she has exceptional taste in men. At least, we share the same type."

I can do without hearing about Noémie's type of man. "Don't you have work to do?"

Wayne taps on his Apple Watch. "Technically, I don't start for another five minutes."

I snort and exit the office with the cash in hand. Out in the front, I load the register.

Noémie slips behind the counter and comes to stand about a foot away from me.

I freeze. My grip on the register drawer tightens. I'm so annoyed by how her nearness affects me that I slam the drawer shut, not meaning to. I side-step to put distance between us. For the thousandth time, I question why I hired her in the first place. What had I been thinking? She's going to be such a distraction, and I seriously doubt that she has the work ethic to cut it at a shop as busy as ours. She's a spoiled rich girl who likely hasn't worked hard a day in her life.

Wayne shuffles out of the back and ties on his apron.

"Can you show Noémie how to work the ovens?" I ask him. "And then show her how to operate the till?"

Noémie pouts. There's a challenge in her voice when she says, "You're not going to show me how to make drinks?"

I grit my teeth. "If you're still here in a month, you'll be taught how to work the espresso machine."

Frowning, she folds her arms.

"You got a problem with that?"

She releases an exaggerated sigh. "Kind of. I want to make drinks."

"Well, you're not going to," I say. "Wayne will show you how to work the till, and that's that."

Noémie looks like she wants to argue some more, but she rolls her eyes and goes over to where Wayne is standing by the ovens. Ugh, what had I been thinking hiring her? The last thing I need to deal with is her piss-poor attitude first thing in the morning.

All in all though, Noémie's first day isn't a complete disaster. Far from it, in fact. The Poutine Princes hadn't lied—she does learn fast. She picks up how to input orders quickly, and during her entire shift, she only errs on two order entries.

The same cannot be said for Corrine, who works alongside me on the Faema espresso machine. Corrine keeps messing up, leaving me and Wayne to deal with more than a half-dozen customer complaints. But even with all her mistakes, the morning rush flies by with relative ease.

In the slow hours, I constantly catch Wayne and Noémie chatting instead of working. Their tones are hushed, like they are conspiring. It makes me think they are talking about me.

My suspicion is confirmed when I happen upon them in the back near the office. I only catch the tail end of their conversation.

"I always get what I want," Noémie says. The confidence behind her statement grates on my nerves. The girl has probably never wanted for anything while most people want for the basics.

Growing up, I learned how to do without or find ways to get things I really wanted. In grade school, when everyone in my class was trading Pokémon cards that my mother couldn't afford to get me, I started drawing pictures of Charizard and Blastoise and exchanged my illustrations for cards. I managed to collect a 120 out of 151 Pokémon without having opened a single pack.

Noémie doesn't know what it's like to have to hustle. She might be struggling a bit now that her daddy has cut her off. But it's only a matter of time before they make up and she's back to her regular program.

"Not with this," Wayne says. "And when I win, you'll have to give me anything I want from your closet. Jay will—" Noticing me, he snaps his mouth shut.

"Jay will what?" I ask, coming to a stop near the shelves that house the flavoured syrups.

Noémie's face goes red—like, really red. She throws Wayne a look that I have a hard time understanding. They both stay quiet.

"Jay will what?" I ask again.

Wayne sighs. "Noémie thinks she can sweet talk you into letting her operate the espresso machine this week, and I bet her that she couldn't."

Wayne and his stupid bets. He loves to gamble on anything and everything. I used to play his stupid games, but I don't anymore. I'm a sore loser, and Wayne almost always wins. I can't quite believe that Noémie would risk losing one of her expensive purses on such a trivial bet. But what do I know? Maybe the girl's got more than one Birkin.

"You're supposed to be training her," I say. "Quit messing around."

"You're such a micromanager," Wayne says.

I roll my eyes and shake my head. "Just get back to work. Seriously."

I'm happy that Wayne listens to me. He trains Noémie on how to operate the panini press, and he shows her how to restock supplies.

For the most part, I keep my distance from Noémie. Being near her makes me feel too much, and I don't want to give myself away.

Apparently, I give the impression that I'm in a bad mood. Corrine asks me more than once if I'm okay, and Wayne tells me that I look like I have a stick up my ass.

I can't put a number to how many gorgeous women I've slept with, but only Noémie and Samira have made me choke on air when they get too close. It's aggravating.

One week flows into the next, and things don't get better. I can't stop thinking about Noémie. I wake up thinking about her. I go to bed thinking about her. I brush my teeth thinking about her.

On a YouTube video, I learned there's a word for this type of unhealthy obsession—limerence.

Is it only because Noémie is out of reach that I want her? Or does the allure come from knowing she's from another world—one of money and privilege? I can't think of any other reason. There's nothing else about her I like. Her personality sucks.

She isn't as bad as I first thought she'd be though—she's far more useful than Corrine—but she distracts Wayne too much. I'm a little jealous of how fast they imprinted on each other.

Used to be that Wayne and I would chat when the rush died down. But now, he's always with Noémie. And I'm avoiding her, so I barely get any time alone with him. Maybe I'm being dramatic, but it kind of feels like I'm losing a friend. And with Sarah gone, I just feel so lonely.

Over the weekend, I view two bachelor apartments. The first place I look at is in the gaybourhood, and it's walking distance from the coffee shop. At 360 square feet, it doesn't have a layout to accommodate my double bed. But on the plus side, the unit recently underwent renovations and features new laminate floors, ensuite laundry, stainless steel appliances, and a dishwasher. I've never had a dishwasher before. Also, the windows are large, letting in so much natural light. I can see myself living there. Unfortunately, the property manager tells me that the rent's been increased from $1,600 a month to $1,900. I can't afford it.

A basement apartment in Chinatown is the second listing I look at. Somehow, it's still not in my budget despite being in worse condition than my current shithole.

I haven't had any luck finding a roommate. I've posted an ad on Facebook Marketplace and Kijiji, but I'm getting no bites. No one is interested in living in Scarborough.

On a Thursday, just after three in the afternoon, the coffee shop is quiet. There are only a few customers in the seating area. Noémie and Kevin are chatting near the cash register. Keeping my distance, I try to instill an outward image of looking cool and disinterested.

Engineer in the making, Kevin Wong used to be one of my favourite employees. He's great at his job. He never drops shifts. He's always on time. And he's got exceptional customer service skills. But he flirts with Noémie at every opportunity and follows her around like a puppy. I hate it.

Wayne emerges from the back, toting a plastic sleeve of purple-branded cups. He sets the stack down on the counter and settles in beside me. "Man, you've got it bad," he whispers with a chuckle.

I glare at him. "I don't."

"Seriously, you should see your face. You're scowling so hard at Kevin right now."

"I'm not—what the fuck do I care if Kevin is making a fool of himself?"

"Yeah, you don't sound jealous at all," Wayne teases.

My eyes dart over to Noémie and Kevin to verify that they hadn't overheard what he said. "Shut up," I say.

Wayne nudges me playfully. "Somebody's got a crush on the Poutine Princess."

"I don't. Go away." I shove him lightly away from me.

Wayne begins to laugh loud enough that Noémie and Kevin look at us and walk over.

"What's so funny?" Kevin asks.

I shoot Wayne a look of warning, silently conveying that I will kill him if he says anything. "I was just telling Wayne about this apartment I went to see over the weekend. The property manager wants $1,900 for a 360 square-foot bachelor pad."

"Doesn't sound funny to me—just sad," Kevin says. He stands very close behind Noémie. I really don't like it.

"Kevin, go wipe down the tables," I say.

My tone makes Kevin wince.

"I wiped them down twenty minutes ago," Noémie says.

"They still look dirty." I pretend to survey the seating area. "Just go and wipe them down."

Beside me, Wayne laughs harder and slaps his knee.

Kevin exchanges a look with Noémie before shrugging. He moves away from the group and grabs the spray bottle and cloth.

Noémie cocks her head to the side, regarding me with interest—like she's trying to puzzle me out. Then, she shoots a look at Wayne, and he sobers immediately.

I wish I could read their thoughts. I've got a feeling they're speaking about me telepathically, but I can't begin to guess what they're talking about.

Wayne smirks and shakes his head.

Abandoning me, he snatches up the sleeve of cups from off the counter and walks over to the espresso machine. He begins replenishing the dwindling stack of purple cups. He isn't too far away. That's on purpose. The devious devil wants to eavesdrop on whatever exchange Noémie and I have.

"So you're apartment hunting?" Noémie asks.

"Sort of," I say. "I either need to find myself a new roommate or find a new place." I opt not to say anything about my best friend U-Hauling across the bloody country. There's no reason to go into details about my life. Noémie and I are not friends.

Frankly, there's no reason for us to be talking now. I motion to turn away when Noémie asks, "What kind of place are you looking for?"

"Something affordable," I say. "If I'm lucky, close to work."

Noémie bites her bottom lip. There's the slightest crease between her brows, and I can tell she's contemplating something. Sliding her hands into the front pockets of her khakis, she rocks back on her heels. "I've been thinking that it might make sense to rent out one of the rooms in my home," she says, and then adds, "I could use the money."

I go really still. I must've misheard. Noémie's not suggesting that I could move in with her—like live together.

I'm probably looking at her like she's sprouted a second head, because her face reddens. Noémie looks uneasy. As I continue to stare at her, I'm not sure what to think. Silence slams between us.

A flash of annoyance registers on her face. "Forget it," she says, crossing her arms. "It'd probably be weird right? Living together? I'm your employee, but I just thought it makes sense. You need a place, and I've got a spare room."

I can't forget it.

An image of the semi-detached home in Yorkville flashes in my mind. Noémie's home isn't that far from the coffee shop. On a nice day, I could even walk to work.

The thought of living with Noémie seems like torture. Hell, I can barely handle working with her. But at the same time, I'm quite desperate. Fact is I can't afford my shitty Scarborough basement apartment on my own, and I'd rather die than move back home with my mom. There's also a part of me that is curious to see Noémie's place of residence. Is it as luxurious on the inside as it appeared on the outside?

"Actually, I wouldn't mind seeing it," I say. "Unless you think it'd be too weird."

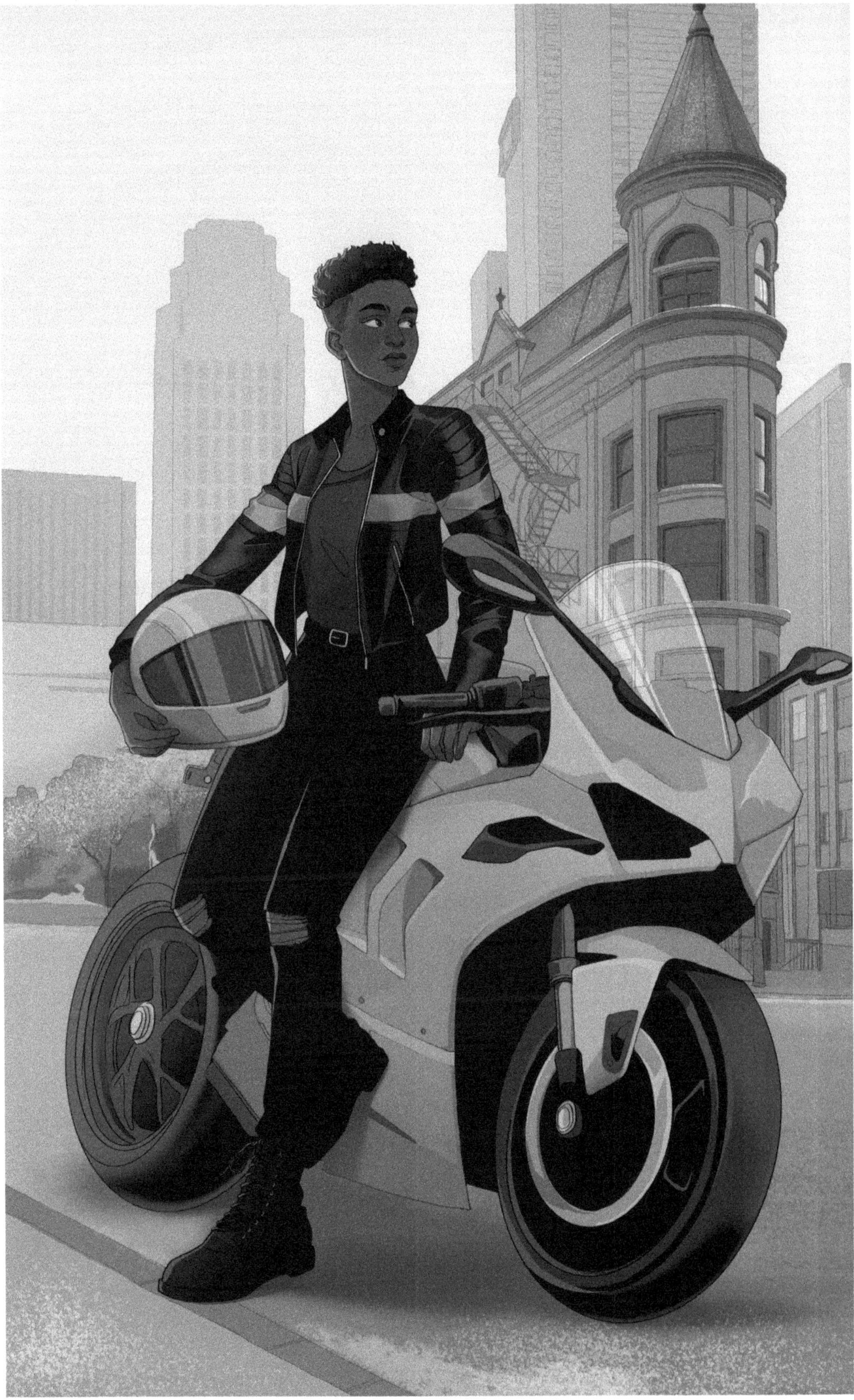

Chapter 8

In the daylight, Noémie's semi-detached Victorian residence exudes charm and timeless elegance. The shutters and front door are painted a wintery shade of green that complements the red brick facade. Wooden shingles line the steeply pitched roof. Neatly trimmed shrubbery edges the driveway that I pull into.

Cutting the engine, I get off my motorcycle. As I remove my helmet and walk up the short concrete staircase, my stomach twists. I question what the hell I'm doing. I should not be at Noémie's place. We could never be roommates.

Biting my lip, I turn and look at my motorcycle. I consider leaving, but only for a moment. Since I drove all the way here, I might as well take Noémie up on her offer for a tour of the home—even knowing I have no intention of cohabitating with her.

I push the doorbell. It's fitted with one of those tiny cameras. A loud whimsical chime plays followed by frantic barking. My anxiety notches up a level. It's not that I'm scared of dogs, but having had very little interaction with them, I do fear getting bit. Growing up, I always wanted a pet, but according to my Caribbean mother, "Dawg and puss fi deh outside."

The front door opens. Noémie stands in the threshold wearing a pair of grey Roots sweatpants, orange slides with Givenchy embossed in crisp white letters, and an oversized white shirt with a collar so wide that it falls off one shoulder. Though she's dressed in clothes that suggest an itinerary of binge-watching sitcoms all day, her makeup is perfection. Her auburn hair is pulled up into her signature ponytail. She is faultless.

The uneasiness in my belly intensifies. I sneak a quick look over my shoulder at my bike.

"Hey," Noémie greets, opening the front door wider. She smiles, waving for me to come inside.

I try to smile back, but the muscles around my mouth aren't working. For a second, I hesitate, but then I step into the bright foyer.

The dog's still yapping. It's a tiny thing with long silky blue-grey hair on its body and brownish-gold hair around its face and muzzle. It pins me with its beady black eyes and barks at me like I'm an intruder.

Jumping on its hind legs, it paws Noémie's calves. "Tais-toi, Céline," she says, scooping the tiny terror up into her arms. "She doesn't bite. Normally, she's very quiet, but visitors make her excited. She's just saying hi."

I can't imagine the dog ever being quiet, but I nod.

I slip out of my Nikes and instantly note how pleasantly warm the glossy-white tiled floor is beneath my socked feet. "Heated floors?" I ask with wonder.

"Yeah, all throughout the house," she says, scratching Céline's head with her French-tipped nails. The dog relaxes and ceases its barking and wriggling.

I imagine Noémie raking those manicured nails down my neck and suppress a shudder. Clearing my throat, I say, "Fancy."

"Just wait until you see the kitchen." Noémie gestures for me to follow her, so I do.

I'm guided away from the foyer, and the white tiles transition to sandy wooden floors arranged in a herringbone pattern.

Noémie points to a room opposite an ascending staircase, "That's the sitting room. It's good for collecting dust."

I give the richly furnished space a cursory glance and can't help but think that it's ridiculous how some people can have rooms they never use. Space is something I've never had enough of. I grew up sharing a two-bedroom apartment with my mother, grandmother, and older sister. Our cramped situation always put us at each other throats. Any little thing sparked an argument, but usually it was an escalating chain reaction. Every weekday began with Amari hogging the bathroom and me banging on the door, screaming at her to hurry up. My screaming and banging always triggered Grandma Janet, who'd start crying out the Lord's name and scripture, and that set off my mother. Before 8:00 a.m., all four of us would be hollering at each other.

I follow Noémie into the main living space. It's an open layout. Natural light pours in from giant windows that overlook a quaint backyard fitted with a canopied deck, grilling station, and what looks to be a hot tub. There isn't much green space, but it's more than most could hope for in the heart of the city. Near a set of sliding doors is a dining area featuring a heavy wooden table that's definitely not from Ikea—probably custom built. The eight adorning high-backed chairs aren't very comfortable-looking.

My eyes go wide when I see the kitchen. It's giving beauty, opulence, and functionality. With its classic white countertops, gold fixtures, and sage green cabinets, it's the kind of kitchen people pin on Pinterest. I've never stepped foot in a kitchen this grand before. I count twelve stools tucked underneath the overhang of a giant kitchen island. A gold range hood hovers over a gas range boasting six burners, a large stainless-steel griddle, and two ovens.

Across the kitchen is a modern living room that looks more staged than lived-in, but there are pops of orange here and there that loan it some of the owner's personality. Noémie being Noémie, I guess I expected her place to have the colour scheme of a creamsicle.

She saunters into the kitchen and walks over to an impressive espresso machine. My eyes narrow on the logo—it's a La Marzocco. Not a machine for beginners. I wonder if it's just for show or if Noémie actually knows how to use it.

"Would you like a coffee?" Noémie asks.

Truth is, I drank a coffee already, but I want to know if the Poutine Princess can operate the espresso machine. "Sure," I say.

"What kind of drink would you like?"

I pull out a stool and have a seat at the island. "How about a latte?"

"Sure." Noémie sets Céline down on the floor. The little dog shakes violently and yawns.

I watch Noémie get to work. She weighs whole coffee beans and spritzes them with water to prevent static during the grind. Before tamping, she whisks the grounds using a WDT tool to ensure even distribution. After tamping, she tosses on a puck screen before twisting the portafilter in place and pressing a button to begin the extraction. I'm thoroughly impressed with her speed and technique, and I know even before she pulls the shot that it will be a perfect golden emulsion.

The machine hums as an even stream of caramel liquid fills a double walled glass. Toasty notes of coffee season the air, and my mouth waters in anticipation. While shift manager at Grind that Bean is not my dream job, I am passionate about coffee. There's nothing quite like a perfectly made cup. Coffee is the one thing in life that will always pick you up.

Noémie steams milk and proceeds to expertly pour it over the shot. When she sets the glass down in front of me, I see that she drew a swan out of the foam. I'm impressed. Latte art is extremely hard. It took me over a year to master drawing a leaf, and I'm an artist.

"Thanks," I say, lifting the cup to my lips. I take a sip. My eyes close. The drink is perfection. It's smooth and chocolaty. The balance between bitterness and acidity is on point. It's possibly the best latte I've ever had.

"C'est bon?"

Not understanding, I look up and blink at Noémie.

"I asked if it's good."

"It's excellent," I say, licking my lips and setting down the glass. "Why didn't you tell me that you knew how to work an espresso machine?"

Noémie folds her arms across her chest and leans against the counter. "Before you hired me, I told you that coffee is one of my hobbies," she says, pinning me with a look that makes me want to hunker down in my seat.

"Yeah, you did," I say. Truth is, I hadn't really believed her.

"And I've been trying to talk to you about it, but you literally go out of your way to ignore me at work," she says. "Do you have a problem with me?"

Yes, I do. You're under my skin. I can't stop thinking about you, and I don't want you to know. "I don't have a problem with you," I lie. "I haven't been ignoring you."

"If you say so." She rolls her eyes.

"I do," I say, drumming my fingers against the double-walled glass of the coffee cup. I sigh. "Look, starting your next shift, I'll put you on drinks." When the words leave my mouth, I want to take them back immediately. I work on the espresso machine. If Noémie works the machine with me, it'd mean we'd be working side by side with each other for almost the entire shift. She's going to be such a distraction. Fuck.

A smile spreads across Noémie's face. She's looking at me like I've just offered her the world. My insides melt. I look down at my cup and tell myself that it's not a big deal. I'm an adult. I can be professional around Noémie.

After I finish my drink, Noémie continues the tour of her home. We walk up a flight of steps, and I'm shown the guest room that she's considering renting out. It's a large room—double the size of my current bedroom and a lot brighter. There's a large bay window with a bench that looks onto the street. The bed looks like a queen. It's richly outfitted with a thick comforter and a pile of pillows and cushions. I bet sleeping on it would feel like sleeping on a cloud. My current mattress has spring coils that dig into my back if I lay on it a certain way.

Noémie pulls open a door that leads to a walk-in closet. I gawk at its size. I don't have enough clothes to take up even a quarter of the space.

She opens another door, revealing an ensuite four-piece bathroom. My mouth hangs open. "Is this the primary bedroom?" I ask.

Noémie chuckles. "No. I told you this is the guest suite. My bedroom is on the third floor."

"I didn't know guest suites had ensuite bathrooms."

Noémie chuckles like I said something funny. "So, you like it?"

Of course, I like it. Who wouldn't? But I'm out of my element here. I don't belong here. People like me don't live in places like this. "Yeah, it's great," I say. "But, I don't think I can afford it."

Noémie frowns. "What makes you think that?"

I gesture at the room. "You have to know what a space like this could go for on the market."

"Yes," Noémie admits. "But I'm not keen on living with a stranger."

"Aren't I a stranger? You don't know anything about me."

"I know you're the type of person who doesn't let drunk girls walk home alone," she says. "I know that Wayne thinks the world of you, and I trust his judgment."

I want to say that she barely knows Wayne, and that she shouldn't put so much faith in him. Wayne is great, but he'd sell his mother to the devil for a designer bag.

"Doesn't change the fact that I can't afford to live here."

She arches a brow. "You don't even know what I'm asking for it."

"And what are you asking for it?"

"What are you paying in rent now?"

"Twelve hundred," I reply honestly, knowing that the pitiful amount is well under what Noémie could possibly want. "I can afford as much as fifteen hundred, but even that is pushing it for me."

A hush falls over the room. Noémie's brows knit together. "Would you be open to renting the room for thirteen hundred?"

"You can get more than double that if you rent to someone else," I say.

"Seriously, why are you fighting this? I already told you that I'm not interested in living with a stranger," she says, annoyance creeping into her tone. "Besides, I am not hurting that bad for money now that I'm working. Thirteen hundred is more than enough to cover the utilities, which is why I'm looking for a roommate in the first place."

"Don't you think it'd be weird—living together?" I ask.

"Because you're my boss?"

"Yes."

She tosses her ponytail over her shoulder. "No, not really. This house has more than enough space for the two of us," she replies.

I bite my lip. Am I actually considering moving in with Noémie? Logically, it would be stupid not to accept her offer. I can afford thirteen hundred dollars a month in rent, and Noémie's place is close to work.

But I can't live with her. It wouldn't be wise, and not just because we work together. Noémie makes me feel things I'd rather not feel. She's a temptation I can never have. Whenever I'm near her, I lose myself a little. I'm not sure how long I'd be able to keep up my front of disinterest if we lived together. And she can never know that I'm interested in her. She's straight—the last thing I want to do is make her uncomfortable.

Sharing a space with Noémie would likely put me in a state of constant sexual frustration. Even now, my fingers itch to drag her over to the bed and have my way with her. Where women are concerned, I'm used to getting what I want. But I can't have her for so many reasons.

Still, I wonder what Noémie would do if I made a move and flirted a little. Would she push me away or pull me closer? I wonder if Noémie is like spaghetti. Some women really are only straight until wet. Nope—not going there. I've been with straight girls before—it's asking for drama. I'm too old for drama.

Noémie stares at me. She's waiting for an answer.

The right thing to do would be to turn down her offer. But when have I ever done the right thing?

Chapter 9

"I'm not going to sleep with her." I shove a cardboard box into Amari's outstretched hands.

My older sister snorts. "You said the same thing about your art teacher," she says. "And wasn't she wifed up?"

It's times like this that I wonder why I tell Amari anything. It's just like her to throw past indiscretions in my face.

"Professor. And I didn't know she had a husband—she never wore a ring," I explain, not sure why I even bother. I've probably told Amari a million times now that I thought Ms. Moretti was single. But Amari always likes to think the worst of me. Trying to convince her otherwise is wasted breath.

Bending, I reach for a box and grunt as I pick it up. It's heavy, and Amari is blocking my path through the doorway.

I glare at her. "Quit being useless. The truck isn't going to pack itself."

"Don't cheese me, fam." My sister rolls her eyes. "You should be nice to me styll—am here doing you a favour."

It's my turn to snort. "You're only *here* because you're nosy."

Years ago, when I'd moved out of our mother's apartment to live with Sarah, Amari had been far too busy sleeping in to assist me. But now that I'm moving to Yorkville to live with Poutine Heaven's founder's daughter, Amari just happens to be free and willing to lend a hand. I don't buy Amari's newfound altruism. Not for a second.

I'm losing my grip on the box. "Seriously, can you move out of the way?"

Side-eyeing me, Amari turns and walks out of the bedroom.

I follow my sister up the stairs and hurry over to Uncle Weston's truck. He'd been nice enough to loan it to me for the day, which saves me the cost of renting a U-Haul—though I'm not sure I have enough things to warrant renting a moving van. Over the course of the last few weeks, I've sold or given away what little furniture I owned along with the kitchen table and sofa Sarah left behind. Now, all my worldly possessions fit into eight boxes and three black trash bags.

Unloading my burden onto one of the back seats of the Tacoma, I let out a sigh and wipe away the sweat weeping down my forehead.

Outside, the air is cool and crisp. Summer is in the rearview. In a week, it'll be Thanksgiving. The leaves are starting to change colours, and it won't be long before the foliage falls, losing colour and brightness to decay. I stare at a giant maple and consider that, in a lot of ways, I'm just like a leaf. I budded and grew, and for a moment, I even shone bright and healthy. But now I languish on the branch of life. It's only a matter of time before I detach and break down. I'm scared I will become my father. I don't want to die alone.

"Who's being useless now, eh?" Amari says, bumping me a little too forcefully.

"Ouch," I say, rubbing my shoulder and shooting daggers at her with my eyes.

Amari smirks.

Thirty minutes later, the basement apartment is empty, the truck is fully loaded, and I'm seated behind the steering wheel. As I back out the driveway, an odd sensation comes over me. Perhaps it is trepidation. Maybe it's more a feeling of moving towards something.

Definitely, moving in with Noémie is not the wisest decision. There's a high chance that things won't pan out well. Like, at any moment, Hugo St. Pierre might welcome his daughter back into the fold. And where will that leave me? I doubt Mr. St. Pierre would approve of his daughter living with a dyke.

And my track record's not the best. I've never been good at denying myself. What if I can't keep my hands to myself? What if I cross a line? What if Noémie lets me? My hands tighten on the steering wheel as I continue thinking up ways that moving in with Noémie can blow up in my face. Sarah would say that I am doom spiralling.

Amari connects her phone to the truck. Cardi B's "WAP" blares through the speakers. The lyrical rhymes about wet-ass pussy are not helping my anxiety, and I'm reminded of the TikTok video of Noémie and her hot blonde friend twerking to this very song. My body tingles.

Shifting in my seat, I lean forward to change the music.

Amari smacks my hand away from the controls. "Not interested in hearing your white-ass music, fam," she says.

My jaw clenches. I hate it when Amari tells me that I'm white or that my interests are so white. I'm much lighter skinned than my sister, and my hair texture is finer. Amari has always held this against me. In my sister's eyes, I am more like our father than our mother. In my sister's eyes, I am a traitor to my race because I enjoy classic rock, refuse to talk like Scarborough mans, and actively avoid going to any parties or cookouts hosted on the block.

Amari knows full well why I keep my distance. She knows why I left home as soon as I could afford it. She knows why I barely visit. But she refuses to acknowledge what happened. Instead, Amari prefers to make ridiculous statements. She likes to tell me that I don't like Black people and that I'm one of those lesbians who hate men. I don't hate all men, and the first statement is completely false.

I'm proud of my Jamaican heritage. But I'm also proud of our Scandinavian roots—our father's roots. My sister, however, rejects that part of herself. From an early age, she wedged a distance between herself and our father, and when he passed away, I don't think she spared a single tear for him.

"Can you just change the song?" I ask. "I'm not in the mood to hear it."

My sister sucks her teeth and turns up the volume. "I don't care what you're in the mood for, fam."

I grit my teeth but don't bother trying to change the song again. There's no point.

Almost an hour later, I turn onto the quiet street leading to Noémie's Victorian home.

Amari whistles. "This hood's a straight up Jeff Bezos flex," she says. "You sure you're trynna live here? Karen might call the boydem on you for trespassing."

Until my sister mentioned it, I never considered how I might be perceived by Noémie's neighbours. While I don't think the police will be called on me, I likely would get the odd stare here and there from the bordering residents. Like hot sauce on ice cream, I don't belong in

Yorkville. Scarborough is written all over me. It's my swagger. It's how I dress. For a long time, it was even how I spoke. I have conflicting feelings about where I'm from. People in general love to hate on my hood, but it's the mecca of Toronto culture. Even big celebrities like Drake adopt our slang.

I pull into the empty driveway, and my sister exits the truck before I cut the engine. She leans against the hood and stares up at the home. I know she's looking for a flaw—something negative that she can point out. But there are none to find. The home is gorgeous.

Amari's face curdles—the lines between her brows and around her mouth deepen. "Deadass, I should start eating pussy too—find me a rich snow bunny with a nice crib to put me up."

"I am not sleeping with Noémie," I say, slamming the truck door.

"Samira says you fuck with everyone."

At the mention of my ex—who is inconveniently my sister's best friend—I tense. "Samira doesn't know what she's talking about," I say, knowing my rebuttal doesn't matter. "And Noémie's straight."

Amari doesn't care about the truth. Sometimes, I think her sole purpose in life is to piss me off. Sometimes, I wish our relationship could be different. It eats at me that she hates me. Kinda pathetic, but even in my thirties, I seek my older sister's approval.

Amari folds her arms and gives me a cutting once over with her eyes. "Samira was straight until you fucked her," she states, her tone pure ice.

When Amari found out about me and Samira, she nearly had an aneurysm—she'd been so angry. And for more than six months after, she'd given Samira the silent treatment—a big deal considering they'd been inseparable since kindergarten. All these years later, my sister still hasn't let it go. She thinks I'm the one who corrupted her best friend. Truth is, Samira's the one who corrupted me.

I was twelve when I realized I was gay. I'd been sitting on the floor between Samira's legs as she braided my hair—a quite common occurrence back then. But for whatever reason, I suddenly became hyperaware of the sensation of her parting my hair with the tail of the comb and the scent of cocoa butter on her skin—the warmth radiating from the centre of her thighs.

When Samira finished, she'd bade me to turn around so she could appraise her work. I remember thinking that the light-blue Baby Phat track suit looked good on her. Without a mirror to see my reflection, I can't say for sure what expression I emoted, but whatever it was made Samira smile devilishly. "You're cute, but too young," she'd said, her words making my heart liquify. And then she'd leaned over and brushed her lips against my cheek before running off to find my sister.

Even all these years later, I still recall my cheek burning from her chaste kiss.

Amari assumed that I'd been Samira's first relationship with a woman, but I wasn't. Before me, she'd been in at least two other sapphic partnerships. But knowing that her best friend wouldn't have approved, Samira had kept her sexuality to herself until Amari stumbled in on us.

I decide not to acknowledge my sister's comment. I decide to push thoughts of Samira away and grab one of the three trash bags filled with my clothes, slinging it over my shoulder.

The front door opens and Noémie steps outside, carrying a wriggling Céline in her arms. My breath hitches, and all I can hope is that Amari doesn't notice. If she notices, she will say something. My sister might say something regardless. The grip I have on the bag tightens.

This afternoon, Noémie is dressed in a tangerine romper. Her auburn hair is loose, cascading past her shoulders.

Amari's gaze darts between me and Noémie. Her lips curve deviously.

"I swear to God, Amari, you better not say anything," I whisper sharply.

"You always think the worst of me."

"I wonder why that is," I mutter.

There's a ball of dread rolling around in my stomach as Noémie descends the short staircase. The little dog is yapping and clawing at the neckline of her romper.

Noémie stops near Amari and extends a hand. "Hi," she says, flashing her perfect smile. "You must be Jordan's sister. I'm Noémie—I work at the coffee shop with her."

Amari shakes Noémie's hand and returns the smile. "Yes, I'm Amari. I must say your home is absolutely stunning," she says, putting on her customer service voice. It's so fake that I almost miss the Toronto slang. "And who is this adorable guy?" My sister coos.

"Her name is Céline," Noémie replies proudly. Her grey eyes dart over to me and to the bag I carry. "Do you need help unloading the truck?"

"No," I say, at the same time Amari says, "Yes."

I glare at my sister and she glares back.

"I don't have a lot to unpack," I elaborate. Why is Noémie offering to help anyways? Seems out of character for her.

"If she's offering to help, why not let her," Amari says, still maintaining an air of politeness.

"It's no bother. Let me just put Céline down," Noémie says, rushing back into the house.

The moment she disappears, Amari whirls on me. "Nyeah eh, that bitch looks like Amy fucking Adams. And you're saying that you're not gonna fuck with her—okay buddy."

Chapter 10

I do up the last button on my collared shirt and debate about going for a more casual look by popping the top two open. I stare at myself in the full-length mirror—the full-length mirror in my walk-in closet. Never in a million years would I have thought that I would have a closet the size of a small office. I feel the urge to pinch myself to check if this is all real. This home—this bedroom, it's more than I deserve.

As expected, Amari hadn't helped me and Noémie unload the truck. Instead, she'd politely asked for the location of the washroom and disappeared for twenty minutes. I doubt she actually used the washroom. It's more likely she spent the time snooping. For whatever reason, she kept up her nice act whenever she was around Noémie. I'm worried about her motivations. My sister is never friendly for the sake of it.

Amari spat her venom only when Noémie wasn't within earshot range. "You dun know she wants something from you. Ah-lie, this is some *Get Out shit*. Don't trust it, fam," she said, screwing up her face as she rubbed her socked feet against the wooden planks. "The floors are heated—Eediat-ting! The utility bills must be mad!" I didn't bother commenting.

Shortly, after all my things were unloaded, Amari took off. I'm glad for it. She's a special kind of toxic that poisons a space by merely stepping foot in it.

Full of surprises today, Noémie volunteered to help me unpack. I'd been quick to turn down her offer to help me. Just the thought of Noémie handling my clothes made my body run hot. But I also just don't have a lot stuff. It didn't take long to empty the boxes and trash bags. My clothes were unloaded in the closet, and I neatly stacked my father's comic book collection on an actual bookshelf. I'm glad to have somewhere nice to finally display them. For the longest time, I kept them piled in a box.

After I finished unpacking, I spent the better part of the afternoon drawing on my tablet before taking a nap on my new bed. It's the comfiest mattress ever. Something tells me that I might not suffer from back pain soon.

Now, it's quarter to eight. I'm freshly showered, spritzed with cologne, and I've applied the barest of eye makeup. As I admire my reflection, I contemplate whether to put on a fitted Jays cap or leave my head bare. I'd gone to my barber less than a week ago —my fade still looks crisp. So I decide against wearing a hat. I also decide to pop open the top four buttons of my black collared shirt. Women love when I show off more skin. Over the years, I've gotten compliments on my collarbones and perky tits.

Tonight I'm in hunter mode. All hot and bothered from being near Noémie, I need to get laid.

Grabbing my leather jacket, I exit my new bedroom. A heavenly scent greets me as I descend the staircase. My mouth waters and my stomach rumbles, reminding me that the last thing I'd eaten was an everything bagel and double-double from Timmies around noon.

The party I'm going to doesn't start until 10:00 p.m., but Kristen wants to meet early at a pub. She's having girl troubles—Hailey's being an ass again. Sometimes, I want to smack some sense into my friend. Why can't she see that Hailey's a loser?

If I don't leave soon, I'll be late. But I'm drawn to see what Noémie's up to in the kitchen.

In the main room, Céline's asleep on the couch. Her tiny body is coiled like a doughnut. Her large dark eyes blink open for a second to register me. I fully expect her to start barking, but she doesn't. Instead, her tail does the most pathetic wag and then she's back asleep.

The overhead lights are dimmed, and the dining table near the sliding doors is set neatly for two. A decanter of red wine sits between the two settings. A large candle is lit, creating an almost romantic ambiance.

I know I have no right to feel irritated, but my skin prickles at the thought of Noémie having a romantic dinner with some dude. Then again, maybe he isn't random at all. While I haven't heard Noémie mention a boyfriend yet, that doesn't mean one doesn't exist. If the guy in the Ferrari shouting for her to get back into the car before peeling off is her boyfriend, she can do better. If I were him, I would never drive off without Noémie. I shake my head. What am I even thinking? I don't do girlfriends. I would never find myself in that position.

My gaze wanders towards the kitchen, and I suck in a breath. Noémie's bent over an open oven. She removes a bright-orange braising pot. Straightening, she nudges the oven door shut with her hip and places the piping hot pot on the counter. Turning around, she removes a pair of orange mitts and tosses them to the side.

When she looks up, she sees me. Her grey eyes widen, and she smiles. I melt. I almost smile back. But I manage not to and direct my attention elsewhere—to the dining table.

Clearing my throat, I ask, "Expecting company?" My voice doesn't betray me. I sound normal. Good.

"No. Why do you ask?"

Frowning, my gaze settles back on Noémie. Sassy, beautiful Noémie. And I hear Amari's words echoing in my head, "*You sleep with everyone.*" Rubbing the back of my neck, I tell myself that I can't flirt with Noémie. I tell myself that Noémie's straight and that it's never a good idea to pursue anything with a straight girl. I tell myself that I can't do anything to fuck up this living arrangement—I can't afford to live anywhere else.

"Is everything okay?"

"Yeah," I say. "There are two place settings. Is one for Céline?"

Noémie chuckles. "She's spoiled, but not that spoiled. I figured you'd be hungry after moving. But no pressure to join me," she says. "Looks like you're heading out."

"I have time to eat," I lie. In less than thirty minutes, I'm supposed to meet up with Kristen in the Village. We have a reservation at O'Grady's. But I'm not in the mood for pub fare, and whatever came out of the oven smells delectable. Also, Noémie set a place for me at the table. It would be rude of me to leave now.

Noémie grins. "Have a seat. I'll bring you a plate."

I shuffle over to the table and sit down. Pulling out my phone, I shoot off a text to Kristen.

> Jordan, 7:55 p.m.
>
> Hey, I won't make it to O'Grady's. Meet you at the party.

Kristen texts back almost immediately.

> Kristen, 7:56 p.m.
>
> Ur joking right?

> Jordan, 7:56 p.m.
>
> Sry. Something came up.

> Kristen, 7:56 p.m.
>
> u suck

> Jordan, 7:57 p.m.
>
> Luv you too :P

Guilt twists my insides, but only for a moment. When a wide-brimmed bowl is placed in front of me, I forget about Kristen and her problems with Hailey. Steam rises off the dish, perfuming the air with notes of garlic, herbs, and seared meat. My mouth waters. It's some kind of stew. Large chunks of beef mingle with root vegetables and pearl onions in a rich brown broth. A sprig of thyme sits on top of it all as a garnish. In its fancy, heavy white bowl, the meal doesn't look home-cooked, it looks professional—like something out of a restaurant or from the pages of a *Food Network Magazine*.

Noémie sets down a basket of crusty bread before taking her seat beside me.

I fiddle with the end of my knife. I'm eager to dive in, but I don't want to start eating before her.

To my dismay, Noémie doesn't reach for her utensils. Instead, she grabs the decanter and pours a glass of red wine for me and then herself. Noémie performs an odd ritual that I've seen on television and film but never in real life. She raises her glass, tilting it slightly to observe the wine. I'm not sure what she is looking for and I don't want to come off as stupid or uncultured, so I don't ask. She swirls the glass and brings the rim to her nose. She inhales deeply and finally takes a sip.

Her grey eyes narrow on me. "Do you not like beef bourguignon?"

"Thought it'd be rude of me to just dig in," I say.

"Take a bite. I want to know what you think," she says, taking another sip of wine. Her eyes are still on me, and the weight of her gaze feels like a caress.

My hand trembles slightly as I reach for my fork. I stab a piece of meat and put it in my mouth. The beef is so tender that I barely need to chew it, and it's well seasoned. I close my eyes and moan my pleasure. "Fuck, this is so good."

Noémie's cheeks colour from the compliment. "Glad you like it."

We eat mostly in silence, and the clinking of metal against porcelain acts as an awkward symphony. So many times, I think about saying something, but each question I form in my mind dies on my tongue. All the questions I want to ask seem forbidden. Like, I want to know what happened between Noémie and her father. What could be so bad that he'd cut her off? I want to probe Noémie about the restaurant she dreamed of opening. I want to inquire about the man in the Ferrari—is he her boyfriend? But Noémie and I aren't close, and I don't want to come across as nosy. So I keep quiet and focus on enjoying my dinner.

Bowl wiped clean with a piece of bread, I pop the last bit of food in my mouth and sit back in my chair. I reach for my glass and finish my wine.

Red wine is not really my thing. I'm more of a rum and Coke kind of girl, but I have to give credit when it's due because the wine Noémie chose pairs so well with the beef stew.

"So where are you off to?" Noémie asks.

"Going to a party in the Village."

"Alone?" She sits back in her seat.

"Nah, with a friend," I reply.

"Wayne says you don't date," Noémie says. "Why is that? I'm sure there are plenty of women who'd want to date you."

Her question is so direct and unexpected that my jaw almost drops. Of all the questions that she could've asked, why'd she have to go and ask this one? There's no way to truthfully answer without going into details about how messed up I am.

Samira tried to convince me to seek counselling or therapy. She told me that I needed to sort my shit out so that I could finally heal. She told me that she needed all of me and not scraps. She told me that crumbs can't feed a relationship.

My ex is right. I probably do need to speak to someone, but there's a tax on healing. Therapy is expensive, and it might not even help. Bringing up my past trauma might just make things worse. Why revisit the issue, if the wound is gone? Besides, I think my scars are here to stay.

Amari is the only person who knows everything. I went to her crying the moment after it happened, and she didn't believe me. My sister shut me down and told me to get over it.

I thought about telling my mom, but I didn't want her to know my shame. Paulette put up with enough bullshit at work at the hospital and didn't need my crap adding to her load.

If a relationship means having to explain myself—why I am the way I am—then I don't want one. Shrugging, I try to ignore the stinging behind the back of my eyes. "Relationships just aren't for me," I lie. "I get bored easily."

Noémie reaches for the decanter and pours herself another glass of wine. "Oh, okay, makes sense." I sense judgment in her tone, but it's subtle.

In a world where marriage is still prized as one of the greatest milestones, many can't conceptualize why anyone would willingly stay single. It bothers me that Noémie likely thinks less of me for my answer.

My phone buzzes and then buzzes again. I don't need to look at the screen to know that it's Kristen.

My chair scraps against the floor as I stand. "I'm so sorry, but I have to get going. Thanks for the meal, it was delicious."

I bend to pick up my dirty plate, but Noémie swats my hand away. "Don't worry about clearing the table. I can do it," she says.

"You sure?"

"Yes," Noémie says. She takes a long drink from her glass. "Have fun tonight."

Chapter 11

Light streams in from the large bay window, leaking in through the gaps between the blinds and painting bars across the bedsheets and my face. I squint and adjust so the band of light isn't in my eyes.

A warm body is draped on top of me. The woman smells like smoke, liquor, and sex. She's got stringy auburn hair and pale skin peppered with freckles. Last night—four drinks in—I thought she looked like a taller version of Noémie. This morning, I see that she's a complete counterfeit to the real thing. I try to recall her name, but it eludes me.

Her brown eyes flutter open. "Morning," she says, her voice raspy. She smiles.

"Morning to you too," I say.

She shifts her weight, laying her body flat against mine. She's completely naked, while I'm topless in a pair of Calvin Klein boxers.

Her breasts feel good pressed against my own. Without the filter of alcohol. She looks nothing like Noémie, but she's still quite beautiful.

She rocks her hips against me, stirring my desire. "You're so fucking hot," she says.

Our lips touch, and I roll her beneath me. I fuck her with one hand

and get myself off with the other.

I don't want her to touch me. I never let anyone touch me.

She cries out my name as she comes and tells me she loves me. It's kind of weird, but it's happened before. Women say things they don't mean when they orgasm. I don't love her. We just met last night, and I'm only just remembering her name—it's Nicole.

About an hour later, we are downstairs in the foyer and Nicole is stuffing her feet into a pair of Vans that look fresh out the box.

"I'm free later if you wanted to grab dinner," she says, shoving her hands down her jean pockets.

I scratch the area behind my ear. "I don't do dates," I say, refusing to meet her eyes. From experience, I already know what I will see in their depths—confusion and hurt. Sometimes, there's anger.

When Nicole slips through the front door without another word, I release a sigh and head for the kitchen. I almost jump when I see Noémie. She's standing by the island, a bright-orange protein shaker bottle in her hand. She's dressed in workout gear—tight-fitting yoga pants and an apricot sports bra. Her hair is bound in a high ponytail. Just the sight of her makes me want to run back upstairs and get off again.

"Good morning," I say with a forced smile.

Noémie doesn't smile back. She does the opposite. Her grey eyes drill into me, and she slams down her protein shake.

I flinch. "Did I do something?"

Instead of answering, Noémie gives me her back. I watch her tug open a cupboard and remove a bottle of what looks to be vitamins. Twisting the top off, she shakes out two pills and tosses them into her mouth.

My heart races. I hear it pounding in my ears. "Can you tell me what's wrong?"

Noémie's lips curl with disgust. "Esti de câlice de tabarnak, c'est pas possible d'être cave de même!"

I have no idea what she just said, but I know it can't be good. Fuck!

"What's wrong?" Noémie points a finger at me. "What's wrong is that I'm not running a brothel. I don't want random women in my home!"

Oh, she's not happy about Nicole. While I understand, I think her reaction is overblown. Still, I realize that I need to tread carefully. The last thing I need is her kicking me out over this.

"Look, I'm sorry," I say. "I didn't think—"

"Maybe you should start."

"I won't do it again."

"Yeah, whatever." Noémie rolls her eyes and storms out of the kitchen with her shaker bottle.

Collapsing onto a stool, I scrub my face with my palms and groan. It's been one day of living together, and I've already fucked things up. I should have asked Noémie if it was okay for me to bring women over. We're definitely going to have to discuss ground rules for this living situation. I need to know what else she's not okay with.

A long drawn-out whine disrupts my thoughts. I look down.

Céline's large beady eyes stare up at me. She paws at the base of the stool. Her nails clink against the metal.

I don't know what the dog wants, but I find myself sliding off the stool and sitting down beside her. The floor is pleasantly warm on my backside. Noémie's hydro bill must be massive. Is what I'm paying in rent really enough to cover her utilities?

Céline climbs into my lap like she owns it and curls up. It's a new experience for me. I've never been so close to a dog before. Lifting a hand, I awkwardly scratch Céline's head. She leans into my touch. I decide that I like Céline. Her presence is calming and nice.

What isn't nice is Noémie's attitude. I've never seen her so bratty. All week, at work, she gives me the cold shoulder. She refuses to speak to me or acknowledge my presence, which is a problem since I'm her manager. It's hard to manage someone who's actively ignoring you.

Wayne's acting as a buffer, filtering our communication to each other. It's so awkward. Not just for me, but for everyone on my team. Wayne isn't on my side, which kinda hurts. In his opinion, Noémie has every right to be angry at me. According to Wayne, I need to give the girl space until she gets over it. I don't even know what Noémie needs to get over. I told her I'm sorry already. And I have no intention of repeating my mistake. What else could she want?

I want to ask her, but she's made it impossible to. After our shifts, Noémie dips out of the coffee shop so quickly, taking off in her Tesla. And at home, whenever I try to talk to her, she stomps upstairs to her bedroom. Usually I'm the one who is childish when it comes to having tough conversations, but I'm nowhere near as bad as Noémie.

I've thought about following her up to the third floor. I've thought about knocking on her door and demanding that she talk to me. But thinking about it is as far as I'm willing to go. I need to tread carefully with her. If I've learned anything in our short time working or living together, it's that Noémie is volatile. You never know what side you'll get—sugar or spice. She really is a Gemini.

The silent treatment is killing me, especially since I've been given a glimpse at just how amazing living with Noémie could be. Our first night together, she made a space for me at her table. I think she'd been trying to befriend me. This last week, Noémie has cooked every single day. She eats and drinks alone. While I don't have any expectations of being fed, it also kind of sucks to see butter chicken simmering on the stove while I prepare my Indomie noodles in the microwave.

By the time our shift ends on Friday, I'm seriously considering changing the roster at work and moving Noémie from mornings to evenings. Wayne says she needs space, but I need space too. I can't deal with Noémie's negativity twenty-four seven. If I can't escape it at home, I refuse to be subjected to it at work.

After wishing Wayne and Kevin a good weekend, Noémie rushes out of the coffee shop, heading home. It's raining, and it would have been nice if she offered me a lift since we're going to the same place. But she isn't considerate like that.

I step out into the cool wet air and unfurl my umbrella. Heading for the subway station, an imaginary argument between us plays out in my head. I tell Noémie that her behaviour is juvenile and unprofessional and tell her that I'm slotting her to work nights. She doesn't like that. She gets angry. She shoves me. And then she kisses me.

I step in a puddle. "Fuck," I mutter. The cold water soaks through my shoe. Is there anything worse than a wet sock? Seriously.

Noémie's white Model X is parked in the driveway when I get home. Normally, she parks it in the garage.

Stepping into the foyer, Céline bounds towards me. She carries a squeaky toy in her mouth. When I bend down to pet her, she turns and runs away.

I chuckle. The dog is really starting to grow on me.

I go to my room, where I strip down and change into a pair of sweatpants, an oversized hoodie, and a fresh pair of socks. Ripping my tablet from its charging cord, I head back downstairs and go to the main room.

While the desk setup in my room is decent, I've always preferred to draw curled up on a couch. And unlike the dark basement apartment, Noémie's living room is bright and her couch has wide arms and cushions that are just perfect. It's my favourite spot to draw.

Usually, it's just me. And it's quiet—so quiet. It's a beautiful thing. I can concentrate in a way I've never quite been able to before. The result: I'm drawing faster than ever. Sometimes, I get so absorbed in what I'm doing that I don't make note of Noémie's presence until she slams a cupboard door or runs the faucet.

Throwing myself down on the couch, I click on the side table lamp and adjust my seating position until it's just right. I enter my flow quickly, transferring the images I see in my mind's eye onto the digital page.

With every stroke of my stylus, Zara Williams and her story become more real to me. As I add layers and depth and shading, I trick myself into thinking that what I'm producing is actually good—something worth sharing.

"What are you always doing on your iPad?"

Startled, I drop my pen. It falls in the crease between the couch arm and seat cushion.

"Nothing," I say, clicking the button on the tablet. The screen goes black.

Noémie leans against the archway leading to the main room.

I'm still annoyed at her for making me walk in the rain. I'm still annoyed at her for making my week hell. But my traitorous heart races the moment our eyes meet. All I can hope is that Noémie can't hear it. If she ever knew how much I wanted her, I'd probably find myself kicked out on the street.

I can't shake the feeling that part of Noémie's weeklong tantrum has everything to do with the fact that my guest had been a woman. Maybe it grosses Noémie out that two women had been fucking under her roof.

With Wayne, Noémie plays the role of an ally well. But she'd been raised in a homophobic household. Her father hates gay people. He's been quoted saying that gay, trans, and non-binary people are mentally ill and need help. Noémie doesn't look much like Hugo, but over the last week I've seen glimpses of him in her glares and dismissive gestures.

This evening, Noémie wears black Lululemon yoga pants and a cropped Billy Talent t-shirt, exposing the smooth plain of her stomach. Billy Talent is one of my favourite bands. In high school, I drove Amari crazy listening to "Try Honesty" on repeat. I doubt Noémie is familiar with any of their songs. In her early twenties, the Poutine Princess is a Gen Z—Billy Talent is way before her time.

Crossing her arms, Noémie approaches the couch. "Seems like it's something," she says.

While I'm happy Noémie's finally talking to me again, I'm not interested in telling her about my passion project. I don't want to talk to anyone about it. Never again. Pitching my first graphic novel had been the hardest thing I'd ever done. All these years later, I still taste the bitter residue of rejection.

Noémie's grey eyes shimmer with curiosity. She's waiting for me to say something. I keep my mouth shut.

"Digital art?" she asks.

I grit my teeth. "Yes, I like to draw," I confirm. "But don't bother asking to see it. I'm not comfortable sharing."

When Noémie nods instead of pushing for me to show her what I'm working on, I almost sigh in relief.

"Wayne mentioned once that you have a degree in fine arts," she says, taking a seat on the thick armrest on the opposite end of the couch.

Wayne talks too goddamn much. What else had he told her about me?

Noémie's gaze drifts upward towards the ceiling, and she leans back on her hands. She bites her lower lip, and her brows furrow in thought. It's the expression of someone who wants to say something but is engineering their sentences.

"The beginning of October is always hard for me," she finally says. "I know that I've been really bitchy these last few days, and I shouldn't have taken my anger out on you."

Now it's my turn to plan my words. I know what I want to say. It's on the tip of my tongue to ask why, but I have enough commonsense not to ask.

"You had every reason to be upset," I say instead. "I should have asked you if it was okay to bring someone over."

"Yeah, you should have," Noémie agrees. "I would have told you that it wouldn't be okay. I don't want strange people in my home."

"Fair enough," I say. "Am I allowed to have friends over?"

"I don't know. Maybe if I meet them first." She puffs out a frustrated breath. "I don't really trust anyone, even people I know. So having people I don't know in my space makes me uncomfortable."

It's my turn to nod. "I get and respect that."

"Do you, though?" she asks.

Our eyes meet. I see vulnerability flickering in the depths of hers.

"Yes," I say, meaning it. If Noémie doesn't want me to have guests over, that's fine. It's not a big sacrifice. I almost never had anyone over when I'd been living with Sarah. But that was mainly because no one wanted to commute back with me to Scarborough.

Noémie looks away first and stands. "I am going to warm some leftover butter chicken," she says. "Do you want some? It's one of my favourite dishes to make, and it usually tastes better the next day."

"Yeah, sure," I say, trying not to sound as excited as I feel. I hadn't been looking forward to the frozen Lean Cuisine I'd planned on warming up for dinner.

"Did you want me to help with anything?" I ask, following Noémie into the kitchen.

"Wanna set the table?"

"Sure."

Noémie pairs our meal with a crisp Riesling. It's the second wine she's selected that I quite like.

The butter chicken is succulent and packed with flavour—the best I've ever had. And the garlic naan is soft and buttery.

"You definitely should open a restaurant," I say, taking a sip of wine. "I'd eat there—if I could afford it."

Noémie's lips curve. She's not quite smiling, but I can tell the compliment pleases her. "Any plans tonight?"

I shake my head. "No."

Usually, I go out Friday nights, but I need to be conservative with my money for the next little while. Winter is coming and I'll need to get my bike ready to sit idle for the cold months. Getting it ready means bringing it into the shop for maintenance—and who knows what the mechanic might find wrong. Just last year, I had to change both tires.

And there'd been something up with the brakes. All in all, it's likely going to cost a lot.

"Do you want to watch something on Netflix?"

Noémie's invitation surprises me. "Was there something you wanted to watch?" I ask.

"No," she says. "But, I am down to watch anything that isn't a rom-com."

I arch a brow. "You don't like rom-coms?"

"You're telling me that you do?"

"I definitely do not watch *How to Lose a Guy in Ten Days* at least once a year."

Noémie coughs up some wine as she laughs. "Oh my God—you don't."

"I really don't see what's so funny."

"You just don't look like someone who would watch a movie like that," she says.

I guess that's sort of true. I'm quite masculine presenting, and I probably come off as someone who's a die-hard fan of the Fast and the Furious series—but I'm not. I can do without watching men measuring their dicks on screen for two hours, thank you very much.

"In my defence, Kate Hudson is a total babe in that movie," I say.

Noémie dabs the corners of her mouth with a napkin. "And Matthew McConaughey isn't too bad himself."

"Sure," I say, rolling my eyes.

Noémie insists on clearing the table. I drop down into my usual seat on the couch while she starts up the dishwasher. Grabbing the remote, I turn on the TV and begin scrolling through the Netflix catalogue.

"Find anything interesting?" Noémie asks, sitting down—right beside me.

My entire body stills. Our thighs are touching, and I can feel the heat coming off her. This close, her citrusy perfume is more intoxicating than the wine I drank with supper.

"I asked if you found something to watch," Noémie says.

I blink. "Ummm … no."

She plucks the remote from my hand. "You snooze, you lose. I'm going to pick."

I couldn't care less about what we watch. With Noémie this close to me, I don't think I'll be able to focus on anything.

Chapter 12

It's Monday, but the coffee shop is closed for the Thanksgiving holiday, which means I get to sleep in.

When I do finally roll out of bed, my first stop is the shower. I'm in the process of towelling off when I hear the ruckus.

Céline is barking at the top of her lungs. A man begins shouting, and then Noémie's shouting back.

Not knowing what to think, I pull on the first shirt and pair of pants that I can get a hold of and hurry out my bedroom and start down the stairs.

Standing in the foyer, a tall man with broad shoulders and auburn hair towers over Noémie. "Why do you care so much about what he thinks?" he yells, fists balling at his sides.

Noémie looks about to answer, but then she notices me and closes her mouth. The man turns his head, following her gaze.

"She's my roommate," Noémie blurts, crossing her arms over her chest.

"Roommate," he repeats.

"We also work together. Her name is Jordan." Noémie pins the man with a look that says he better play nice.

I take that as my cue to descend the last few stairs and introduce myself. I extend my hand to the man. "Nice to meet you."

I notice that his eyes are very much like Noémie's. Perhaps slightly darker grey. He looks me up and down. His gaze is a scale, weighing my self worth and value.

"Jordan," he says, taking my hand in his own. His grip is firm. "I'm Claude—"

"My brother," Noémie chirps.

"Nice to meet you, Claude," I say, dropping his hand.

Claude smirks. "You should bring her to Thanksgiving dinner."

Noémie purses her lips. "Like I said, I'm not going to dinner unless I'm invited." Bending, she scoops up Céline who's still yipping and whining.

Her brother rolls his eyes. "We both know Hugo's not going to do that, but you know our mother wants you there. She misses you."

"Then she should be the one asking me to come, not you."

Claude releases an exaggerated sigh. "Can't say I didn't try." He turns towards the front door. Before leaving, he smiles at me. It's a predatory smile full of teeth. "It was a pleasure meeting you, Jordan."

When the front door clicks shut, Noémie walks over to the front window facing the street and opens the blinds slightly. She watches her brother slide into a red Ferrari—I recognize it as the one she'd stormed out of weeks ago.

Claude reverses out of the driveway and peels off.

Noémie closes the blinds. I don't think she realizes that I'm still around because she sags against the wall and slides down to the floor, burying her face in Céline's coat.

I move in her direction.

She looks up at me. Her grey eyes sparkle with unshed tears. She looks so small and sad. This is a side of her that I've never seen.

I want to wrap her in my arms and hold her tight. But doing that would cross a boundary. We aren't friends. So I don't.

Céline squirms in Noémie's arms until she's free. The dog shakes its body violently and takes off down the hallway.

Noémie hugs her knees. I drop down beside her and hug my own knees. Our shoulders brush.

"Do you want to talk about it?" I ask.

Noémie shakes her head.

I don't press for an answer. I don't move. I just sit with her in the silence.

A sad sigh escapes Noémie's lips, and she leans to rest her head on my shoulder. The scent of her shampoo makes me dizzy.

"Claude hates our father so much," she states, "and he's always looking for ways to punish him. I'm so sick of it."

I frown as I digest what she just told me. "Don't you hate your dad for cutting you off?"

"No, he has his reasons," Noémie says. She doesn't elaborate.

I nod and try not to notice how our bodies touch at multiple points, how hot I feel all over. My fingers itch to comb through her hair, so I sit on them.

A hush ferments between us. I can't say what is going on in Noémie's mind. Her gaze seems so distant. Me, I'm trying to think of something to say to tether her back to reality and make her smile.

"So you're not celebrating Thanksgiving with your family … Did you want to join my family dinner?" I ask.

Noémie lifts her head from my shoulder. Her lips curve up slightly. "Sure, if it won't be too weird."

I don't tell her that it might be weird. I've never brought a friend over to meet my family—not even Sarah. My mother always took that to mean that I was embarrassed of where I grew up. She wouldn't be wrong. Also, I can't say how my mother and grandmother might react to seeing Noémie. I can't bank on Amari being polite. I can't rule out that my cousins won't be jerks. But it's too late to take back the invitation.

At quarter to four, I climb into the passenger seat of the Model X and fasten my seatbelt. Noémie starts the car, and we are off, heading out of the city core and eastward towards Scarborough.

Noémie's playlist is a blend of new music and early 2000s hits that take me back to high school. It surprises me that she's familiar with The Used and Evanescence.

"Aren't you a little too young for this music?" I ask, rotating in my seat to look at her.

Noémie's hands visibly tighten on the steering wheel. "The Used was my sister's favourite band …" She clears her throat. "And she had an unhealthy obsession with Amy Lee."

I hadn't known Noémie had a sister. Then again, I just learned today that she had a brother. There's so much about her that I don't know.

"She has great taste in music," I say.

"Yeah, she did," Noémie whispers.

Fuck! "I'm so sorry."

"Don't worry, it's okay," Noémie says, sparing me a brief glance before turning her attention back to the road. "She died years ago …"

"That doesn't mean it doesn't still hurt," I say, thinking about my dad. "The hole of your grief might get smaller with time, but it never goes away."

"Isn't that the truth," she agrees. "October fifth was the anniversary of the ... the incident. Antoinette got hit by a car. When that date rolls around, it's like I feel everything all over again. If that even makes sense."

"It does," I say. "My father overdosed three years ago around Christmas, and I can't find it in myself to feel merry around that time."

"I guess we have something in common."

"Guess so," I say. I'm not sure why I told her about my dad. It's not something I usually share.

"Were you close with your dad?" she asks.

I blink. "It's complicated," I say. "Before my parents divorced, my dad was always around. He was the one who picked Amari and I up from school and made us dinner. My mom's a nurse, so she's always worked crazy hours. After the divorce, my grandmother moved in, and my dad's visits became more infrequent with time."

"That sucks, I'm sorry."

"It's okay. It is what it is." I sigh. It crosses my mind that now is the perfect opportunity to ask the question that's been weighing on my mind. "What's the deal with your parents? Why'd your dad cut you off?"

"There's nothing much to say. My family is dysfunctional. It's always been that way, even before my sister passed," Noémie says. She pauses for a moment, and I assume it's because she's trying to choose her words carefully. "My father has expectations of me and Claude, and if we don't fall in line ... it's a problem. And even if my mother doesn't agree with him, she always takes his side."

"I hate that for you."

"It's okay. It is what it is," she says, parroting my earlier words.

Noémie turns up the music. I take that as a hint that she doesn't want to talk anymore, and we don't speak for the rest of the drive.

Arriving at the apartment complex, Noémie parks in a visitor parking space. The shiny Model X stands out amongst the other vehicles in the lot.

When I exit the car, I examine the weathering orange brick building with its rusting grey balconies. Parma Court is one of the rougher places in the General Toronto Area. But as a kid, I never felt unsafe running around the neighbourhood. In fact, I often look back fondly on the days when my cousins and I played tag in the narrow alleys that were always peppered with brown and green glass from shattered beer bottles. I remember summers filled with reggae and R&B, and the aroma of barbecue mingling with the sweet notes of marijuana.

It had been a time before smartphones and unlimited streaming. Adults spent the better part of their days drinking, smoking, and slamming down dominos. Teenagers tended to congregate around the rec center or at the basketball court that had hoops without nets and cracked asphalt. Generally, kids were left alone to wander and explore. The only rule had been that Amari and I needed to be back inside before the streetlights came on.

Yeah. Sometimes, I remember the good things—the laughter, the camaraderie, the adventure. Mostly, I only recall the bad things. Like how the apartment building is infested with roaches that happen to find their way into everything—even the ice cubes in the freezer. Like how rowdy the neighbours are and how often fights breaks out. There were too many nights to count where I was awoken by the ring of sirens and a show of flashing red and blue lights leaking through the sheer curtains covering my bedroom window.

But nothing turns my stomach more than the groups of young men chilling on the block, who holler at girls the moment their boobs start showing—it's disgusting. As a teenager, I often had to outmanoeuvre being grabbed or fondled. And then there was the time I wasn't so lucky.

"You okay?"

I blink and look at Noémie. "Yeah, I'm good," I say, scratching the back of my neck. "Maybe, I'm a little embarrassed. This isn't Yorkville."

Noémie rolls her eyes. "I know what you think of me, Jordan, but I'm not a rich white girl who expects everyone I interact with to come from money," she says. "I would never judge my friends for where they come from."

She called me her friend. She thought we were friends. I smile at her, and she smiles back.

Chapter 13

We step off the janky elevator into the dimly lit hallway. One of the few working lights flickers. A fusion of cigarette smoke and cooked food flavours the air. Behind one of the doors, a baby wails. Once upon a time, the carpet was red. Now it looks brown. I eye the peeling wallpaper and feel ashamed.

We reach my mother's apartment, and for a second I just stare at the door. Sighing, I lift my hand and knock.

Noémie adjusts her hold on the bottle of French wine she brought from her collection. I told her that she didn't need to bring anything. She insisted, saying that it'd be rude to come to dinner empty handed.

Paulette cracks the door open.

Today, my mom's wearing a dark-blue house frock and one of her signature satin bonnets. A smile begins to blossom on her lips, but it wilts upon seeing that I'm not alone.

"You didn't tell me you were bringing a *friend*," she says flatly.

I silently curse myself. I should have given my mom a heads up that Noémie was coming.

Stepping back, Paulette swings the door open wide.

Noémie and I shuffle inside. The apartment smells like Jamaican food—pimento, Scotch bonnet peppers, and sautéed onions.

While my mom never openly voiced disapproval of my sexuality, I know how she feels about me being a lesbian—she doesn't like it one bit.

My mom's not good at controlling her face. If she doesn't like someone or a situation, her eyes and the set of her mouth lets you know exactly what she's thinking. Right now she's thinking that I have some nerve. Paulette's dark-brown eyes pinball between me and Noémie. She's wondering if we're together. She decides we must be. She isn't impressed. She doesn't want me to go to hell.

I clear my throat. "This is Noémie, my roommate," I say.

My mom's expression doesn't soften.

"Very nice to meet you, Ms. Alexander," Noémie says. Then, unexpectedly and before I can stop her, Noémie leans over and brushes her cheek against my mother's, making one of those kissing noise.

Every muscle in my body seizes as I watch the exchange. Generally, my family isn't touchy. We barely hug. Greetings are usually reserved to fist-bumps.

My mother stares at me with a look that says, *Is this girl mad?*

"She's French," I explain.

"French," Paulette repeats with a huff.

If Noémie detects the strain in the atmosphere, she doesn't show it. Grinning wide, she holds out the bottle of wine. "For you. It's a Bordeaux—pairs well with beef and lamb."

My mother accepts the offering, sticking the bottle under her arm. "Thank you, Noémie. Make yourself comfortable. Dinner will be ready soon." With those words, she leaves us, disappearing behind a green, yellow, and black beaded curtain that leads into the kitchen.

Noémie nibbles her lower lip. "That could have gone over better. I'm sorry."

"Don't worry about it. I should have warned you about my mother. She isn't always the most welcoming," I say, holding out my hand. "Give me your coat, I'll hang it up."

Noémie removes her taupe peacoat and hands it to me. She bends to unzip her boots.

I try not stare, but Noémie looks stunning this evening. She's got on a cream cable knit dress, which she's styled with a thick gold buckle belt that cinches her waist. Her auburn hair is down. Orange maple leaf stud earrings glint in her ears, matching the glossy polish on her neatly trimmed nails.

Usually short nails are a flag, signalling that woman might not be quite straight. I've never seen Noémie sport those fashionable acrylic talons that are favoured by most chicks. But because of Wayne, I know that Noémie prefers short nails for practical reasons. During a slow hour at the coffee shop, they'd been talking about nail art. Wayne asked Noémie why she wore her nails so short.

"They aren't very hygienic," Noémie responded. "Can you imagine trying to knead dough with those things on?"

Wayne looked at her like she'd turned into a gargoyle. Before that conversation, he hadn't known that Noémie is a master chef in the making.

After hanging up our stuff, Noémie and I move over to the living room and sink down in the larger of the two red corduroy couches.

Noémie crosses her legs. My eyes follow the movement, and when I realize that I'm staring at her legs, I drop my gaze to my lap. I clear my throat. "So, I know I said dinner starts at five, but … it never does."

"That's fine," Noémie says.

I scratch the back of my ear. "If you're hungry, I'm pretty sure the soup's ready. I can get you a cup. Have you had Jamaican yellow soup before? It's pretty good."

"No, I haven't tried it before," she says, "but I'm good for now."

"Okay."

Beres Hammond's smooth voice fills the space. The song, "Tempted to Touch," feels a little too on the nose for this moment. God must have a sick sense of humour.

I resist groaning. I resist looking at Noémie. But my bouncing knee gives away my anxiety. I scan the living room, picking out things I hope Noémie doesn't notice. Like the fine dust coating the picture frames and the base of the TV stand. The rug has seen more years than I've been alive. It looks its age—stained and fraying. The parquet floors have seen better days too. Much of the varnish has flaked off.

Noémie speaks, but I don't catch her words. I look at her. "Sorry, what'd you say?"

"Artist in the family?" she repeats, cocking her chin towards the wall displaying more than a dozen of my sketches and paintings—a timeline of my progress.

Looking at my past work makes me cringe. My first attempts at realism were really, really bad. I've tried to get my mother to take them down, but she's stubborn. Paulette will only remove something if I give her a replacement, which is not happening. I only draw for myself now.

"Yes, my Jordan is so talented," Grandma Janet says, coming from out of nowhere.

Both Noémie and I rise from the couch.

I enfold my grandmother in a hug. Yes, my family isn't touchy feely, but Grandma Janet is the exception. "This is my roommate, Noémie," I say, pulling away. "Noémie, meet Grandma Janet."

Having learned from her encounter with my mother, Noémie only extends her hand in greeting. "Very nice to meet you," she says. "I have to say, before today, I didn't know just how talented your granddaughter is. Jordan refuses to show me her drawings."

"It's nice to finally meet one of Jordan's friends," my grandmother says, clapping Noémie on the back. "Oh, let me get you some soup. It will do your belly good." She leaves and returns moments later with two steaming Styrofoam cups brimming with soup.

Noémie and I take a cup.

From the kitchen, my mother calls out for my grandmother.

Stiffening, Grandma Janet yells back, "Lawd, nuh cry out me name suh." She tuts her irritation. "Better go and see what she wants."

When my grandmother disappears behind the beaded curtain, I blow on my soup and try to ignore the weight of Noémie's eyes on me. She stirs her soup with a plastic spoon slow and methodically. I choose to ignore the spoon and silently slurp some of the fragrant yellow broth. The broth is flavourful in the best way, with notes of pumpkin, thyme, and pimento. But it's far too hot and I burn my tongue a little.

Noémie moves towards the wall of my artwork. I follow her. I don't want to talk about my cringey sketches and paintings, but I want to be close to her.

Noémie's fingers fiddle with the plastic spoon as she assesses a sketch I did of Amari. "You are really talented," she murmurs.

The compliment makes my heart skip, and it's times like these that I'm grateful to be melanated. My face is hot, but Noémie won't be able to tell that I'm blushing.

Lifting the spoon to her lips, Noémie takes a dainty sip. "Ah, c'est délicieux," she says, closing her eyes. "I will have to ask for the recipe."

"I'm not sure my mother will give it to you," I say. I like that Noémie likes the soup.

"I can be very persuasive."

"Is that so?" I arch a brow.

"I usually get my way," she replies, smirking.

I'm about to say something, but I get distracted when the apartment door opens. My sister steps inside—with Samira.

The world slows for a moment. Samira's gaze darts between me and Noémie. She scowls. Even though we've been broken up for forever, I think Samira is under the pretence that I'm still hers—that I'll always be hers.

Amari, who's holding a large box of Popeyes chicken, notices Samira's dark expression and shoots me a look meant to maim. I brush it off.

My ex looks good this evening. Her locs are so much longer now, passing well past her shoulders. She's dyed the tips blond. I wonder who she's fucking now. Do they know Samira likes her hair pulled right before she climaxes? Do they know how wild she gets when her sides are nibbled? It's always easy to forget about Samira when she isn't around. Out of sight, out of mind. But whenever I see her, the memories come flooding back, along with the heartache and wanting.

Samira and I were so good together. We should have been end game, but apparently, I never loved her—if I actually loved her, I would have let her touch me.

"You're selfish and you are broken, and you don't let anyone in, Jordan," she said. Even all these years later, it stings recalling her words.

Still standing by the door, Samira kicks off her Timberland boots and slides out of her Canada Goose puffer jacket, revealing a black turtleneck dress that clings to her taut body and sizeable tits like a condom.

Samira looks up at me before I can look away. I don't like that she caught me staring. I turn away from my ex, deciding that I need fresh air.

.

Chapter 14

It's windy on the balcony. I light up a cigarette and lean against the rusty railing.

Behind me, the door squeaks open and clatters shut.

I smell Noémie's citrusy perfume before I see her. "You okay?" she asks.

People only ever ask that question when it's obvious that someone's not okay. It's such a dumb question, but my hearts skitters all the same. It's nice to know that Noémie cares—or is pretending to care.

I don't respond. Mainly because I'm not sure what to say.

I take a drag from my cigarette and stare down at the parking lot. The view is bleak—kind of like my life.

"You know you can talk to me," Noémie says, nudging her elbow into my side.

Can I really? Noémie doesn't know me, and I barely know her. She said we are friends, but we aren't actually. Still, in the span of a few days, we've gone from not talking to each other to conversing about loved ones long departed. I never talk about my dad. Never brought him up to Sarah or Wayne, even when probed. But I opened up to

Noémie about him. Maybe that means something?

"There's nothing to talk about," I say.

"I'm not buying that, but if you don't want to talk about it, I get it." Noémie sighs. "Lord knows there's a lot I refuse to talk about." She holds out her hand, gesturing for the cigarette.

I pass it over.

Noémie takes a long pull. The end smolders red. She blows out a breath of smoke and hands it back. Her lip gloss left a mark on the filter.

Possibly, I'm a sicko, because I feel a bit giddy when I suck on the end that was just in her mouth.

"I wasn't expecting to see Samira," I confess.

"The woman with your sister?"

"Yeah."

Noémie's brows draw together. "You guys have history?"

"You can say that," I say, drumming my fingers on the balcony railing. "She's that person for me, you know? The person I can't shake—like a piece of me will always belong to her." I'm saying way too much, more than I usually would, but it's too late to take back my words.

Noémie's nods like she understands.

A gust of wind whips her auburn hair about her face, and I catch myself almost reaching out to push the strands back out of her eyes.

"So you're in love with her," Noémie states, folding her arms across her chest.

I shake my head. "No, not anymore." I stare back down at the parking lot. The streetlamps have come on. It gets dark so early now. I hate it. "It's more like, when I look at her, I remember. And sometimes I wish things were different … that I was different."

"I get that," Noémie says, leaning her back against the railing. "My ex did a number on me—turned my life upside down. Looking back, I wish I could have done things differently too. But maybe things are supposed to happen the way they happen. Maybe we have to go through the tough shit to appreciate something good when it comes along."

I'm not entirely following Noémie's bit of sage wisdom, but I nod because I want her to believe that I get it. Also, I'm happy that we've moved away from talking about my drama and that we're talking about her.

"Is this a recent ex?" I ask, stamping the cigarette out in an ashtray.

"Yes."

"What'd he do?" I want to know what kind of dumbass fool would let a woman like Noémie slip through his fingers.

She nibbles her lower lip. "I'd rather not talk about it."

I don't press for more information. I want to, but I don't. Instead, I shrug, feigning indifference.

If there's anything I've learned about Noémie, it's that I don't know anything at all. She keeps her cards closer to her chest than I do. But I want to know everything about her. It's such a stupid thing to want. I need to get over my crush.

"We should probably head back inside," she says.

I nod.

When we step back inside, Uncle Weston walks into the apartment, followed by his two sons, Ezra and Samuel.

Ezra is the same age as me. He's built like a basketball player—strong and tall. He's handsome and always carries himself well. His cornrows are always tight, and his goatee is always neatly trimmed. As kids, we'd been inseparable, but in our teenage years we grew apart, which is kinda sad. There are times when I miss him and the bond we once shared.

Ezra hitched himself to a rough group of friends since high school. For years, he hasn't been on a good path. He's gone to jail more than a handful of times—all his charges were drug related. But, according to my mother, my cousin is finally trying to turn a new corner. I love that for him. I hope he succeeds.

Uncle Weston's younger son, Samuel, is the exact opposite of his brother. He's all bones, acne, and awkwardness. He dresses like a Pokémon trainer. Despite only being five years apart, Samuel looks so much younger—perhaps because he can't grow a beard to save his life.

I move towards the group and sense Noémie following closely at my back.

Uncle Weston beams at me. "Wagwan!" he says, holding out a fist.

I commit to the greeting ritual, bumping his fist. "Nottin' much. Am good, Uncle Weston."

I turn towards my cousins and give them props as well.

Their gazes focus behind me—on Noémie. I can tell they're very interested to know who she is and what she is to me. Though, Ezra's black eyes glint with something that reads more like hunger than intrigue.

I tense.

Again, I'm regretting my decision to invite Noémie. The last thing I want to see is Ezra turning his charms on her. Noémie deserves better than what he can offer her.

Where women are concerned, Ezra's track record for breaking hearts is a thousand times worse than my own. At least, I've always been honest and upfront with the women I sleep with. I've always made it clear as crystal that I don't do relationships. I've never strung anyone along. But Ezra, at any given time, has at least three women he's talking to. Women who think he's serious about them.

Ezra grins. "Who's your friend?"

"Noémie," I say.

"And she's with you?" Ezra asks, arching a brow.

I grit my teeth.

Besides Ezra's seedy friends, another reason for our rift is the fact that he consistently denies my sexuality. He thinks that a lesbian is just a woman who hasn't found the right man yet. When Samira and I were dating, that didn't stop him from throwing game at her every chance he got. I still hate him for that.

I'm half tempted to tell him that Noémie is with me, but before I can even think to utter something, Amari pushes her way into the conversation, stating, "Nah, they're just roommates."

I drill my sister with a hard look. Amari grins like the devil she is.

Ezra stretches his hand out toward Noémie. "Nice to meet you, Noémie," he says in a deep and buttery voice.

Noémie shakes his hand, and when her face flushes, my stomach curdles. I taste something sour in my mouth.

"I need to use the washroom," I say, skirting around my family to get to the narrow hallway. I walk past the two bedrooms and yank open the bathroom door, shutting it behind me. I flip down the toilet seat and sit on the lid, holding my head in my hands.

My heart's beating fast like a hummingbird's wings. I'm hot all over. I'm being so stupid. So what if Ezra wants to flirt with Noémie? So what if she likes it and flirts back?

The doorknob turns.

"Occupied," I say, bolting to my feet.

But my ex walks in despite my warning. She's the last person I want to be alone with right now.

"I'll be out in a bit," I say, blowing out a breath. "You can leave."

Samira ignores me. She closes the door and turns the lock.

I swallow. "What the fuck are you do—"

"Shhh," Samira says, pressing a finger to my lips. "Don't tell me you've forgotten this game. We need to be quiet."

"Seriously, Samira—"

She encircles my neck with her arms, cutting my words off with a kiss.

Like an idiot, I kiss her back. Like an idiot, I push her up against the wall and force my leg between her thighs. Like an idiot, I graze my lips down her neck and suck at her beating pulse.

"Fuck, I missed you," she purrs into my ear. "You look good."

Samira smells just like I remember, like coconut body butter. The familiar scent dislodges a thousand memories from wherever the hell they'd been stuck. They float to the surface of my mind, and I'm reminded of all the mornings we spent together wrapped in each other's arms. And of the nights we went clubbing and danced until the overhead lights were flipped on, signalling that the party was over. I remember the laughter, the fights, and the passion.

I'd thought she was my ride or die. I saw us getting married. I'd even been saving for a ring. But Samira craved something more than I could give her. She wanted all of me—heart and body. She wanted me to surrender to her, and I just couldn't. I don't like to be touched. Samira believes there's something unnatural about touch-me-nots.

"You're so broken," she told me more than once.

The memories are sobering. I pull away. "We can't do this."

"Why not?" She pouts, trying to tug me back.

"Because nothing's changed," I answer.

Frankly, I'm surprised she came after me in the washroom. For five years, we've circled each other cautiously without exchanging more than a few sentences. I'm not entirely sure what her agenda is for being here right now. Whatever it is, I want no part of it.

"There's no point stirring shit back up between us," I say.

Samira shoots me with a dark look and folds her arms over chest. "Maybe I've changed," she says with a huff, her nostrils flaring. "But maybe you're right. Maybe there's no point in stirring this shit back up again. From what Amari tells me, you only go for chicken nuggets now—you're all about that white meat."

My jaw clenches so tightly that my teeth hurt. So that's her agenda—she's jealous of Noémie. It grates on my nerves that her dig at Noémie involves race. Why does it always have to be about race with my sister, Samira, and my family?

Not wanting to have it out with her in the bathroom, I throw open the door and nearly collide with Noémie.

"There you are," she says, wringing her hands. "Dinner's ready."

Samira steps out of the bathroom and makes a big deal of righting her dress.

Noémie's eyes grow wide as her gaze flickers between me and my ex.

"It's not what it looks like," I say, although I'm not sure why I feel the need to explain.

Noémie blinks and stands a little straighter. "Sorry, I have to pee," she says, sliding past me. The bathroom door clicks shut behind her.

Samira chuckles. I glare at her.

My ex pinches my cheek. "You've always been so adorable when you're pissed."

I bat her hand away and return to the living room.

Minutes later, everyone is gathered around the oval table. Dishes of curry goat, oxtail, jerk chicken, rice and peas, steamed fish, and fried plantain are set out. Turkey isn't a thing in our Caribbean household.

The room is stifling and humid, and I'm itching for a cigarette. But I can't disappear outside until after the food is blessed and I have eaten.

Grandma Janet stands at the head of the table where a stack of disposable paper plates and plastic cutlery mark the beginning of the queue for food.

Back from the washroom, Noémie sidles up beside me just as the prayer starts.

I'm not sure I believe in God, but we are expected to close our eyes and bow our heads, so I do it when Grandma Janet starts to speak.

"Father God, blessed almighty, may you lay your hands on this food before us so that when we eat it, it does our body good," she says. "For you are the lord of lords and the king of kings. And to you we give all of the praise …"

The hum of my grandma's prayer fades into the background as I crack an eye open to look at Noémie. Not only are her eyes clammed shut and her head bowed, but her hands are clasped together too. Considering her religious upbringing, I shouldn't be surprised that Noémie is taking the prayer as seriously as Grandma Janet, my mother, and Uncle Weston.

Across the table, Amari and Samuel are snickering about something. Samira's eyes are half-closed, and I can feel her gaze on me. Ezra's focus is entirely on Noémie.

I scowl at him. The bastard winks at me.

"Bless and sanctify this food!" Grandma Janet finally cries out. "In God's name we pray. Amen."

Everyone does as directed and says amen.

Grandma Janet is encouraged to grab the first plate, and a line forms behind her. Noémie and I are at the back of it.

Amari doesn't bother lining up. She won't be eating any of the prepared food. My sister has always been the pickiest eater I've known. Ever since she landed her first job, she stopped eating anything home-cooked, preferring to buy takeout. Her diet mainly consists of pizza, McDonald's, and Popeyes chicken—she's lucky we've inherited great metabolisms.

Naturally, both my mother and Grandma Janet are hurt by Amari's refusal to eat anything they prepare. "Scarnful dawg nyam dutty pudding," they'd often tell my sister. The Jamaican idiom loosely translates to "people who act haughty are soon humbled."

I keep waiting for the day to come when Amari is finally humbled. I'm starting to lose hope.

I pile my plate with curry goat and rice and peas, spooning on some gravy from the stewed oxtail. Personally, I'm not a fan of oxtail meat, but the gravy is bomb.

It pleases me to see Noémie take a bit of everything. Has she ever had Jamaican food before? She's such a foodie. I wonder if my mother's and grandmother's food will meet her high standards.

The two couches are full, so Noémie and I perch against a wall to eat.

"Is it good?" I ask after she's taken a few bites.

When Noémie nods curtly, I wonder if she's lying, if she actually dislikes everything she's putting into her mouth. But she's making a huge dent in her plate. I've never seen her eat so fast. So maybe she does like it. I hope she does.

For some reason, I get the sense that she's mad at me. The atmosphere around us just feels off again, like all the progress we've made towards building our friendship today is corrupted. I'm not sure what she could be mad about. Does she think I lied to her about Samira? Out on the balcony, I'd told her that I was over my ex, and pretty soon after Noémie saw us exiting the bathroom together.

Having inhaled everything on his plate, Ezra gets up from the couch, tosses out his plate and makes his approach.

He leans in very close to Noémie. His musky cologne is too much, and I bite my tongue before I can say anything about it.

My cousin asks Noémie what she does for a living, and how she knows me.

Noémie beams at him. It's the same smile she gave me when I offered her a job. I hate that she's looking at him like that.

My cousin and Noémie hit it off, and it's not long before their conversation dips into flirting territory. Noémie is touching his arm and leaning in close.

It makes me sick. I seethe.

I run off to the balcony for a smoke.

Chapter 15

Noémie barely speaks to me the rest of the night, and I'm fine with that. The drive back to Yorkville from Scarborough is quiet, minus the drone of the music.

I go to bed convinced she's mad at me. I'm mad at her too, even though I have no right to be.

I'm fully expecting to go through the same silent treatment bullshit as before. So imagine my surprise when I find Noémie waiting for me by the front door the next morning. She smiles at me, rousing the butterflies in my stomach. All the anger I feel swirls down an invisible drain.

"It's raining," she says, tucking her hair behind an ear. "I thought you might wanna ride into work with me."

My tongue ties and I'm tripping over my words. "Umm … yeah, thanks."

The rain isn't coming down hard. It's a sad, pathetic dribble. It's the kind of weather that extinguishes my motivation to do anything.

Noémie pulls up to a curb and parks. I swing open the car door and step out into the cold.

Wayne's huddled under an umbrella near the front doors to the shop. He waves at Noémie and makes room for her to join him under the canopy. The two of them dive into a conversation that I can't quite hear as I fiddle with the store keys.

Once inside, our ritual begins. I rush to disarm the alarm, Noémie starts arranging the seating area, and Wayne does nothing until I remind him that he should be working.

I'm just finishing loading the cash register when I hear Wayne screech, "Jay has never extended me an invitation to meet her family." He pops a tray of frozen croissants into the oven and slams the door.

I snort. "Like you would even want to."

"You know that I'm dying to meet Amari," he says. "I have a hard time believing half the things you say about her. She can't be that bad."

Noémie chuckles and sets down a spray bottle she'd been using to wipe down the front counter. It's sticky for some reason, and whoever mopped the floors Sunday night did a piss-poor job. There are shoe prints all over the place.

"Whatever Jordan told you about her sister, it's probably an understatement," Noémie says.

I arch a brow at her. "How do you figure that? You two barely spoke." Also, Amari continued being extremely polite to Noémie, for whatever reason.

"She brought Popeyes for herself when there was an entire spread of delicious home-cooked food. I don't think she ate anything that was prepared. Like, your mother and grandmother must've been so upset."

"They've gotten used to Amari's particularities," I say. "My sister hates Jamaican food. She hates anything that isn't McDonald's, pizza, or Popeyes." I pick up a syrup bottle and frown because it's empty. And where the hell is the whole milk? There's none in the fridge beneath the counter.

I make a mental note to have a chat with Gordie, the evening shift manager—the night staff are not carrying their weight.

"I don't know how anyone can hate Jamaican food," Noémie says. "C'est délicieux."

I like it when Noémie speaks French. It's sexy. But I know the reason my chest suddenly feels warm is because Noémie voiced that she enjoys Jamaican food—a part of my culture.

The coffee shop opens and the rush starts almost immediately. But it isn't chaos. The shift passes by smoothly—too smoothly. There hadn't been a single complaint or slip up, and I can't remember another time of that ever happening.

Noémie's quick on the espresso machine. We work well together, almost operating like a fine-tuned engine, pumping out americanos, lattes, and macchiatos like we're competing in the barista Olympics.

After work, I stay back fifteen minutes to give Gordie a piece of my mind. When I exit the shop, Noémie is outside scrolling through her phone, leaning against a wall. She looks up at me and grins, and I want to bottle up her smile to preserve it forever.

"Thought you might want a drive home," she says, pushing off the wall and sliding her phone into her pocket.

The warmth I'd felt earlier spreads throughout my entire body like a fungus. Why is Noémie being so thoughtful? I can't quite believe she waited for me. Part of me wishes she was the complete bitch that I once thought her to be. How will I ever get over my stupid crush if she's nice to me?

Once home, Noémie swaps her work clothes for work out gear and heads down to the basement gym.

After a fast shower, I slip into a black hoodie and a pair of baggy sweatpants before collapsing into my favourite spot on the couch. I get comfy, arranging the cushions in the way I like, and begin to draw on my tablet.

I'm in the process of sketching out one of the last scenes for the third volume of *The Diaries of Zara Williams* when Noémie struts into the main room. Fresh out of the shower, all the makeup is scrubbed from her face. Still wet, her hair looks more dark brown than auburn in its ponytail. She wears an oversized grey cardigan that looks almost like a robe, a white camisole, orange leggings, and her favourite Givenchy slides.

Noémie is so fucking beautiful it hurts. Like, I actually fucking hurt. There's a painful ache developing between my thighs. I'm not someone who usually uses words like yearn, but that's what I feel. I yearn to touch her, even if it's just trailing a finger down her cheek, even if it's only for a second.

I bite down on my lower lip.

"You ever going to show me what you're working on?" she asks.

I turn the tablet face down in my lap. "I'm not working on anything."

"You're such a bad liar," Noémie says, moving into the kitchen.

She begins rummaging through the fridge and cupboards, and I go back to drawing. Or, at least, I try to. I'm feeling self-conscious.

The scene I'm working on depicts Zara Williams and Detective Pamela Cross kissing after barely escaping a shootout that broke out in an abandoned warehouse. Zara isn't a hundred percent match for me—her hair is much shorter than my own and she's a tad more feminine, with her pop of red lipstick and thick eyelashes. Pamela is also not a carbon copy for Noémie, with her green eyes and mole just above her lip. But there are enough similarities between us and my characters for me to be anxious about Noémie getting the wrong idea if she were to catch a glimpse of the drawing.

I peer over my shoulder. Noémie's deep in concentration chopping up some vegetables. Deciding the coast is clear, I go back to my sketching.

There's something relaxing about drawing to a background soundtrack of sizzling oil and pots and pans clinking. Back at the basement apartment, I hated the constant reminder of living with someone and neighbours above me. But I don't mind Noémie's noise.

A heavenly aroma fills the space, making me salivate. My stomach growls, and I take that as my queue to warm up some instant noodles.

I try not to get in Noémie's way as I reach into the cupboard to grab the red-and-white package of Indomie.

"What are you doing?" Noémie asks, flipping her ponytail over her shoulder. "Dinner will be done in a bit."

I blink. "Oh." I shut the cupboard.

"If you wanted to help to set the table, I'd appreciate it," she says with a smile.

After I nod, Noémie gives me clear directions—I guess I set the table wrong the last time. I arrange the mats and flatware as specified.

Around seven, dinner is ready, and we sit at the table together. Seared salmon with a citrus breadcrumb crust is the star of the dish. According to Noémie, the side is made up of sautéed peppers, shaved fennel, preserved lemon, parsley, and olives. A thick orange sauce decorates the side of the heavy white plate.

Failing to remember my table manners, I dip a finger in the sauce and lick it off. When I look up, Noémie is staring at me oddly. Her lips part, and a subtle crease forms between her brows.

"It's good, what is it?" I ask, trying to make conversation.

This is the third time we're sitting down for dinner together, and I feel more nervous than ever. Why is that? I'm not sure, but I'm hyper-aware of how domestic the atmosphere is.

Growing up, it was a rare event for my family to eat a meal together. More often than not, I ate off cheap plastic plates with mismatched cutlery in front of the television or at my desk.

Noémie pours us each a glass of white wine and she responds to my question. "It's a saffron orange butter sauce. Pairs well with most fish."

"Cool, cool, it's very good," I say, nodding like an idiot. My ears burn. My face burns. I just burn all over. I hope Noémie can't tell.

"I'm glad you like it." She reaches for her wine, her long fingers wrapping around the stem. She takes a long-measured sip, and my gaze dips to the movement at her throat as she swallows. I stare down at my plate and decide that I won't look back up until I've finished eating.

Noémie's a hell of a cook, and it takes effort not to wolf everything down. But even trying to eat slowly, Noémie's only halfway through her meal by the time I've cleaned my plate.

I'm on my second glass of wine, and the alcohol makes me feel looser, more relaxed. Setting down my knife and fork, I lean back in my chair. I'm feeling chatty all of a sudden. "I hope Thanksgiving dinner wasn't too awkward last night," I say.

"It was wonderful—magnifique." Noémie pops a small forkful of fish in her mouth. She chews.

"Really?"

"Yes, I loved the food. You'll have to get me the recipe for the soup and that oxtail dish."

I scrunch my nose. "I hate oxtail. Love the gravy though."

"Why?"

"It's slimy and there's barely any meat."

Noémie laughs. I really like it when she laughs. "I'll try to remember that," she says.

"So, just to confirm, you didn't feel too awkward." Yes, I'm probing, which is weird for me to do, but I can't shake the feeling that she'd been the slightest bit upset with me last night.

"I had a good time," Noémie confirms. "I'm happy you invited me."

"I'm happy you're happy. But … it just seemed to me like you were a little annoyed towards the end." I really don't know why I can't let this go. Usually, I'm not the type to push for information.

Noémie's lips press firmly together. "I guess I was a little irritated that you didn't find a way to break me away from Ezra. I was clearly giving you signals to get me out of there," she says. "Somehow, I ended up giving him my number, and now he's texting me. Ugh …"

I frown. She's kidding right? She's got to be gaslighting me. She had totally been flirting obnoxiously with my cousin, laughing at all his stupid jokes and touching his stupid arm.

"I thought you were enjoying Ezra's company," I say.

"He's so not my type," Noémie states. "And if you were paying any attention, you would have realized that I was pretty much begging to be whisked away."

"I was paying attention," I argue. "But whatever signals you were flashing weren't loud enough."

Noémie rolls her eyes. "My signals were obvious. I couldn't have been more obvious without coming off as rude."

Was that true? Had my jealously skewed my vision, making me see things that never happened? It's possible.

"I'm sorry. In the future, I will try to be more observant."

Noémie grins over the rim of her wine glass. Her grey eyes sparkle. "Thanks."

"So if Ezra isn't your type, what is?" I ask. It's a bold question. I'm not sure I want to hear the answer, but I want to know.

Noémie frowns as she contemplates her answer. "Naturally, an appreciation for good food and wine is a must. I like confidence, but not cockiness—"

"Ezra's one cocky bastard. He's definitely not for you." I chuckle.

There's a flash of a smile on Noémie's lips, but it doesn't reach her eyes. Her expression sobers, and she stares down into her wine glass. "Trustworthiness is probably at the top of my list," she says.

Clearly, that comment is directed at her ex—the one who did a number on her, turning her life upside down. I wonder what he did to break her trust. Had he cheated? Men always cheat. On a balance of probabilities, that's likely what happened. It's hard to believe that anyone would cheat on Noémie. Then again, even Beyoncé got cheated on—Beyoncé! Most men are dogs. I'm thankful that I'm hopelessly gay and never have to deal with the opposite sex romantically.

After dinner, I insist on tidying up. It's only fair since Noémie cooked. It takes me half an hour to load the dishwasher, scrub the pots and pans, and wipe down the counters. While I clean, Noémie sits on the couch with a second glass of wine and Céline curled in her lap.

Noémie pivots in her seat and looks at me over the back of the couch. "Did you want to watch something?" she asks.

"Yeah, sure," I say.

A minute later, I plop down on the couch on the opposite end from Noémie. It's a calculated decision. I want to be near her, and that's why I need to stay far away.

Chapter 16

Noémie and I fall into a routine of sorts. Weekday mornings, she drives us to work. For the most part, our shifts fly by easily, and then once home, Noémie works out while I put the final touches on the third instalment of my graphic novel.

Almost every night, we eat something different. I'm getting exposed to so many different cuisines and wines. I try duck breast for the first time. I'm so hesitant to try it. The meat is pink and that trips me up. But Noémie assures me that's how it's supposed to be. All my life, I've been told not to eat meat that's not cooked through. I've also been led to believe that white people don't season their food. Noémie's food never tastes bland—she's testing my beliefs. Duck breast is now my favourite thing in the world—that crispy skin, it's bomb. Tastes kind of like Hickory Sticks.

After dinner, I make it my job to get the kitchen in order while Noémie relaxes on the couch with a second drink. Before heading off to bed, we usually watch Netflix. Currently, we're watching The *Haunting of Hill House* since it's spooky season.

I'm not quite sure when the change happened, but I now sit beside

Noémie on the couch, our legs touching. It's bittersweet. As we spend more and more time together, I adjust to being constantly aroused. It's somehow both easier and harder to be around her—if that even makes sense.

The Saturday before Halloween, I'm at the shop getting my motorcycle serviced for the winter when Sarah video calls me for the first time since she's left.

"Hey, it's been a while," she says. "Whatchu saying?"

I turn up the volume on my phone to hear her better and step out of the noisy shop. "Nothing much, just at the bike shop."

"Cool, cool," Sarah says.

There's something off about Sarah's tone. "Everything good?"

Sarah sighs. "Veronica and I just got into a fight—a big one."

"Fuck, sorry to hear that." I sit down on a bench just outside of the wide garage doors. "Wanna talk about it?"

"Not really."

"Okay."

"I'd rather hear what's up with you. What's it like living with the Poutine Princess?" she asks.

"Not sure we can keep calling her that," I say. "Her father cut her off, remember?"

"You find out why yet?"

I play back the conversation we had in her car on Thanksgiving. "She says that her father has expectations of her, and if she doesn't fall in line, it's a problem," I say.

"So she basically didn't tell you."

I frown. When Sarah puts it that way, it does sound like Noémie skirted the question. Thinking about it, there are a lot of questions she hasn't given me a straight answer to. Meanwhile, I keep going into greater specifics about myself and my past. It doesn't sit well with me that I'm opening up and she's refusing to bud.

Our new friendship is lopsided. Noémie won't let me in, while it seems like she tells Wayne any and everything. At work, the two of them are always whispering and sneaking off to the stockroom to have secret conversations. I've been trying to let it slide. Things with Noémie are so good at home now, and I don't want to break the peace. But I feel left out.

"So what's it like?" Sarah asks, breaking me from my thoughts.

I slump down a bit on the bench. I don't know what to say. What I should say? Frankly, I'm dying to talk to someone about Noémie. Usually, I go to Wayne with girl problems, but I can't now, not when the source of my problems is his new bestie. He's compromised and can't be trusted to keep his mouth shut. I can't risk my truth getting out. I don't want to make Noémie uncomfortable. I don't want to be kicked out.

I end up telling Sarah everything.

"Sounds like you're catching feelings," she says.

"It's not that serious."

"You just told me that you haven't gone out in forever. You also said you're planning to stay in on Halloween instead of partying in the Village? Like, who the hell are you? Where's Jay? This straight girl is changing you, buddy."

"I've gone out every Halloween for years," I say. "Honestly, I'm looking forward to dressing up and handing out candy to kids."

Sarah snorts. "You hate wearing anything that isn't black, and you hate kids."

I don't bother denying it. Sarah knows me too well.

"Bruh, she's domesticating you and you guys aren't even smashing. Seriously, Jay, you need to get laid. Don't wrap yourself up in this straight girl. You know you're just asking for trouble."

"I'm not wrapping myself up in anything. She's my friend."

"And you were my friend …" Sarah goes silent for a beat, and then I hear her sigh over the phone. "Like, I can speak about it easy enough now, but when I was deep in my feelings for you—fuck, it hurt so much. I don't want that for you."

"I hate that I hurt you," I say.

"You never hurt me. I hurt myself. I knew we couldn't be together, but I put myself in a position where I was always around you."

I slump even farther down the bench. Propping the back of my head on the wooden back rest, I stare up at the sky. It's a somber grey. There aren't clouds. It's just haze.

∽

I don't go out for Halloween.

While I totally agree with Sarah about needing to put some distance between myself and Noémie, I lack willpower. Besides, I already promised Noémie that I would stay home with her and hand out candy. I can't back out of a promise, right?

Not to mention that Noémie would kill me if I ditched her. She takes Halloween very seriously. At least, more seriously than anyone I know. She went all out, decorating the interior of the Victorian with glittering orange pumpkin banners and fake cobwebs. Outside, three cartoon gravestones stick up from the tiny patch of lawn. A skeleton with glowing eyes hangs on the green door.

A week earlier, Noémie coerced me into carving pumpkins with her. Noémie's jack-o'-lantern turned out picture perfect while mine boasted a lopsided grin with teeth that were too small. I should have used a template—I shouldn't have winged it. According to Noémie, my carved pumpkin looks far better than hers, but I disagree. Both our pumpkins sit on the stairs that lead up to the entrance.

It's almost 6:00 p.m., and I know that it's just a matter of time before trick-or-treaters start ringing our bell. Noémie's in the kitchen reheating leftovers for dinner while I sit on the couch, reviewing the third volume of the Zara Williams series one last time. The plan is to start outlining the fourth instalment next week.

The bell rings. Céline goes ape-shit and runs towards the front door. I hope her barking doesn't scare the kids off.

"I can get it," I say, tossing down my tablet.

I rise and tug back on the thick red cap with the M emblem on it that completes my Mario costume. I look fucking ridiculous and can't take my reflection seriously. I've never dressed up before. Not even as a kid—but that had more to do with my mom deeming Halloween a pagan and ungodly holiday.

When Noémie first proposed the idea of us dressing up as Mario and Princess Peach, I laughed it off, thinking she'd been joking. The joke was on me. A couple days later she presented me with my costume and she'd been so fucking excited. I didn't know how to say no to her. So I'm stuck feeling stupid and sporting the bristly faux moustache and the blue overalls with its large gold buttons. I can put up with a bit of discomfort if it makes Noémie happy.

"Trick or treat," a group of six kids shout when I open the front door. There's a little girl dressed up as Elsa and a boy dressed up as Buzz Lightyear. The other costumes are lost on me.

As directed, I drop two full-sized chocolate bars into each of their outstretched bags and wish them a good night.

Closing the door, I set down the candy bowl and shake my head. In grade school, some of my classmates bragged about getting full-sized chocolate bars on Halloween. Not once had I ever witnessed or received that miracle myself.

There'd been a few years where my dad secretly took Amari and I out trick or treating. My Halloween haul had mainly consisted of stale tootsie rolls, rockets, and those cheap lollipops that are always chipped or completely shattered.

But here I am, more than twenty years later, distributing two full-sized chocolate bars to each kid who knocks on my door. It must have cost Noémie a small fortune to buy all this candy. I wonder how she can afford it.

The doorbell rings again, and I pick the candy bowl back up. I get stuck at the front door for the next twenty minutes. There are so many kids! Where the hell did they all come from? I hadn't known there were any children in the neighbourhood. The evidence of their existence isn't anywhere to be seen. No bikes litter front lawns. No basketball nets hang over driveways. No chalk drawings paint the sidewalk. As I distribute the chocolate bars, I wonder when Princess Peach will make her grand appearance— she's the one who suggested we do this together.

Finally, there are no kids in sight, and I'm able to escape my post at the door. I hurry back to the living room and discover what kept Noémie.

I go very still for a moment before my hands clench at my sides. I see red. "What are you doing?"

My tablet slips from Noémie's fingers, dropping to her lap. She bites her lip.

Not waiting for an answer, I rush over and snatch the device and click the screen off. Anger and embarrassment ripples through me like a gong. If I were a cartoon character, I'm sure steam would be whistling from my ears.

I point a finger at Noémie. "What the actual fuck—you had no business going through my shit."

Noémie has the audacity to roll her eyes. "Je m'en fous. I don't get why you're so pissed."

"I'm pissed because you know—you know that I didn't want you to see …" My words trail as my anger mixes with panic. How much did Noémie read? Did she see the resemblance between Zara and myself—Pamela Cross and herself?

Noémie shakes her head. The movement makes her crown topple. She's quick to right it. "Look, I'm sorry if I made you upset. I guess I shouldn't have looked," she says. She stands and comes over to me. Her dress makes her look like Pepto-Bismol threw up all over her. Somehow, she's still so fucking hot.

Our eyes meet, and I look away.

"I really don't get what the big deal is. Why do you insist on hiding your work? I read about two chapters and it's so fucking good. You're so talented, Jordan. You're doing a disservice not sharing your art with the world." She tries to take my hand in hers, and I pull it back.

I give her my darkest look. She stares right back at me. There's an electric current between us. Can she feel it too?

Noémie licks and bites down on her lower lip. My eyes follow the movement. Feelings overload my system. I'm pissed off, anxious, and horny. The room is too hot.

The doorbell rings.

Céline starts barking. Noémie takes a step back, blinking. She adjusts her crown and runs her hands down the puffy skirt, smoothing it out. Rushing out of the main room, she dismisses me like I don't matter.

Gritting my teeth, I fling off the stupid red cap and stomp upstairs to my room. Fuck Noémie. She can hand out candy by herself. I'm done for the night. I tear off the fake moustache and trade in the overalls for a black tee and a pair of sweatpants.

Throwing myself down on my bed, I stare up at the ceiling. My hearts thumps so hard in its cage that I fear it might escape. Scrubbing my face with my palms, I groan. I should have listened to Sarah—I should have gone out tonight. But maybe it isn't too late. The night's still very young. A spark of bad judgment makes me text Audrina.

Jordan, 6:57 p.m.
Whatchu saying tonight?

Almost immediately, three little dots pop up on the screen. They disappear as fast as they came. Twenty minutes pass, and I decide that Audrina has finally had enough of me. Not surprising. It's about time.

I tap onto the TikTok app and scroll. For how long, I don't know. Sometimes, I'm grateful for the time portal that is social media. Other times, I hate that hours will fly by in a wink—a whole day gone.

There's a knock on my door. I sit up.

"Jordan, can we talk?" The door muffles Noémie's question.

It's only after I reply, "Yeah, sure," that it dawns on me that I don't want to talk. I don't want to see her.

Noémie steps inside my bedroom. She looks absolutely ludicrous in her bubble-gum pink dress with its puffed sleeves. But she only looks ludicrous because she's out of character—not smiling. Princess Peach shouldn't look miserable.

She takes a seat on the edge of the bed and turns to face me. "Look, I've been thinking, and I'm sorry that I snooped," she says with a sigh.

I snort. "You don't sound sorry."

"Well, I am sorry." Her cheeks colour. "Clearly, I overstepped, even though I don't get what the big deal is."

"I draw for myself, nobody else."

"And why is that?"

I don't owe Noémie an answer. Not when she's been tight-lipped about herself. A friendship shouldn't be one-sided. She doesn't need to know that I reached for my dream once only to crash and burn. She doesn't need to know that I gave up drawing for years only to pick it back up to escape my grief. I miss my dad so much. Even though we barely saw each other towards the end, I never questioned that he was my biggest fan. If he was still around … maybe I could try to dream again.

A ball forms in my throat. I sniffle.

"Jordan?" Noémie whispers. She rests her hand on my leg.

"Why do you even care?" I say, moving so her hand falls onto the mattress.

Silence steeps as seconds tick by.

"You know … Antoinette was really into comics and manga," she says finally. Her voice wavers. Noémie stares down at her lap. There's a glimmer in her eyes. I don't think I've ever seen her look so sad and small. "She was gay—I don't think I told you. And you know how my father is …"

I do know how her father is—homophobic.

Once, Noémie called him confused, but I have seen enough of his interviews to know that he's an awful, hateful man.

I remember how Noémie's voice faltered at the coffee shop when she identified herself an ally. Had she been reminded of her sister then? Is that why she stumbled over her words?

While I'm super glad Noémie's opening up, I question her disclosure. Why now? What's changed? Is she only opening up because she fucked up and went through my shit?

To date, our deepest conversations happened on Thanksgiving. Our friendship is surface level—as deep as thin-crust pizza. We stick to safe subjects. We talk about TV shows and movies. We talk about food and fashion. We talk about work. We don't talk about anything that really matters. I don't know Noémie's position on the conflict in the Middle East, and she doesn't know mine. I'm a Liberal, but I don't know if Noémie's a Conservative like her father. I don't know if we have shared values. I have no insights into her past relationships beyond the tiny morsel she fed me on the balcony. She never mentions her friends or family.

Sure, I don't offer much up either, but I've definitely shared a lot more.

Noémie clears her throat. "My sister used to complain so much, and Claude was so annoyed. I don't remember being annoyed, but I didn't get her constant need to talk my ear off about the lack of queer representation or feeling forced to stay in the closet. She whined so much about having to hide her *L Word* DVDs and Batwoman comics," she says. Wiping her eyes, she stares up at the ceiling. "I'd give anything to hear her complain again."

A magnetic force pulls me towards her, I scoot down the bed until we are sitting side by side.

Noémie tenses when I place my hand on top of hers, giving it a gentle squeeze.

She locks eyes with me. "I'm sorry that I looked at your artwork. I didn't mean to, I swear. It's just that the display was on, and I glimpsed an image of two women holding hands, and I was reminded of Antoinette's obsession with Batwoman. And I just …" Noémie releases a breath with her entire body. She goes quiet for a beat. "You're so talented, Jordan, and the world needs more stories like yours. There aren't enough."

I don't know what to say to that. It's hard to think when she's looking at me with pained intensity. In the dim light of the bedroom, Noémie's eyes look more blue than grey—she's so fucking beautiful.

I'm not angry anymore, but I'm not sure I fully forgive her. I don't like that Noémie has seen a side of me that I've reserved for myself. Still, I hate seeing Noémie so upset even more. I want to pull her into my arms and hold her until the hurt in her eyes recedes. It occurs to me that I can do that. I wouldn't be crossing any lines by hugging her. We're friends. Right? Friends comfort friends. Right?

Deciding to go for it, I lean forward.

My phone vibrates. I look down at the screen. There's a message from Audrina.

Audrina, 8:47 p.m.

Heading home around 10pm

Want to come over tonight?

I'd love for you to tear my nurse costume off with your teeth

"I didn't know you were still talking to Audrina," Noémie says. There's a bite to her tone. "At least ...Wayne mentioned something about her being crazy and not being able to take a hint."

I turn my phone over face down. "You really are such a snoop," I say, almost playfully.

"I guess I am." Frowning, Noémie rises to her feet. "It's been a day. I'm going to sleep."

"You don't want to finish watching *The Haunting of Hill House?*" I ask. I'm in the mood to watch it, and we only have one episode left. We decided to save it for tonight. I want to sit close to Noémie on the couch. I want to talk some more. I want something more than I can have.

"No," she says. "I'm exhausted."

I nod and try to hide my disappointment when I say, "Okay."

Before she leaves, Noémie pauses in the doorframe. She looks over her shoulder at me. Her mouth opens like she's about to say something. But she doesn't. She exits my room, closing the door behind her.

My phone vibrates again. I flip it over. I'm met with a selfie of Audrina looking every bit the part of a naughty nurse in her white corseted outfit.

I heart the photo, and then reply to her last message.

Jordan, 8:51 p.m.
Yeah, sure. Can you pick me up?

It's probably not a good idea to keep stringing Audrina along like this, but if I can't be with Noémie, I might as well be with someone else tonight.

Chapter 17

It's fucking cold outside. Wind slices down the narrow cobblestone streets of Toronto's Distillery District, but I barely feel it. My insides burn hot like lit coals—all because Noémie's arm links through mine as we stroll past the various vendors at the Christmas market.

Items for sale line tables. I spot hand-painted ornaments, sweaters knit from alpaca wool, and maple syrup—lots of maple syrup.

There are long queues behind the mulled wine stand. There's an even longer tail of people waiting to be served gooey raclette shovelled over roasted sausage and potatoes.

A few weeks ago, Sarah told me that I was catching feelings for Noémie. And now, I can't deny it—it really is that serious.

The epiphany came two nights back. Noémie and I were watching some guy restore paintings on YouTube. I like his videos. The restorer's voice is soothing, and there's something oddly relaxing about watching someone clean old varnish off a painting with cotton swabs. There's a special beauty in repairing an object once thought to be unsalvageable.

I don't know when I went offline, but when I woke up, a sleeping Noémie was curled in my arms with her face nestled against my chest, her breaths even and soft. Afraid that the slightest shift might wake her, I stayed motionless. It was within that stillness that I realized I had fallen flat on my face in love with my straight roommate.

I've been trying really hard to not let my feelings impact how I treat or act around Noémie. I think I'm doing a good job. But even before my revelation, Wayne caught on that I liked Noémie a lot, and he didn't like it one bit.

Since Halloween, not a single shift goes by without Wayne cornering me when no one's around. "Don't do it—just don't. I swear if you pull game on my Noémie and break her heart, I will fucking kill you," he warned me more than once.

Each time, I deflected, saying, "What game? We're just friends, seriously. And I think you keep forgetting that she is straight."

"When has that ever stopped you?" he countered, sounding very much like Amari.

That Wayne thinks so poorly of me gnaws at me. Sure, I get that Noémie's his new favourite person, but aren't I his friend too? It feels like he's picked a clear side and labelled me as some kind of predatory lesbian, which I am not. I've never pursued anyone who didn't show interest in me first. And even if Noémie expressed interest in me, which she hasn't, I like to think that I'd shut that down. After all, we live and work together. I know it's never smart to shit where you eat.

There is also the fine detail that I'm in love with her. I can't sleep with someone I have romantic feelings for. I'm not putting myself through hell again. I'm not interested in getting close to someone just for them to realize that I'm broken and break things off with me.

So I'll be keeping my feelings and my hands to myself. Wayne's got nothing to worry about. All I can hope is that the day comes soon when I can look at Noémie without my heart pirouetting.

At this moment, I can feel Wayne's eyes burning holes into my back. He isn't thrilled that Noémie invited me to tag along to the Christmas Market. There's also a palpable tension between him and Noémie, but I can't guess what they're beefing about.

It's a quarter past seven at night and the historic site sparkles from the millions of lights hanging over our heads and encasing art sculptures.

The main Christmas tree is in the square. At fifty feet tall, it towers over everything, glittering like distant galaxies. Both Noémie and Wayne snap a bazillion photos of the tree while they wait in line to take an unobstructed photo of themselves in front of it.

Personally, I'm not interested in having my picture taken. In the last few years, I've become somewhat of a grinch around Christmas. But when Noémie grabs my hand, I become putty and allow her to steer me towards the base of the giant fir.

Wayne glowers at us as he takes our picture. Noémie definitely notices his ire, but she doesn't comment. So I decide not to either. They're acting so weird.

Staple jingly holiday music peppers the air. To me, it's as pleasant as screeching car brakes. Once upon a time, Christmas had been my favourite time of the year. But after my dad died, I started hating the entire month of December.

Despite being cold enough to turn a person's legs into popsicles if they don't move for a minute, the Distillery District is more crowded than ants on a dropped sugar cube. We aren't free to walk and have to shuffle with the herd.

Noémie stops at a vendor's table, eyeing tiny silver trinkets and jewellery.

Wayne picks up a pair of snowflake dangle hook earrings with inlaid white and blue stones. "These are giving Elsa in her frozen castle realness," he says. Flipping them over and peering down at the price tag, he dramatically rolls his eyes and sets them back down. "I will have to hold off on my *Frozen* fantasy until I'm rich."

"I can get them for you," Noémie says, "if you want."

The two friends exchange a look. I can't quite believe it when Wayne says, "Thanks, but I will pass on that offer."

I've never known Wayne to turn down anything he wanted. I'm even more curious to find out what they're quarrelling about.

"Oh look, they're giving out free samples," Noémie says suddenly, snatching Wayne's hand and tugging him away from the table. They hurry off without me. My guess is that Noémie wants a moment with Wayne alone to talk about whatever it is that's going on.

Without Noémie's nearness, I become aware of just how cold it is. The tips of my fingers burn, and I can't feel my toes. I look over my shoulder and watch Wayne and Noémie weave through the crowd, heading towards a woman carrying a tray of what looks to be miniature smores.

My eyes go back to the table. I spot a necklace with a maple leaf pendant set with orange stones that I think would be perfect for Noémie. The seller sitting behind the table monitors me closely as I pick up the necklace. When I look at the price tag, I'm sure my eyes bulge. Two hundred dollars!

It kind of kills me a bit that I can't afford it. Christmas is two weeks away, and while I don't celebrate the occasion anymore, I want to get Noémie something nice. I want to watch her unwrap my gift and shriek with delight.

I put the necklace down on the table and then pick up the earrings Wayne had been coveting. They were even more expensive at three hundred dollars. Could Noémie even afford them?

It's a question I've been asking a lot lately. For someone who's cut off, Noémie doesn't spend like she's hurting for cash. She goes shopping a lot, and Amazon packages are always showing up on our doorstep. I hope she isn't taking on debt to fund her lifestyle. I've thought about broaching the topic of money with her, but I don't want to overstep.

With a sigh, I head in the direction Noémie and Wayne rushed off to.

Despite the crowd, I find Wayne easily enough. Mainly because he's wearing the most ridiculous toque, with a pompom the size of a grapefruit.

And then I see Noémie and … the entire world drains of colour and sound.

A tall man holds her by the hips. Noémie's mittened hands are twined behind his neck. Their bodies are pressed together. They are kissing.

I am repulsed but unable to look away. My heart shrinks, becoming two sizes too small. My knees wobble. How long I stay rooted there, gaping at the tableau in front of me, while people shove and brush past me, I can't say. It's probably only a second or two, but the moment stretches out like chewed bubble gum in a child's hands.

The man and Noémie pull apart. Their mingling breaths cloud together.

A giggle erupts from Noémie mouth. "I can't believe we just did that," she says.

"Blame the mistletoe," the man says, rubbing the back of his exposed neck.

He isn't wearing a hat, and his tousled brown hair falls into his very blue eyes. The black Moose Knuckles parka he's wearing is unzipped down the front, and I decide he must be crazy because it is freezing. What kind of person doesn't zip up their jacket when it's like minus twenty outside? I also decide that I hate him. Men that look like him are always trouble. With his chiselled jaw and broad shoulders, he's far too attractive to be safe.

Turning slightly, Noémie notices me. She smiles.

I try to smile back. I can't. Every fibre of my body wants to bolt. Sarah always liked to joke that running is my default.

My fingers itch for a cigarette. But I have none. I'm trying to quit again. Reaching into a pocket I withdraw a pack of nicotine gum. I pop one in my mouth and chew.

I stumble forward until I reach the group. I can't begin to guess at what expression is on my face, but I hope it reads as neutral.

Wayne looks irritated. He shoves his hands deep into his pockets.

"This is Felix. He's an old … friend." Noémie says. "Felix, this is Jordan, my roommate."

Felix assesses me for longer than what's socially acceptable. There's a competitive glint to his blue eyes.

He holds a hand out. "Nice to meet you, Jordan."

"Same," I lie, taking his hand. He squeezes. The bones of my fingers mash together. We stare intently at each other. It's a pissing contest. Whoever blinks first loses. I'm not entirely sure why he feels the need to compete.

Someone clears a throat—Noémie. She is giving Felix a look that's colder than the weather.

Felix drops my hand.

Wayne grumbles something I don't catch, and Noémie shoots him a glare.

Chapter 18

When we get home from the Christmas market, I rush off to my bedroom so fast that I forget to take off and hang up my jacket in the coat closet.

Whatever.

I'm going a little insane, to be honest. The image of Noémie kissing Felix plays over and over in my head like a bad song, and each time it does, a cocktail of emotions braids a barbed rope tighter around my heart.

To my dismay, Felix stuck around for the rest of our time at the market, clinging to Noémie like she was a helium balloon and he was a kid scared to loosen his grip on her string. All fucking night, I'd been haunted by the timbre of his voice and Noémie's responding laughter.

I learned a lot about their relationship that I could've have gone without knowing. They'd met four years ago on a first-class flight to Vegas. Noémie had just turned twenty-one and she'd been flying to Sin City with friends to celebrate. It was supposed to be a girls trip but, after uncovering that Felix and his buddies were also staying at The Venetian, the two groups merged.

Specifics of what exactly they'd gotten up to in Vegas weren't provided, despite Wayne's constant probing. Each time, Felix was about to say something damning, Noémie interrupted him with a spearing look, resulting in Felix saying, "What happens in Vegas stays in Vegas."

Over the years, the two friend groups linked up for other events like attending Tomorrowland in Belgium or hitting up Paris for fashion week. These were the experiences of the rich, and Felix's connection with Noémie really hammers it home just how out of my league she is.

I throw my jacket on my desk and strip down to my sports bra and boxers. There's a headache building behind my eyes. Collapsing on my bed, I rub my temples.

Noémie knocks on my door. "Hey, Jordan, do you have a sec?" I rise up on my elbows and stare at it.

I don't have a second. I want to be alone. But for some stupid reason, I say, "Yeah, sure come in."

The door creaks open, and Noémie steps inside. She looks at me and goes still. Her face flames as she diverts her gaze.

If she was someone else, I might interpret her reaction to be attraction. But it's more likely that she's never seen a woman in boxers before. I consider grabbing the oversized shirt laying on my nightstand and pulling it over my head, but I decide not to. All night, I had to endure Felix's presence. Noémie can stand to be a little uncomfortable for the duration of this exchange.

"What did you want to talk about?"

Noémie bites her lip. "I just wanted to check on you."

"Why?"

"You seemed off tonight."

Great, I failed at coming off as neutral. My head pounds. "I hate

Christmas," I say. It's not a lie.

"Because of your dad?"

I nod, but don't offer up much else.

Noémie wrings her hands. "I'm so sorry," she says, meeting my eyes. "I guess it was inconsiderate of me to ask you to come out."

"It's okay." I shrug.

Noémie shakes her head. "It really isn't."

"It is—I'm a big girl. Besides, my dad's passing is just one of the many reasons I hate the holidays."

"There are others?" Noémie frowns.

"Yeah, the holiday season has never been a merry time for me," I confess.

Noémie inches closer to the bed. "Can I ask why?"

I take a moment to consider whether I want to tell her. Funny enough, I do. "My mother usually works during the holidays to get the pay bonus. And for the longest time, Amari and I celebrated Christmas with my dad's side," I explain.

There's more to say, but I'm not quite sure how to put into words what I experienced growing up. How can I explain the feeling of not belonging? My father's ancestry is a blend of Norwegian and Scottish. The Alexanders are tall, blond, and blue-eyed. The Alexanders are all dentists, lawyers, or engineers. The Alexanders all drive BMWs and own homes that can almost rival this townhome, but not quite. In other words, they are whiter than Wonder Bread, and Amari and I are not.

I clear my throat and stare down at my lap. "I think Amari and I were only ever tolerated—not ever really considered as family," I say, trying to ignore the lump forming in my throat. "We never had a seat at the main table. No one ever went out of their way to talk to us. And it was always so exhausting trying to pretend to want to be there. Of course, you know my sister—she never pretended. Maybe that's part of the reason the invitations stopped coming the moment my dad died."

Crossing the room, Noémie sits on the edge of the bed near me. Her grey eyes have a glossy sheen of empathy. She places her hand on top of mine and squeezes.

And just like that, the braid unravels and my stupid heart's soaring again. I should probably pull my hand away. I'm playing with fire, and it's only a matter of time before I get cooked.

"You should come to the chalet," Noémie blurts.

"Huh?" I blink at her.

Noémie gives my hand another squeeze. "For Christmas—come to the chalet with me. The change in scenery might be just what you need." Her expression is pure excitement. "The view is to die for. We can roast marshmallows by the firepit. We can even go skiing or snowboarding. You'll have so much fun."

I cringe internally at the thought of engaging in any type of winter sport. "I wouldn't want to intrude—"

"C'est tiguidou. You wouldn't be," she says. "It'll just be me, my brother, and his fiancée. There's plenty of space. You'd have your own room. And I know you've been looking for inspiration for your next graphic novel … maybe you can find that inspiration in Québec. You know I'm dying to read the next chapter, especially after that cliff-hanger."

I still don't know how Noémie managed to talk me into letting her read my graphic novel series. I feel like I should still be mad at her for invading my privacy. Sometimes it feels like I can't say no to anything she asks for.

To my utter mortification, Noémie immediately clocked that Detective Pamela Cross looks like her. "You definitely designed her after me. Admit it," she teased me a few days ago.

"A narcissist like you would think that," I countered. "Pamela's modelled after Amy Adams."

Pouting, Noémie shook her head. "No, I don't see it. Amy's whole milk wholesome. Pamela's a margarita—she's got sass and style like me."

"No, you're not a margarita. I like those. You're a negroni and burn like lighter fluid," I said with a chuckle.

"Take that back," she said, shoving me. Not hard, but hard enough that I instantly reacted, grabbing her wrists and pushing her back down on the couch.

It was such a stupid thing to do. In that moment, I was so tempted to kiss her. And I got the sense she would have let me. There'd been a charge between us. I'm pretty sure Noémie felt it too.

Luckily, I had enough sense to let go of her quickly and scuttle away. It would have been very bad if I kissed her. We live and work together. I can't do anything to jeopardize our friendship. I can't kiss someone I have feelings for.

Now, Noémie's looking at me with the biggest doe eyes—like she actually wants me to go with her to Québec. Like she isn't just making the offer to be nice.

I meet her gaze and feel pulled in two different directions. Part of me wants to go the chalet, but only because it means being with Noémie, which is the exact reason why I shouldn't go. Time away from her is what I need to reset. I need to squash my feelings, not strengthen them. But

Chapter 19

My jaw drops as the car rolls up the steep and winding drive that leads to the chalet. I envisioned it being quaint and cozy—not a timber and glass mega McMansion construction.

Perched on the edge of a snow-covered cliff, and overlooking a near-frozen lake, it looks more like a resort than a family vacation home. The architecture is a stunning collection of peaked roofs, wooden beams, and grand archways. The double-doored entrance is so large an elephant could walk through it.

Despite my tiredness, my fingers itch to sketch the place. I determine that I will before we leave. Perhaps, in my next volume, I will have Zara assassinate someone in a chalet.

Parking the car, Noémie turns in her seat and smiles. "We're finally here," she says, sounding more exhausted than victorious. Stretching her arms over her head, she yawns. I yawn too.

Including the stop to recharge the Tesla and another stop to use the washroom, the drive from Toronto to the Laurentian Mountains of Québec took almost eight hours. We took turns driving. I did the first stretch of the trip, and Noémie took over the wheel when we arrived in Kingston.

I click out of my seat belt. "I have to admit, this is not what I pictured when you said family chalet."

"Years ago, they added on to the place. It wasn't always this ..."

"Over the top?" I offer.

She nods.

We exit the car. As we are grabbing our bags from the trunk, another vehicle pulls in behind us—a gleaming silver Mercedes G-Class.

"Câlisse!" Noémie says. I don't know what that word means, but the way she's glaring at the car makes me think it's a curse.

"What's wrong?" I ask.

"Seems like my brother extended invitations," she replies.

The driver's door of the G-Class swings open, and a man with a glorious red beard hops out. "Salut, Noémie, c'est bon de te voir," he says. "Qui est ton ami?"

"Hey, Paul," Noémie greets with a tight grin. "This is my roommate, Jordan. She doesn't speak French."

"Very nice to meet you, Jordan," Paul greets. His accent is thick, and his brown eyes sparkle with what appears to be genuine interest.

The passenger door of the G-Class pops open and a fashionable blond woman slips out into the cold. Her expression is the exact opposite of Paul's—dark and stormy. "Tabarnak! C'est froid," she says, hugging her arms around her torso.

"This is Angel, my girlfriend," Paul says, gesturing at the blond. "Angel, rencontrez Noémie, la soeur de Claude et Jordan, son ami."

"Salut," Angel says. Her blue eyes are as frosty as they are bright.

I feign a smile and wave at her. "Hello, nice to meet you."

Noémie tugs on my arm. "It's cold. We'll continue this greeting inside, Paul," she calls, pulling me towards the entrance of the chalet.

"He seems nice," I say as we climb the steps leading to the palatial set of doors.

Noémie snorts. She seems annoyed.

I look at her inquisitively. "I sense there's a story."

"Not now. I'll tell you later," she says, motioning to slide her key into the lock. But before she can, the door is opened by an older man with a composed demeanour. He wears a tailored black suit complete with a black bowtie and waistcoat. The white shirt underneath it all is a crispiness I've never been able to achieve with an iron. The toes of his dress shoes are polished to shine.

All at once, Noémie's expression becomes joyous. "Henri!" she exclaims, dropping her bags to the floor and throwing her arms around him.

For a split second, the man smiles before regaining his controlled countenance. "Bienvenue, Mademoiselle St. Pierre. Bienvenue, Mademoiselle Alexander," he says, taking a step back and bowing slightly.

He takes our bags and ushers us inside. Setting our things down away from the entrance, he assists Noémie out of her coat, and before I know it, he's at my side. "May I take your coat, Mademoiselle?" he asks. His English has the slightest accent.

"Yeah, sure," I say, shrugging out of my jacket.

Henri flits away with the lightness of a butterfly to hang up the coats, and I take in my surroundings. My jaw hangs open for a second time. The foyer boasts soaring ceilings with exposed wooden beams. A giant chandelier glitters above my head. Intricate stonework makes up the floors and crawls halfway up the walls. Where there isn't stone, the walls are panelled wood that adds warmth to the space.

"How did Claude manage to steal you away from our parents?" Noémie asks.

"Business sees Monsieur et Madame St. Pierre in the U.S.," he replies.

Nodding, Noémie looks at me. "Henri is our butler—my parents' butler," she explains, before turning back to the older man. "That still doesn't explain why you are here. Didn't you want to take the holidays off?"

"There's no place I'd rather be than here with you and Claude," Henri says.

"Always the charmer," Noémie says, shaking her head. "Where is my brother?"

"I believe he is in the study."

"Of course, he is," she mutters. "Claude never knows when to give work a break."

If Henri agrees with Noémie's statement, he gives no indication. Instead, he turns and says, "Follow me, I will show you both to your room."

Noémie freezes. "You mean rooms?"

"Unfortunately not."

"Putain," Noémie says, rubbing her temple with a hand. "Don't tell me Claude invited all of his friends."

"He did," the butler confirms. "So you and Mademoiselle Alexander will be sharing your room."

My pulse quickens. This is not good. I can't share a room with Noémie. We can't sleep in the same bed.

Noémie is suddenly very red. Her hands ball at her sides. She says nothing more though.

We are escorted down a hall, passing by a large living space with even higher vaulted ceilings and an open concept kitchen. My gaze darts everywhere as I try to map our steps, but I get a little distracted by the artwork lining the walls. There's a small fortune worth of oil paint landscapes adorned in gilded frames.

Henri begins climbing a flight of stairs, and we follow. Upon reaching the second landing, I jump at the unexpected sight of a towering taxidermy bear.

Henri stops at a door, setting down our bags to open it. He waves for us to enter. I walk in after Noémie. Henri places our luggage down next to the dresser and makes to depart.

"Thank you, Henri," Noémie says.

"Thank you," I parrot.

Spinning slowly, my eyes drink in the magnificent room with its floor-to-ceiling windows that look out over the waterfront. There's a massive fireplace and seating area at the far end of the room. The bed looks made for a king, piled high with cushions. But even as large as the bed is, I fear it's not big enough. According to Sarah, I'm a serial cuddler—what if I do something stupid in my sleep?

"Did you hear what I said?" Noémie asks.

Blinking, I shake my head. "Sorry, no."

"I was just apologizing. It was just supposed to be me, you, my brother, and his fiancée." Noémie sighs. "But Claude invited all his friends."

I shrug. "It's okay." It's not actually okay. Sharing a bed with Noémie might be disastrous.

"It really isn't," she says, echoing my thoughts. Noémie grits her teeth and makes her way to the door. "I'm going to go and give my brother a piece of my mind."

"You really don't have to."

"I really, really want to though," Noémie says. "Make yourself comfy, I'll be back in a bit." She exits the room, leaving me alone.

Not really knowing what to do with myself, I begin unpacking my things. Then, I circle the room, inspecting the furnishings. I open a door that leads to a bathroom that looks as if it belongs in a Scandinavian spa.

I change into some fresh clothes—trading in my sweats for a pair of loose-fitting jeans and a black-and-grey plaid shirt.

Throwing myself down on the bed, I take out my phone with the intention of scrolling TikTok or Instagram. Unfortunately, the reception is horrible, and I don't have the password to access the Wi-Fi.

Minutes tick away. I think about drawing on my tablet, but then think better of it. Noémie will be back soon, and I don't want to get into a creative flow only for it to be interrupted.

Ten more minutes pass, and then another ten. I close my eyes, trying to take a nap. Unfortunately, despite feeling the exhaustion in my bones, my brain is wired.

I rise off the bed and begin to pace. I walk over to the windows and stare out of them, but there's nothing to see. In the short time that elapsed since arriving, the sun set. It's very dark outside. I wonder if I'll be able to see the stars if I go outside later. In the city, only the brightest stars are visible.

Turning away from the windows, my eyes go to the bed. In a few hours, I'll be sharing it with Noémie. The thought of laying next to Noémie sends a rush of blood and heat to my depths—not good. I'm worried about doing something stupid in my sleep. Or even worse, what if I say something?

Wayne already seems to think the worst of me—that I'm some kind of predatory lesbian. He's been exceptionally terse towards me lately. I don't want Noémie thinking the same. Sure, I might want her in the worst way, but I'd never do anything to purposefully jeopardize the friendship we've built over the last few months.

Fuck! I shouldn't have come here.

I pace some more. Another ten minutes pass. When I can't take it anymore, I crack the heavy bedroom door open and peer into the hallway. A symphony of chatter greets my ears.

Leaving the bedroom, I descend the staircase and follow the sound of voices and laughter. I'm brought to the large living space I spied earlier. I'm shocked to see that it's now full of people. I spot Paul's red beard and Angel's cold face. There are five others—three men and two women. None of whom I recognize.

Paul is deep in conversation with a man wearing a trendy sports jacket and a flashy Rolex. Angel stands about a foot away from her boyfriend. She seems very uninspired by what an animated brunette is sputtering. As if to tolerate the woman better, Angel swallows back the last bits of her wine.

There's a bald man with a goatee seated alone in an armchair. He scrolls through his phone. For some reason, he looks familiar—like I've seen his face before.

At the far end of the room, leaning against the kitchen counter is a man so pretty that he looks like he just left a shoot for *GQ*. He has black hair styled to look messy, and his piercing blue eyes have a hungry look as he sips from a glass holding amber liquid. He's chatting up the last woman, who looks related to Noémie with her curly auburn hair and legs for days.

Where is Noémie? My eyes dart around the room again. I don't see her or her brother.

"Mademoiselle St. Pierre is in the study."

I jump. I hadn't heard Henri's approach. The butler stands on my right, holding a decanter of red wine.

"Is that it?" Angel says, strutting towards Henri and holding out her empty glass.

"I've only just opened it. We should give it at least thirty minutes to breathe," he replies.

"I don't care." Angel thrusts her empty wine glass towards him.

Not one to argue, Henri fills the glass. "Did you want a drink, Mademoiselle Alexander? We have an assortment of wines, spirits, and refreshments."

"I'm good. Thanks, Henri."

The butler dips his head slightly and walks away.

Angel, surprisingly, doesn't go back to Paul's side. Instead, she focuses her gaze on me. She's eyeing me like how I imagine mathematicians inspect complex equations. I wonder what she's trying to figure out.

"So how do you know Noémie?" she asks, taking a sip of wine.

"We work together, and we're roommates."

"Roommates—interesting," Angel says. "And where is it that you work? It's my understanding Noémie quit her line cook position at that fancy establishment that just got a Michelin star. Why that girl chooses to work, I will never understand."

I almost correct her. I almost say that Noémie isn't choosing to work. But the truth is, I'm not entirely sure Noémie's been super honest with me about her financial situation. Either she's not as broke as she's led me to believe or she is broke and stacking on debt.

A couple of days ago, I went with her to the butcher shop and watched her drop sixty-four bucks on two Berkshire bone-in pork chops. When I asked if she could afford it, she got all weird and refused to talk about it. While I get that her financials are none of my business, I wouldn't want her to get into a situation where paying back her credit cards is an issue.

"We work at Grind That Bean. It's a coffee shop in Toronto's financial district," I say, answering Angel's question.

"Noémie serving coffee?" The woman snorts. "How dreadful."

My jaw clenches. I don't like Angel. I know her type—she's just like my father's side of the family. She's the type to think less of me because I'm not a lawyer or a dentist or a fucking engineer.

"I will need to swing by one day and see it for myself," Angel continues, either oblivious or uncaring that I'm scowling at her.

"Do you know where the study is?" I ask, changing the topic.

"Yes, down the hall and make a left," Angel answers.

I don't thank her, I just leave.

Angel's directions take me down another lengthy corridor flanked by solid wood doors.

Behind the door at the end of the hallway, two people are arguing. One voice belongs to Noémie. The other I recognize as Claude's. I don't understand what they are screaming about. They are speaking in French, and my fluency in the language doesn't extend past introducing myself or asking to go to the washroom.

It's none of my business, but I wonder what Noémie is so pissed about. It can't only be about her brother extending an invitation to his friends to come to the chalet. Then again, maybe that's exactly what she's angry about. Maybe Noémie is unnerved about sharing a bed with me. Or maybe I have it all wrong and her vehemence has more to do with the displeasure I saw etched on her face the moment Paul and Angel arrived.

What's Noémie's beef with Paul anyways? He seems nice enough.

Deciding that I over-extended my stay in the corridor, I pivot with the intention of heading back to the main room.

A door creaks open, and Noémie calls my name. "Jordan?"

Every muscle in my body tenses, and heat burns up the back my neck. I don't want Noémie thinking that I was eavesdropping.

I stop walking and turn to face her. "Hey, I was looking for you."

Noémie's face is very red. Her grey are eyes glossy, like she's on the verge of crying.

I go to her. "You okay?" I squeeze her shoulders.

At that exact moment, Claude steps out of the study. Unlike his sister, he doesn't look perturbed. There's a smug tug to his lips.

"Salut, Jordan, very nice to see you again."

Noémie throws him a look of warning over her shoulder. I'm not sure what she's warning him against, but he seems to understand. He smiles, but it's more predatory than kind. Were they talking about me? I'm back to thinking that I'm the cause for their argument. My stomach boils with unease as the two siblings share a silent conversation with their eyes.

"Good seeing you as well," I say.

Noémie grabs my wrist and pulls me away from her brother. I let her drag me away.

When we round the corner, I ask, "What was that about?"

"It's nothing."

"Your tight grip tells me that it is something."

"Oh, I'm sorry," Noémie says, letting go. She runs a nervous hand through her loose auburn hair. My eyes follow the movement. I can't help myself.

"It's okay," I say. "But I just want to let you know that you can talk to me. If you ever want to vent to me about your brother, I'm all ears." I want her to talk to me. I want her to open up.

Noémie forces a smile. "Thanks. I appreciate that. But seriously, it's nothing. I'm just irritated that he invited all his friends without giving me a heads up." She bites down on her lip. "Can you do something for me?"

"Yeah, sure. Anything."

"Try not to be alone with my brother."

I frown. "Is he dangerous or something?"

Noémie snorts. "No, no, he's just a dick. And I don't want him upsetting you. I invited you here to get away from it all, not to suffer through his bullshit," she explains. "Anyways, have you had a chance to meet everyone yet?"

I shake my head.

"Let's get these introductions over and done with then."

Chapter 20

Dinner is catered. While it looks appetizing, the arrangement of meats, salad, and sides are a far cry from the fancy meals Noémie lavishes me with at home.

Claude insists that I sit beside the man with the goatee—the gentleman I'd seen earlier on his phone.

The moment I'm told his name, I discover why he looked so familiar. François Lafontaine is an uber successful digital artist and YouTube influencer. I've seen his videos before, and I know his story.

Sitting beside him makes me nervous.

He's got the type of resumé I can only fantasize having. He's worked for big companies like Ubisoft and CD Projekt Red. Early in his career, he designed characters for popular console games. Now, he makes a living uploading videos and selling prints of his work directly to his fan base. François's got a following in the millions, and a little over a year ago he launched his first Kickstarter campaign to fund the release of a comic book series. Within minutes of going live, his Kickstarter surpassed all its stretch goals.

I'm a little envious of him, but I try not to let it show in our interactions.

Noémie sits directly across from me, slathering too much butter on a slice of crusty bread.

The conversation around the table is about François's latest project, which he is describing as being a cross between *Macbeth* and *Resident Evil*. It sounds really interesting; I would read it.

"You know, Jordan is also working on a graphic novel," Claude says.

I nearly choke on my wine. My gaze snaps to Noémie's. Our eyes meet for the briefest second before she glares at her brother.

"Is that so?" François asks, sounding genuinely interested.

And suddenly all eyes—except for Noémie's—are on me. I feel the flame of embarrassment on my cheeks. But I don't just feel embarrassed, I'm hurt. How could Noémie betray me like this? She knows how I feel about talking about my art. And she doesn't even like her brother, so why would she tell him about my graphic novel series?

I realize that François is still waiting for an answer. I say, "Ummm … yeah."

"What's it about?" he asks, picking up his glass of wine and taking a sip.

I reach for my own drink. The crystal feels heavy in my hand. It wobbles. I decide to abort and set the glass back down.

The table is hushed, all forks and knives hovering over plates as everyone awaits my answer.

God this is awkward.

I clear my throat. "It's about a woman …who works as an accountant by day, but secretly she is one of the country's deadliest assassins. And … there's, like, a detective investigating her crimes, so the assassin snuggles up to the detective to sabotage the case." I feel sweat dripping down my spine. My heart is thundering. "Anyways, it's like my version of a queer *Death Note*, minus anything supernatural."

"You've sold me, I love *Death Note*," François says.

"It's really, really good," Noémie exclaims from across the table.

I scowl at her, and all I can think is that I should have never given in. I should have ignored all her begging and pleading. I shouldn't have allowed her to read all three volumes.

The table goes back to eating. Cutlery clinks and scrapes fine bone China. The hum of conversation picks back up. Paul mentions something about the weather being perfect for skiing, and there are a few agreements.

"I really would love to read it," François says.

I really don't want him to. He's like really, really incredible at drawing, and I'm … good but not great. He's probably just being nice. There's no way François Lafontaine actually wants to see my work.

Wagering the likelihood of him actually looking at my graphic novel is zero, I say, "Yeah, sure, I can send you a digital version of the first volume."

"Awesome," he says.

I ask him for his email, and he pulls a business card from his wallet. I didn't know people still carried business cards.

After dinner, I grab my jacket from the closet and venture outside for a smoke. I bought a fresh pack the night my heart broke watching Noémie kiss Felix. I bought another the day I almost kissed Noémie. My most recent pack, I bought after going out to a party with Kristen and Hailey and finding all the women there lacking. When I got home around 2:00 a.m., Noémie was still up and she was plastered. We got into the stupidest fight over me leaving the dirty French press on the counter. Noémie's not a nice drunk. Noémie's not good for my lungs.

The cold air feels surprisingly good on my skin. After burning through a cigarette, I immediately light another. Alone on the porch, I stare up at the night sky. It is very dark and a smattering of stars twinkle back at me. It's a sight meant to be admired, but I don't. The weight of my emotions is cutting off my ability to marvel at the beauty above me. How could Noémie betray me like this?

I pull out François's card. His name and contact information are engraved in a shiny red cursive font. I should probably crumple the card and toss it in the nearest trash bin. But a small part of me doesn't want to. A small part of me wants François to look at my work.

Hope is stupid, but I end up shooting François an email on my phone with the first volume attached. I got the Wi-Fi password earlier. Outside, the signal is weak, so it takes minute for the email to send.

I only go back inside when I can no longer stand the cold. Not in the mood to mingle, I retreat to the bedroom. I get ready for bed, and then slip under the covers. The mattress is softer than a cloud, and the cool sheets feel like velvet against my skin. Letting out a sigh, I feel some of the tension seep out of my muscles. In that moment I register just how tired I am.

I'm just about to turn off the bedside table lamp, when the bedroom door opens and Noémie steps inside.

"Hey," she says.

I don't say anything.

Noémie wrings her hands. "Are you mad at me?"

I'm not in the mood to fight with her now. I'm exhausted. "No," I say flatly.

Noémie exhales a loud breath. "Okay."

I roll over so that I'm facing away from her.

I hear the bathroom door click shut and then the sound of running water.

Reaching over, I flick off the light and close my eyes. I start to drift to sleep, but my brain turns back on the moment the bathroom door opens and a beam of concentrated light spears the darkness.

Noémie flips the switch and the room is once again black.

The bed dips as Noémie climbs into it.

I'm hopeful that she will think I'm asleep. Of course, I'm not so lucky.

"Jordan," she whispers, moving past the middle of the bed, past her section of the mattress. "Are you awake?"

I let silence hang in the air between us, almost ignoring the question. I want to ignore it. The last thing I want to do is talk, but I mumble, "Yes."

Noémie moves even closer. She's so close that I can feel the heat of her body and smell her perfume—citrus and spice.

"Don't be mad at me." Noémie slings an arm around me and tugs me to her. Her breasts press against my back. My breath hitches.

I hope Noémie can't sense how hard my heart pounds. It's pretty much all I can hear.

"I'm not mad," I manage to squeeze out. Please let me go—never let me go.

"You are, I can tell," she says against my neck. Her breath on my skin feels too good. "I get that you have every right to be angry with me, but I was trying to help."

"I don't see how telling your brother helps anything."

Noémie sighs. "You underestimate your talent, Jordan. I couldn't put your graphic novel down, it's so good," she says. "And I'm not just saying that because Pamela is based off me."

"She's not. You're so conceited," I say. "You shouldn't have told Claude. I draw for myself. I make stories for myself."

"So you're really telling me that you never once thought about getting your work published?"

I did once. I don't respond.

"You never once thought about putting your work out there?" she pushes.

"Why does it even matter?" I squeeze my eyes shut.

"Because it does," Noémie says. "If it's what you want, you should do it."

I try to pull away from her, but she wraps her arm tighter around me.

"I know it's scary, putting yourself out there," she says. "Especially when it's something you're so passionate about."

I feel the sting of tears in my eyes. I'm recalling the rejection. Recalling being told that no one wants to read a story about a dyke.

Sniffling, I wipe my eyes.

Noémie senses my sadness and rubs my arm.

"I can't do it again," I say when I'm sure my voice won't break. "I can't put myself back out there."

"You can," Noémie says.

I shake my head. "It's not so simple."

"It really is," Noémie says. "It won't be easy. Nothing worth having is ever easy. But if it's what you want, you need to go for it."

Right now, what I want more than anything is to kiss her. But that would be a huge risk. Going after something also means being okay with the possibility of losing something.

"I don't think I have it in me to …" I sigh. "It's just, like, I put so much of myself into my work. What if nobody wants to read it? What if people hate it? What if nobody cares about a story with a dyke for its main character?"

I feel Noémie stiffen. "Did somebody tell you that?"

"Pretty much."

"Whoever told you that is a homophobic asshole, and they're wrong. I loved it, and I'm sure François's going to love it too," Noémie states. She sounds so confident.

I don't say anything.

"Look, I didn't mean to say anything to Claude. But after I finished reading it, I just—je ne sais pas. I wanted to help, and François is literally my brother's best man, so I asked my brother if he could introduce you to François. Of course, I never imagined that his idea for an introduction would be to invite François here for the holidays—merde."

"You shouldn't have underestimated him," I say with a sad chuckle. I feel lighter. "I really shouldn't forgive you—you're the absolute worst."

"Really, I'm the bad guy for pushing you to reach for your dreams?"

"Yes, yes, you are. I kind of hate you for it."

"Shut up. You love me, and you know it," she says.

I do know it.

Clearing my throat, I say, "Since you are forgiven, you can go to your side of the bed now."

"Is it okay if we stay like this?" Noémie asks, nestling her face against my neck.

I should say no, but I say okay. I'm dancing on a dangerous ledge. There's a part of me that wants to fall off.

Chapter 21

It's still dark outside when Noémie nudges me awake. "Hey, Jordan," she whispers.

"Hmmm?" I'm so tired. It took me forever to fall asleep. Exquisite torture best describes the experience of being spooned by Noémie for the better part of the night. While she succumbed to sleep almost immediately, a combination of anxiety and desire kept me up.

"Did you want to come skiing?" she asks. "I forgot to ask you last night, but a bunch of us are heading out in an hour."

Shaking my head, I pull the sheet over her face. "I don't do winter sports."

"Come on." Noémie chuckles and nudges me again. "You're missing out. It'll be fun."

"I don't do cold."

She sighs. "Suit yourself."

I fall back asleep, and when I wake up next, the sun is shining on my face. Rubbing my eyes, I roll over and reach for my phone to check the time. It's 11:00 a.m. I slept in, and yet I feel like I can nod off again.

I flip onto my stomach and bury my face in the pillow. It smells like her—spice and citrus. I sniff the pillowcase like it's a line of coke. Just like a bump, I feel the high.

My mind carries me back to last night—Noémie's breasts pressed against me and her hot breath on my neck. I rock my hips into the mattress. Last night, I was wet, and I'm getting wet right now as I start to think about all the things I want to do to Noémie. I want to trace her entire body with my tongue. I want to nip her inner thighs and hear her gasp. I want to fuck her and feel her tighten around my fingers as she comes apart.

If things were different—if we didn't live together, if we weren't friends, if she wasn't straight—I would've tried my hand at fucking her last night. I would have brushed kisses down her neck, making her shudder. Her nails would scrape against my back as I sucked on her nipples and licked a path down past her belly button.

"Fuck, Jordan," she'd moan, arching her back off the bed. "Please, I need …"

"Tell me what you need," I'd say.

"I need you inside me," she'd say.

Groaning, my hips rock harder against the mattress. I shove my hand down the waistband of my boxers and rub my clit.

"How bad do you need it?" I'd ask.

"I'm going to die if you don't put your mouth on my pussy and thrust your fingers inside me," she'd say.

I rub faster and faster. The friction feels so delicious. I'm so close. Very close—

The door to the bedroom opens.

My hand shoots out from my boxers, and I sit upright in bed. My heart races.

"I can't believe you're still in bed," Noémie says, stepping into the room.

She's wearing a white ski jacket that has an orange stripe running down both sleeves and matching ski pants. The tip of her nose and her cheeks are still red from the cold. Her auburn hair hangs loose and dishevelled about her shoulders.

"I had a hard time sleeping," I say.

Noémie's brows furrow. "Because of me?" There's real concern in her voice, and I'm not sure where it is coming from.

"No, no," I say, shaking my head. "I just have a lot on my mind."

"Like what?" Noémie unzips her jacket.

Like you. "I'd rather not talk about it."

Noémie accepts my response with a nod. She's unlike Wayne in that way. If I say I don't want to talk about something, most times she drops the issue—maybe because she's the same way.

She slips out of her jacket, throws it on the coat stand near the door and goes to the bathroom. The moment the door clicks close behind her, I consider finishing what I started before I got interrupted.

I decide against it. I get dressed quickly, tugging on a pair of loose-fitting jeans and an oversized cable knit sweater.

When Noémie steps out of the bathroom, I exchange places with her. I wash my face and brush my teeth. I massage a glob of coconut scented curl activator into my hair. The hair product defines my short black curls, making them shine. Staring down my reflection, I admire my new fade. Two days ago, I visited Tyrone—my barber for the last five years. Like always, he hooked me up. My line up is perfection. The edges are crisp and the mid-fade is fading.

Exiting the washroom, I discover Noémie's gone. I find her downstairs in the main room. It seems like everyone, except Claude, is present.

Noémie sits at the kitchen island. She's deep in conversation with the chatty brunette woman, Amelia—Claude's fiancée. Hate to say it—Amelia is pretty, but she doesn't strike me as Claude's type. Maybe I am stereotyping Claude, but I see him with a super skinny model with killer legs and razor-sharp cheek bones. Frankly, I see him with someone like Angel. Amelia is athletically built with broad shoulders and a tapered waist. Her face is full and round and jovial. Though we barely spoke yesterday, I get the sense that Amelia is a warm and kind person. She just exudes that vibe.

"Salut, Jordan," François says. He steps towards me and holds out one of two steaming mugs. "Cider? It's delicious."

I like apple anything, so he doesn't have to ask me twice. I take the offering and sip before I consider the hazard. "Shit," I say, spitting out the burning liquid. "I one hundred percent burned my tongue."

"Sorry, I should have warned you that it's hot," he says. "If it's okay, I'd like to continue our conversation from yesterday. Come, let's sit by the fire." He waves a hand for me to follow him.

I do.

François sinks into one of two armchairs near the wood burning fireplace. I drop down into the second one. The radiant heat coming from the fire is delightful.

I blow on my drink. "So what did you want to talk about?"

"I read your graphic novel," he says. His brown eyes sparkle.

My mouth drops open. I blink. "But … I sent it last night."

"Oui, and I devoured it," he says, leaning back in his chair and taking a sip from his drink. "Yes, there are areas where the story and dialogue can be improved. But overall, it's solid. Where you truly shine is with the artwork. The level of detail you put into each panel—very impressive."

It's a lot of praise coming from someone like him, and I don't know what to say. I have to be dreaming. This is unreal.

I clear my throat and try to keep my cool. But I can't stop the smile that breaks across my face. "I'm glad you liked it."

"So tell me, are you interested in getting it published?" he asks.

I almost say no—it's what I've been telling myself forever. But maybe Noémie's right. Maybe, for once in my life, I should try running towards something instead of running away from it.

"Yes, I am interested," I finally say.

François beams at me. "Well, I understand that it is the holidays and you'd rather not talk business right now, but please give me a call in the new year. I would love to discuss the possibility of us working together," he says.

Once again, I am speechless. François Lafontaine wants to work with me!

Chapter 22

Early Christmas morning, I awake to see that Noémie's not in bed. I find her in the kitchen with her apron on and dozens of pans, bowls, and utensils around her. It's organized chaos. She's in the process of measuring and chopping all her ingredients. The name for this, Noémie taught me, is mise en place—everything in its place.

The sun is just starting to poke its head through the window, streaming thin ribbons of light into the kitchen.

My stomach roils like the Atlantic in a storm as I cross the main room. My fingers bite into the thin wrapping paper. I clutch Noémie's gift to my chest. It's not the necklace with the orange stones that I saw at the Christmas market. But it's something I think Noémie will appreciate, and for me it's kind of a big deal. The mixed media artwork that I slaved hours over is the first piece of artwork that I've made for someone in a long time.

The last person I painted for was my father—almost a year before he passed. I'd done a portrait of him because he begged and guilted me into doing it. I can still recall the way a smile broke out over his face when he saw his portrait. He'd been so impressed by it. I hope I can hold on to the memory forever. I hope I won't forget the brightness of his light-brown eyes or the dimples that pierced his cheeks.

According to Noémie, the Christmas gift exchange is scheduled to take place after dinner, but I don't want her opening my present in front of an audience. I don't want people calculating the time it would have taken me to cut out each printed letter and picture. I don't want people diving in to skim their fingers over the varnished impasto. And most importantly, I don't want anyone reading between the lines and seeing my love for Noémie written out in every chaotic brushstroke.

To be quite honest, I thought about destroying the piece upon completion. But I couldn't bring myself to take a palette knife to Noémie's painted face. And she'd been so nice inviting me to the chalet, I felt obligated to give her something special. As broke as I am, the only thing of value I can offer is my time and my art.

I near the kitchen and catch the scent of nutmeg, cloves, and cardamom. Deep in the flow of things, with her AirPods in and her head bopping to music, Noémie doesn't see me. Her auburn hair is pulled back into a neatly plaited ponytail. Flour lightly dusts her red apron that reads, *Keep Calm and Merry Christmas.*

I don't understand the "Keep Calm" craze. I'm not sure I want to understand it.

Noémie picks up a French rolling pin and begins beating the shit out of some whole pistachios in a Ziploc bag. She frowns as she punishes the nuts.

Watching her, I feel a pang of longing in my heart. I want her so badly, and I'm starting to think that I will never be able to shake off my feelings for her. If anything, they grow a little more each day.

When Noémie catches sight of me, she jumps. "Câlisse," she says, clutching her chest. She taps her phone, muting the music. "I didn't expect anyone to be up yet."

"I thought I could help out," I say, scratching the back of my neck.

Noémie's gaze drops to the gift that I'm holding, and she smirks. "That for me?"

"Maybe." My heart hammers in my ears.

"We will be exchanging gifts after dinner," she says, wiping her hands off on the towel tucked in her apron. "You should put it under the tree."

I shake my head. "Yeah, I know, but I'd rather you open it now." I pretty much shove the package at her.

Noémie raises a questioning brow but takes it. "This wrapping paper is great," she says.

The paper is red with cartoon Yorkshire terriers wearing Santa hats and sunglasses. When I saw it at the store, I knew I had to buy it.

"I thought you'd like it," I say. "Any Céline status updates from Wayne?"

Apparently, the dog gets nauseous during long car rides and hates the chalet. I didn't know animals could be so finicky. Lucky for Noémie, Wayne was more than happy to house sit and watch over Céline.

"She's doing good, Wayne sent me a video of her yipping in her sleep last night. I'll send it to you."

I chuckle. "You better." Over the last few months, I have gone from never interacting with a dog to being super obsessed with them. A couple of times, I joined Noémie at the local dog park and found myself striking up conversations with dog owners, and not because I was just being polite, I was actually interested to know about their pets.

"Are you sure you want me to open it now?"

I nod. "Yeah."

Biting her lip, Noémie slides a finger under the tape, and I hold my breath as she extracts the framed portrait. The wrapping paper floats to the floor.

Noémie frowns.

Why is she frowning? I get a little lightheaded and reach to brace myself on the counter. "You don't like it?"

Noémie blinks, stopping her inspection of the portrait to meet my eyes.

I forget how to breathe as I wait for her response. I'm drowning under the current of Noémie's stare. My lungs burn.

"No, I love it," she finally says. Her voice is thick with an emotion I can't name.

"Oh … awesome, great." I let out a breath.

Noémie takes a step towards me. We're only a few inches apart, and I feel that charge again. I'm compelled to bridge the gap between us. I gaze down at Noémie's lips. It hurts to know that even this close, she's still so out of my reach.

I'm startled when I look back up and see a strange look on her face—I'm not sure I'd call it desire. But she isn't moving away from me. In fact, she seems to be leaning in.

Someone coughs.

Both Noémie and I jerk apart.

Claude is standing by the fridge with his arms crossed. His expression is only shades away from anger.

"Bonjour, Jordan. Noémie," he says.

I force a smile. "Merry Christmas, Claude."

The siblings stare intently at each other, holding a silent conversation that I can't follow. They do that a lot. It's annoying.

Claude breaks eye contact first and yawns. "I need coffee," he says, motioning towards the coffee station.

I'm about to echo the sentiment when Noémie grabs my hand, tugging me out of the kitchen, up the stairs, and down the hall. I don't understand her urgency. I ask her to tell me what's up, but she doesn't.

It isn't until we are in our room that Noémie drops my hand. She begins to pace a bit before sitting on the edge of the bed. She gently sets the portrait down on the mattress beside her.

"I thought I told you to stay away from Claude," she says.

Okay, now I'm super confused. Where is this even coming from? "Besides saying hello, I've barely said a word to your brother."

Noémie blinks. "Oh, I thought …" She scrubs her eyes with her palms and sighs. "Sorry. Forget it."

"Sorry about what? What did you think happened?"

"It's nothing."

"It doesn't sound like it's nothing," I huff, approaching the bed.

Noémie wrings her hands. "My brother is just very protective of me. He's never liked any of my friends," she explains, her expression shifting from irritation to sadness. "I just don't want him upsetting you. I invited you here to relax, and it just seems like the opposite is happening …"

I think she's deflecting, not telling me what the actual issue is, but I can't even guess at what the actual issue could be. Noémie doesn't tell me anything. She keeps me at arm's length. I'm so sick of being shut out. I want to be let in. But I don't want to whine about it. I want her to want to tell me things.

Sighing loudly, I rub my forehead.

"How long did it take you to make this?" Noémie asks, so softly that I think she never meant to voice the question aloud. Her fingers glide over the painting's textured surface.

"Not long," I lie.

"I love it," Noémie says for the second time. "It's possibly the most beautiful thing I've ever seen."

The praise makes my stupid heart flutter. "That's because it's your face, and you're full of yourself."

"Anyone who looks like me would be full of themselves," she replies. Rising to her feet, Noémie moves towards the closet. "Close your eyes."

"Why?"

"Because I told you to."

I exaggerate rolling my eyes before closing them.

There's some rustling, and then I sense Noémie's presence in front of me. "Okay, you can look now."

I open my eyes. Noémie's holding out an exquisitely wrapped gift with a large red bow. "Joyeux noël," she says.

"I thought gifts were going to be exchanged after dinner?"

Noémie shrugs. "I got to open my gift, so you get to open yours early too."

I take the box—there's some heft to it. Sitting on the floor, I put it on my lap. Noémie kneels across from me.

It's my turn to carefully pick off the tape. The wrapping paper is thick and patterned like a candy cane.

Upon uncovering the Shoei brand name, my hands still. I stare at Noémie with disbelief.

"Do you like it?" she asks. "It's the same size as your current helmet. I wasn't sure what colour to get, but since you always wear black, I got you black. But if you don't like it or if it doesn't fit, there's a gift receipt—you can exchange it."

Shoei is top of the line. It's like the Gucci brand of motorcycle helmets. They aren't cheap.

I shake my head and push the box towards her. "I can't accept this."

Noémie's eyes narrow on me. She pushes it back. "Why not? You've been complaining nonstop that you need a new helmet."

"I know, but …"

She grits her teeth. "If you don't like it, you can exchange it."

"It's not that. I love it. Like, this is possibly the nicest gift I've ever gotten. But it's too much."

With a dismissive wave, Noémie says, "It really isn't."

"It is," I say. "Can you even afford it?"

Silence hangs between us for a beat until Noémie severs it. "Merde," she says, exhaling a loud breath. "Jordan, if I couldn't afford it, I wouldn't have bought it for you. Why are you so difficult? You're like one of my best friends. I hate knowing that you ride around on that death trap with that banged up helmet. Also, it's rude to turn away a gift."

I want to ask her where she got the money from, but I know the question won't go over well. So I don't. I don't want to get into it with her right now. It's Christmas. We shouldn't be fighting.

"Fine, I'll accept it," I say.

"You say that like you have a choice," she says, leaning back on her hands. "Put it on. I want to see it on you."

"You're so bossy."

"You love it," she says.

I really do. Ugh.

I open the box and remove the sleek black helmet. It slides over my head like a glove—the fit is perfection. "How do I look?" I ask, flipping up the visor.

"Very cool," Noémie replies. Pulling out her phone, she snaps a quick photo of me before I can stop her.

"Delete that." Ugh, she better not post a photo of me. Noémie's back on her social media game, but instead of posting get ready with me videos, her content is mostly about food now.

"No, I don't think I will," she says with a grin. "How's the fit?"

"Comfortable. Thank you."

"I'm glad you like it," she says. Her gaze drops to her watch. "I really need to get back to the kitchen. I'm on a strict schedule."

I pull off the helmet. "I'm happy to help."

Holding up a hand, Noémie shakes her head. "Nope. I appreciate the offer, but if I let you help then Amelia will also insist on helping, and my brother's fiancée should never be near anything edible."

I chuckle. "Is that so?"

"Yes."

When Noémie leaves, I put the helmet back on and check myself out in the mirror. While I absolutely fucking love it, it doesn't sit well with me that she must've dropped at least a grand. Where is her money coming from? Didn't her father cut her off?

Chapter 23

I'm sitting in an armchair by the fireplace, exchanging text messages with Sarah, when Henri approaches me. Bending towards to my ear, he whispers, "Monsieur St. Pierre wishes to have a word—privately."

My gaze darts to the kitchen where Noémie is still working on dinner. I know she doesn't want me alone with her brother, but at the same time, I don't need her to protect me from him. In my thirty-plus years, I've dealt with my share of assholes, and I'm a survivor. I can handle Claude. I'm also curious to know just how bad he can be. So despite knowing how Noémie feels, I rise from my seat and follow Henri out of the main room and down the long corridor.

Upon reaching the study, Henri opens the door and gestures for me to enter. He makes his exit once I'm inside, closing the door behind him.

A lit cigar in hand, Claude sits behind a giant mahogany desk with a varnish that gleams in the dim lighting.

I take a quick look at my surroundings. Fully stocked bookshelves line two opposing walls. Retreating sunlight drips through giant windows overlooking the water. The room is large, but Claude's arrogance fills the entire space. He stares me down like he's a cat and I'm a mouse.

"You wanted to talk?" I say, folding my arms.

"Yes, have a seat." He waves at a chair and rises to his feet. Walking over to a shelf, he pours out two drinks of amber liquid. Rounding the desk, he holds out a heavy crystal glass for me to take.

I don't care much for liquor on its own, but not wanting to be rude, I take the offering.

Claude leans against the desk. "Please have a seat," he says again, taking a sip from his glass.

Because he said please, I oblige him and sit down in a leather armchair a few feet away from the desk.

Silence stretches between us. Claude takes a pull from his cigar. Smoke billows around him like a curtain.

I stare down at the amber liquid and trace the thick patterned groves in the glass.

Finally, Claude says, "What is my sister to you?"

Every muscle in my body tenses. I look up and meet Claude's eyes. His are grey and appear so much like his sister's that it's unsettling.

It's an odd question to ask. Then again, perhaps it makes perfect sense if he's as protective as Noémie indicated. This morning Claude walked in on me and Noémie in the kitchen. I'm not sure what my closeness to her looked like to him, but he hadn't been happy about it. Maybe he's also a homophobe—just like his father. Maybe he sees me as some predatory lesbian threatening to turn his sister. Or maybe he can see the truth—that my worthless ass is hopelessly in love with Noémie.

Deciding that I do need a drink, I lift the glass to my lips and take a sip. It's smoother than any liquor I've ever had, but it burns down my throat all the same. "She's my friend and my roommate. And we also work together," I reply.

"And how long have the two of you known each other?"

I frown. "Why does that matter? What's this about?"

Claude takes his time answering. He takes a final inhale from his cigar before stomping the glowing end in an ashtray. "Noémie has never been a good judge of character," he says. "And I know your type."

"My type?"

"Yes, your type," he says. "I've done a little digging, and you're a deadbeat womanizer intent on weaselling your way into Noémie's good graces, taking advantage of her and her connections."

My hand tightens on the glass. I grit my teeth. "You don't know the first thing about me."

"I know you have a price—everyone has a price," he states, finishing off his drink and setting it down on the desk with a thunk. "What's yours?"

"What?" The world spins as I digest his words. I couldn't have heard him right.

Claude reaches into his sports jacket, removing a pen and a cheque book. "What's your price?" He clicks the pen.

"For what?" I ask, even though I'm sure I know the answer.

"To get the fuck out of my sister's life."

My shock prevents me from answering. I really can't believe the fuckery coming out of his mouth—that this conversation is happening is unreal.

"How about ten thousand dollars?"

Anger boils inside me. I'm hot from the tips of my ears to my toes.

"That too low for you? I will bump the number to twenty-five thousand, but you would have to leave tonight," he says, dropping his focus to the cheque book. He begins filling out a check. "I'll even pay for your commute back to Toronto."

My fury bubbles over. I fly out of my seat and fling the contents of my drink on him. The liquor hits him in the face and drips onto his white collared shirt.

"Câlisse!" He glares at me.

"You don't know fuck-all about me! But know this: I don't want your fucking money and I don't have a fucking price. Noémie's priceless."

I slam my glass down on the desk and don't stick around to hear any more of his bullshit. I retreat to the bedroom and cocoon myself in the bed and switch off the lights.

The conversation with Claude repeats in my mind over and over. My eyes burn, and a ball forms in my throat. I start to cry, and I hate that I'm crying. But it's to be expected, I guess. Christmas is not meant to be a happy time for me. This is what I get for thinking that it could be. I start to think about my dad, and I'm wrecked by even more tears.

The door creaks open. "Jordan, are you in here? Dinner's going to be ready in about fifteen minutes."

I suck in a breath and let it out slowly. I can't let Noémie see me like this. I can't talk about what happened with Claude—not now. I just need to be alone.

"I'm not feeling well. I think it's a stomach bug," I say. "I won't be coming down for dinner." I drag the bedsheets over my head. I'm praying Noémie leaves me be.

"Oh ... okay," Noémie says, sounding both disappointed and sad. I hear her moving towards the bed, and then feel the mattress sink. "Do you need anything? Tylenol? Advil? I can make you some soup …" She rubs my shoulder over the blanket.

I squeeze my eyes shut and pull the blanket tighter around me. "I just—I just need to be alone," I croak. And now she knows that I've been crying. Great.

"Jordan, I …"

"Please, leave me alone. I just need to be alone." I sniffle. "Please."

"Jordan—"

"Please go."

Noémie doesn't say or do anything for a long time. She just sits in the dark with me. And just when I start to think she's never going to leave, she does.

Chapter 24

"You need to talk to her Jay—tell her what that asshole did already," Wayne snaps.

I shake my head.

"You know Noémie thinks she did something wrong. She's mad with worry and blaming herself. Be a fucking adult for once and stop shutting her out."

For the millionth time, I curse myself for telling Wayne about what happened with Claude. Frankly, it's surprising the traitor hadn't gone to her immediately with the news. Then again, I think I told him to do my dirty work for me. But he wants me to tell her, and I don't want to—it's a difficult conversation I don't know how to broach.

"I don't see the point in telling her. She might not even believe me," I say with sigh. Too many times in my life I've not been believed. Closing my eyes briefly, I push back a painful memory.

The office chair I sit on has a foam armrest that's cracking. I pick at it.

"You need to tell Noémie," Wayne repeats.

"Tell me what?"

Both Wayne and I look towards the office door—the very open office door. Crap.

Noémie stands in the door frame hugging an empty ice bucket. Her grey eyes are wide, her brows knitting with confusion. She steps into the office, her gaze flitting from Wayne to me. "Tell me what?" she asks again.

"I just remembered that I need to check the oven," Wayne says. He pushes past Noémie and shuts the door.

Fuck Wayne. I know him well enough to know that he's likely eavesdropping just outside.

I slouch in my seat and avert my gaze from Noémie's. I itch for a cigarette, but my need to bolt is even more intense. I don't want to have this talk. Noémie might not be on the best terms with her brother, but he's still her brother. If it comes to my word against his, I don't think she'll believe me. So why even bother bringing it up?

I pick off a chunk of armrest foam and flick it to the ground.

In a way, I know Wayne is right. I do need to talk to Noémie. I've been pretty much ignoring her since Christmas. On the ride back into the city, I pretended to be asleep for the time Noémie drove, and then, when I took over the wheel, I feigned a headache, shutting down any attempt on Noémie's part to have a fruitful discussion with me.

Things have only gotten more awkward between us over the last couple of days. At home and at work, I try to stay out of her orbit. I can't look her in the eyes. I hate that I'm worrying Noémie, but I don't know where to begin.

Noémie sets the ice bucket down a little too hard. "Jordan, is this about the helmet? Are you really that weirded out about it?"

I blink up at her.

Red tinges her neck and cheeks. Her hands are clenched at her sides. "The store opens in ten minutes, but I swear I won't let you leave this office until you tell me what's up." She crosses her arms over her chest and leans her back against the door. "I'm so fucking tired of tip-toeing around you. Just tell me what I did already."

I exhale a deep breath. "You didn't do anything."

"Then why are you ignoring me?"

Seeing Noémie like this—this upset—it's breaking my heart.

"You didn't do anything," I repeat, leaning forward and rubbing my temples. "But I don't know how to start to explain."

"You need to. This silent treatment is killing me."

I look up at her. Noémie's eyes sparkle with a mix of frustration and tears. She turns her head to the side, wipes her eyes, and sniffles.

Against my better judgement, I go to her. I pull her in my arms. She's warm and soft and everything I want that I can never have. Her perfume makes my mouth water. Holding her like this feels like I stuck my finger in an electrical socket. My heart jackhammers against my ribcage. Can Noémie feel it?

"Jordan …" she whispers.

I take a step back, withdrawing from her. I clear my throat and decide to rip off the wax. This conversation is going to be difficult. Better to just get it over and done with. "Your brother offered me money to stop being your friend," I say.

I wait for Noémie to start screaming at me. I wait for her to call me a fucking liar. She doesn't though. Instead, tears spring from her eyes and run down her cheeks.

"How much?" Her words come out choked. "And let me guess, you took the money, but now you regret it?"

I scowl. "Of course not. Our friendship doesn't come with a price tag," I say. "He offered me twenty-five thousand, but there's no amount of money I'd take."

Noémie blinks with surprise, as if she couldn't have possibly heard me right. "You turned down the money?"

"Of course, I turned down the money. Who the fuck wouldn't?"

"My ex," she says, hugging her arms around her stomach. She looks down at the vinyl tiles.

My mouth drops open. "Your ex did what?"

Noémie chuckles, but it isn't a happy sound. She wipes her eyes and sniffles. "My father paid my ex to dump me," she says, trembling. I can tell she's trying so hard to keep herself together, but sometimes the only way to become whole again is to break apart first.

Noémie slides her back down the door until she's sitting on the floor. She squeezes her knees and curls her head to rest on top of them as she sobs.

"Shit, I'm so sorry." I settle down next to her and rub her back. "You're priceless. He's a fucking idiot." *If you were mine, I'd never let you go.*

Noémie peels her head away from her knees. Her eyes are red, and her cheeks are puffy. Still, she couldn't be more beautiful.

I want to kiss away the tears balancing on her eyelashes and tell her that I will always be here for her if she needs me. Of course, I can't do that. But I can sit here with her until she puts herself back together. Our customers can wait.

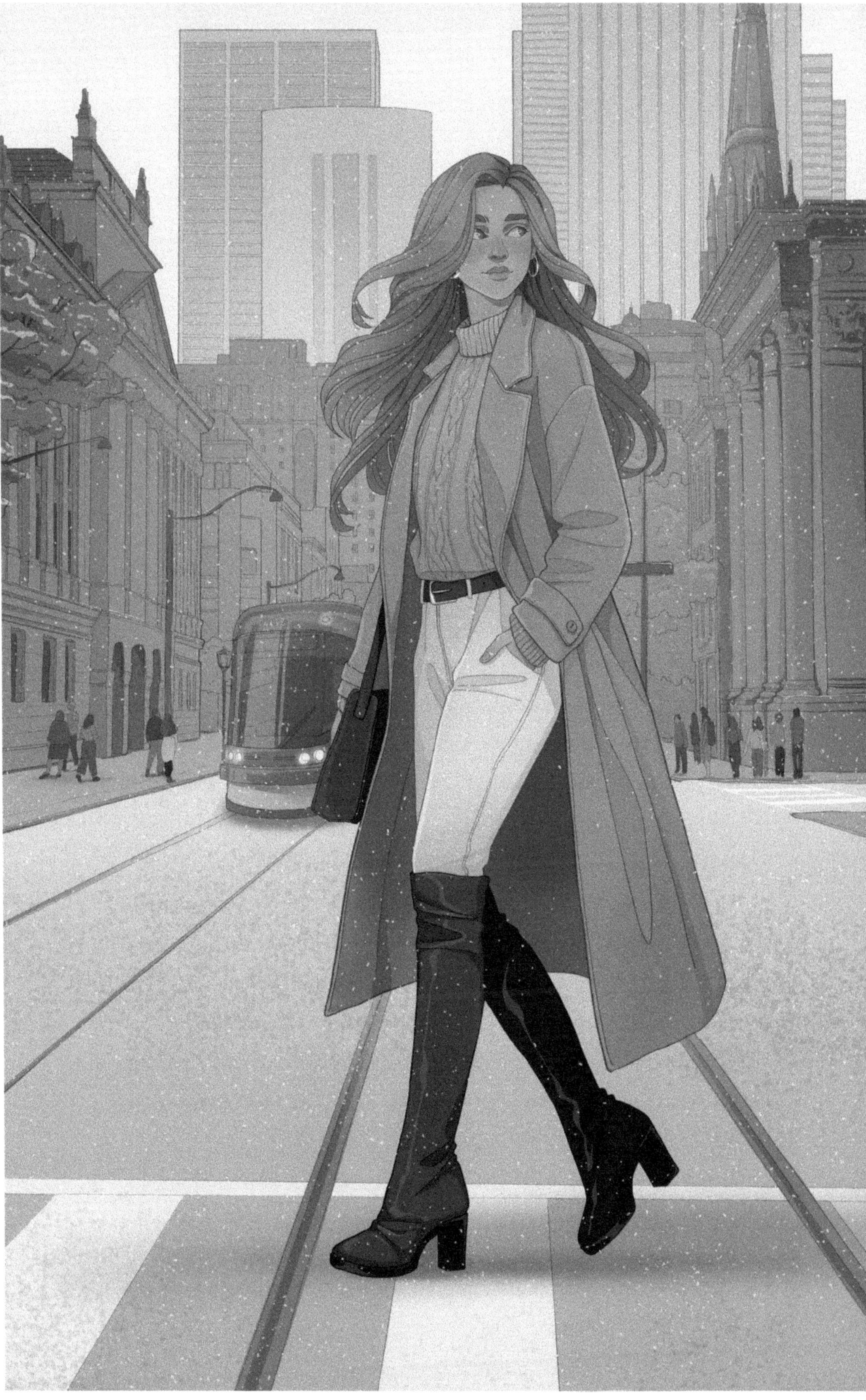

Chapter 25

The New Year is four hours away. Noémie descends the staircase looking like a goddess.

I shouldn't gawk the way I'm gawking, but I can't help it. Noémie is heartbreak wrapped in orange, and I'm starved for what she's serving. The dress is the same strapless one she'd been wearing the night of Sarah's send off—the night I walked her home.

Wayne elbows me in the ribs. I glare at him, even though I'm thankful for the distraction.

Reaching the foyer, Noémie smiles. "Ready to go?"

We're all dressed to impress. We're going to hit up a queer bashment in the Village to ring in the New Year. The event mainly draws a Black—Caribbean centric—crowd, but everyone is welcome. Even straights show up sometimes. All in all, it's always a good time.

I have mixed feelings about Noémie's attendance. While I want to celebrate the New Year with her, I'm also horny as fuck and want to hook up.

So the question is, do I have the willpower to quit simping for Noémie long enough to make a connection with someone else tonight?

"Yeah, I'm good to go," Wayne says.

I nod. "Me too."

"I'll call the Uber then," Noémie says, reaching into her Chanel purse to retrieve her phone.

Five minutes later, our trio steps out of the Yorkville residence and into the cold night air. The Uber is a black Honda Civic. Wayne takes shotgun, and Noémie and I slip into the back.

For the duration of the car ride, I keep finding myself staring at Noémie and then internally chastising myself. Sometimes, I feel like I can stare at her forever and never grow tired. It's hard to imagine how anyone could ever give her up. Whoever that sucker is, I curse him to always step in a puddle after putting on a fresh pair of socks.

Toronto's city streets are alive. Rambunctious partygoers clog the sidewalks, and the traffic is so bad that it feels like we're being transported via tortoise instead of vehicle. A part of me considers calling for the driver to stop and walking the rest of the way, but it's winter and I'm not trying to freeze my ass off.

Finally, we arrive. There's a line wrapping around the block to get into the venue. But lucky for us, Corie, Kristen, and Hailey arrived earlier and are holding spots for us near the front of the queue. It's their first time meeting Noémie. They eye her with appreciation—even Corie, who as a rule isn't into feminine women like herself.

I dive right into the introductions. "Everybody, this is Noémie." I nod at Corie. "Noémie, meet Corie, the resident femme of our group."

Noémie greets her with a kiss on both cheeks. "Very nice to meet you. I love your outfit."

Corie blushes, and it's got nothing to do with the cold. "I'm so glad to finally be meeting the infamous Poutine Princess. I've heard so much about you."

The colour drains from Wayne's face.

Noémie drills me with a scalding look. "Poutine Princess?"

I raise my hands in defence. "Hey, that was Wayne's nickname for you."

Noémie directs her ire at Wayne.

He glares at me. "Thanks for throwing me under the bus, Jay." To Noémie he says, "I'll have you know that the nickname was retired the moment you started working with us when we realized you weren't the spawn of coffee Satan."

"Spawn of coffee Satan?" Noémie repeats in a serious tone. And then she chuckles, breaking the tension. "I wasn't that bad. It's not my fault that you guys kept messing up my order."

"Your order was fucking ridiculous. Who the hell mixes whole milk and almond milk?" I say with a laugh.

"And exactly half a pump of vanilla syrup and hazelnut syrup," Wayne adds.

"Are you guys done?" Noémie flips her hair over her shoulder. She smiles at Hailey and then Kristen. "I didn't catch your names."

Hailey speaks first, thrusting her hand out. "I'm Hailey, and this is my girlfriend, Kristen."

Noémie shakes the outstretched hand. Kristen doesn't offer hers. Instead she gives Hailey a dose of side-eye, which tells me something is up. I wonder what they are fighting about this time.

The line moves, and the cold is really starting to seep into my bones. I'm not Canadian enough for winter in Toronto.

Wayne and Corie begin talking about sports, of all things. Corie says something about Caitlin Clark being able to beat Steph Curry in a shootout, and Wayne is having none of it. "Gurrl, you've no idea what you're talking about," he says.

The line creeps up some more, and finally we're the next group to be vetted by venue security.

"This is so exciting," Noémie says, latching onto my arm. "I haven't been out in ages."

My stomach flips. "This your first queer party?"

"Nope," Noémie replies, not offering up anything else.

Noémie detaches from me when she's called up by a female bouncer built like a football player. After handing over her I.D., Noémie is frisked and a flashlight gets beamed into her purse. All clear, the venue door is opened for her and she disappears inside.

It's my turn next. I go through the motions that I know all too well, and a part of me feels like I'm getting too old for this crap. I'll be in my mid-thirties soon, and then I'll be just a hop and a skip away from the graveyard.

I guess I'm happy to be out tonight. But to be honest, it might have been nicer to be at home with Noémie. We could've binge-watched the Lord of the Rings trilogy and ordered pizza. Noémie could've cracked open a bottle of champagne from her collection. We could've celebrated the end of a turbulent year together.

"You're good," the bouncer says.

I blink out of my thoughts and step through the door being held open for me. I climb the staircase leading to the party.

Noémie and the rest of the group are waiting for me by the ticket seller. The woman behind the register is a cute Southeast Asian woman with a wolf cut mullet. Her name tag reads *Sabrina*. I smile at Sabrina, and she smiles back. And for a moment, I feel reinvigorated, more in my element. I can't have Noémie, but there are plenty of other fish in the sea, and I know how to lure them. I can be funny and interesting. I can be suave and mysterious. But it also doesn't hurt that I'm a pretty stud—and there aren't many of us.

We all buy our tickets and check our coats, and then Sabrina stamps the insides of our wrists.

"I like your haircut," I say as she stamps a blue star onto my wrist.

Sabrina meets my eyes and grins. "I like your vibe," she says, biting down on her lower lip.

I consider asking for her number. Someone tugs on my arm, pulling me away from the ticket stand. I'm slightly irritated, and then I see that it's Noémie dragging me away and I become jelly. We slip past the satin red curtain and enter the club. Everything is black—the walls, the sticky floors, the couches that rim the area. The main dance floor is only half full, but it's only a matter of time before it gets packed. Dancehall music blares so loud that I feel the vibration on my skin.

Noémie guides us towards the nearest bar and gestures for the others to follow. She orders a round of tequila shots for the group and drops my hand to grab a few twenties from her purse. Six shot glasses are lined on the bar top and filled with a sloppy flourish. The bartender tops each with a lime wedge.

"Tequila. I see you're looking to get wild tonight," I say in Noémie's ear.

She forces a shot glass in my hand. "Hell fucking yes!" She reaches for the salt, sprinkling some on the back of her hand. She licks it off, downs her shot, and bites down on the lime.

Mesmerized, I watch her. I shake myself out of it to perform the same ritual. The tequila makes me shudder. I hate tequila—I'm more of a rum and Coke or beer person. And I guess, Noémie has turned me into a wine person now too.

"Not a fan of tequila?" Noémie asks.

"Nope."

"I am," she says, signalling for the bartender. Noémie orders another shot for herself and downs it after clinking glasses with Wayne.

I order a bottle of MGD.

Corie sets off for the middle of dance floor and begins swaying to the music. I stare at my friend in wonder. I don't know how people do that—go out on to a dance floor alone and sober. I'd say that I'm a pretty good dancer, but I need liquid courage do to something other than a one-two-step or a lean-with-it-rock-with-it.

"Let's dance with Corie," Noémie says.

Still waiting for the alcohol to hit, I shake my head. "I don't feel like dancing yet. You go."

Pouting, Noémie latches onto Wayne, a willing victim, and pulls him out onto the dance floor.

Hanging back with Hailey and Kristen, I lean against the bar and sip my beer. I try not to focus on Noémie, but she's like a beacon of light in the dark and I'm a pathetic fly—I'm drawn to her despite knowing that getting too close will get me zapped.

"You fuck her yet?" Hailey asks.

Kristen frowns. "You don't have to answer that, Jay, but have you? Just curious."

"No, she's my friend."

"Sarah was your friend. Weren't you fucking her?" Hailey says with a cackle before taking a swig from her own bottle of beer—Molson Canadian. She's got terrible taste in beer.

Kristen elbows her girlfriend, but Hailey doesn't take the hint. Instead, she doubles down. "I don't know how you live with a piece like that and not go insane, especially when she seems down."

Noémie down? I shake my head. "She's straight."

"Spaghetti's also straight until it gets wet."

"Seriously, Hailey, shut the fuck up," Kristen snaps.

Hailey rolls her eyes and doesn't shut the fuck up. "If Noémie was my roommate, she'd get it."

"She wouldn't want your fat ass. I'm going to get some fresh air." Folding her arms, Kristen turns and walks away.

"You should go after her," I say.

Hailey grunts and makes no move to leave. I really, really despise her.

Downing the rest of my beer, I slide the empty bottle on the bar and chase after my friend. Outside is freezing, and the line to get into the party is longer. I'm not sure that everyone who wants to get in will get to. The city streets buzz with chatter, laughter, and frequent car horns. I find Kristen bumming a cigarette from a group of thick-built studs sporting intense expressions and snapbacks. The group makes both me and Kristen look femme. Normally, Kristen isn't a smoker. She must be very upset.

I sidle up beside her, offering up a lighter. Kristen pops the cigarette in her mouth, and when I spark the flame, she leans in close to light the tip. Smoke whirls around her in the cold winter air.

Kristen sags against a wall. I light a cigarette too and go to stand beside her. "Want to talk about what's bugging you?"

"Do I even have to say it?"

"Hailey is an asshole," I guess.

"Yup." Like me, Kristen is a pretty masc. She's even lighter skinned than myself, and she's got the neatest dreadlocks I've ever seen. Considering how women are constantly stumbling over their words around her, I really don't know why she chooses to anchor herself to Hailey's dead weight.

"For real, why are you guys still together?" I say.

"I really don't know," Kristen mutters, staring down at the cigarette between her fingers.

"Want to talk about it?" I ask again.

Kristen shakes her head. "Nope."

"Okay." I rub my arms. It's really fucking cold.

"I am curious though," Kristen says, puncturing the silence.

"What about?" I ask, taking a final drag from my cigarette. I crush the butt under my heel and exhale a cloud.

"You and Noémie—you really haven't hooked up?"

"Why is everyone so surprised?"

"You don't have the best track record, and Noémie is … gorgeous."

"She's also straight."

"And when has that ever stopped you?" Kristen raises a brow.

Everyone keeps saying that and it's really starting to grate on my nerves. I've never had an active agenda to turn straight girls. It's been my experience that curious women are the ones to make a move on me, not the other way around.

"We work together. She's my roommate. She's my friend. There are so many reasons why it'd be a bad idea to even try to pursue anything with her," I say, shoving my hands down my front pockets in an attempt to warm them back up. "But most importantly, Noémie isn't interested in me—I would know if she was. If there's one thing that I'm good at, it's reading women."

"You didn't know Sarah was in love with you."

I frown at my friend. "You knew about that?"

"Everybody knew. It was kind of hard to miss."

My jaw clenches. "Noémie's not Sarah."

"You sure about that? I swear, when you aren't looking, she stares at you like you hang the moon. And you stare back at her the same way. It's disgusting."

Kristen's got to be wrong. Sure, there'd been a few sexually charged moments between us, but it's likely that I was the only one who felt anything. Noémie doesn't want me. She can't want me—that would make things too messy.

"Let's go inside," I say. "It's fucking cold out here."

Chapter 26

The venue is packed. Every flavour of queer makes up the thick mob on the dance floor. Twinks twerk in their tight booty shorts. Glamorous femmes with forty-inch lace front wigs and acrylic nails herd together. Fly studs wearing fitteds, glinting chains and fresh pairs of Js edge the perimeter.

I head for the bar, deciding to get another drink now while the line isn't too hectic.

Vybz Kartel's voice booms so loud over the speakers that I barely catch Kristen saying, "I'm going to find Hailey."

Nodding, I watch her disappear into the crowd. I order another MGD. The bartender cracks a bottle open for me. I slide a ten on the counter and move out of the way. I scan the area, looking for a pop of orange, but I have no luck. It's very dark and very busy. Head bopping to the music, I navigate through the horde of gyrating bodies. I can feel the alcohol working its magic. I'm feeling looser.

Halfway through my beer, I've circled the large room twice, and still there's no sign of Noémie, Wayne, or Corie. I'm thinking about texting them when arms encircle my waist. A woman's mouth presses against my ear. "You didn't tell me you were coming out tonight."

I recognize the voice. Turning around, I face Audrina. Tonight, she's wearing grungy jeans with a studded belt and a cropped purple Raptor's jersey. A floppy toque sits atop her shoulder-length curly hair. Usually, Audrina's style leans towards hot secretary, which I dig. But I have to say, she's looking hella fine in masc attire.

"I missed you," she says, brushing her lips over mine. Not one to be subtle, she grabs my crotch and pouts. "Not packing tonight—what a pity."

I roll my eyes. "That's all you ever want me for."

She reels me in until our foreheads touch. "You know I want so much more than that," she murmurs against my lips.

I don't say anything to that, and she doesn't expect me to. We start kissing and dancing. Her hips grind into me, and I match her movements to the beat of the reggae music. It feels good, so good to be wanted. My hands slip up her shirt, and my thumbs caress the skin of her stomach as I nuzzle her neck. Audrina's fingers dig into my back.

We've always had amazing chemistry. If it weren't for my hangups, perhaps we'd be a perfect match for each other. But I do have hangups, and I don't do relationships. Since the summer we've been fucking—I can't remember the last time I've kept a fuck buddy around this long. In a way, I'm probably leading her on, which isn't fair to her.

Guilt makes me pull away. Audrina tries to pull me back.

"We can't keep doing this," I say with a shake of my head. "You want and deserve so much more than I can give you."

Audrina looks at me with eyes wide and hurt. She opens her mouth to say something.

"There you are!"

My gaze darts over Audrina's shoulder. Noémie is in the process of shimmying her way through a group of friends chatting in the middle of the dance floor.

Audrina looks in the direction I'm staring. She scowls, her hurt morphing to anger and hot possessiveness.

Noémie doesn't seem to notice Audrina. Arriving at my side, she laces her fingers through mine. "Wayne and I have been looking all over for you."

"Jordan, who's this?" Audrina asks, crossing her arms.

Noémie smiles a little too sweetly at Audrina. "I'm Noémie, Jordan's roommate." She holds out her hand. "Nice to meet you."

Audrina's eyes ping-pong between me and Noémie. She ignores Noémie's outstretched hand. Her jaw clenches. "You never mentioned a roommate," she says, giving Noémie a dirty look. "Then again, we don't do too much talking when we're together."

Noémie's smile drops. "I need to go to the washroom," she says, squeezing my fingers.

"And I'm going to get a drink," Audrina says, arching a brow. "Coming, Jordan?" I know what she is really asking—she's asking me to choose her and ditch Noémie.

Scratching the back of my ear, I divert my gaze. "Maybe I'll catch you later," I say.

Audrina's nostrils flare. "Don't bother." Whipping around, she forces her way through the web of dancers.

Though we were never official, it kind of feels like a breakup. I don't think I'll be getting texts from her anytime soon—the revelation weighs surprisingly heavy in my chest.

Noémie leads us off the dance floor and down a narrow staircase.

The queue to use the toilet extends out of the washroom. We take our spot at the back of it. I find it odd that Noémie still hasn't dropped my hand, but I'm not going to say anything. I love the feeling of our fingers intertwined.

Down in the venue's dank basement, the music is drowned out, allowing for more practical conversation. Neither me nor Noémie says anything though. I'm a bit surprised that she's not asking about Audrina. I wonder what's on her mind. She's frowning the slightest bit.

We shuffle forward as the line moves. Behind us someone says, "Gawd, you guys are too fucking cute."

It's Noémie's blush that makes me realize that the comment is directed at us. Eyeing the woman standing behind us, I force a grin. She's short and curvy with tousled hair dyed pink and sweat beading her forehead and upper lip. Clipped to her shirt is an enamel pin shaped like a PlayStation controller with *Gaymer* printed on it.

"We aren't together," I say. While I don't mean for my words to sound bitter, they do. I hope Noémie doesn't notice.

"Shame. You'd make the cutest babies," the pink-haired woman comments.

"That's not even possible," Noémie says dryly, clearly showing her disinterest in the conversation.

I'm not interested in it either. Sometime between arriving at the club and this moment, my mood soured. I just want to go to bed. Lifting my beer bottle to my lips, I finish it off. There are a few empty bottles on the floor. I set mine down to join them.

"Yes, it is. I read it somewhere …" The woman taps her chin and frowns. "I can't remember. Too drunk."

"Aren't we all," Noémie mutters.

"How much have you had to drink?" I arch a brow at her. I hope she hasn't had too much. Drunk Noémie is a diva.

"I don't drink and tell," she replies. Her tone is off—she sounds tired.

Finally, we reach the front of the line. A stall door opens and two women stumble out. One of them is Hailey, and the other is one hundred percent not Kristen.

"What the actual fuck?" My feet move on autopilot. Before I know it, I'm in Hailey's air space. "You're fucking disgusting," I snap, shoving her.

Hailey stumbles into the garbage can. The grey plastic bin turns over with a thump, scattering crumpled and damp brown paper towels onto the stained concrete floor.

"I'm not the one who's a homewrecker," Hailey claps back, straightening. Her eyes glint like the edge of a polished blade.

For a moment, I think Hailey's going to retaliate and come at me. I don't think I can take her if she does. She's a police officer. She knows how to take people down. But Hailey doesn't come after me. Instead, she grabs the woman—who she'd been doing only God knows what with—by the elbow and rushes them out of the washroom.

Dozens of eyes are focused on me. Noémie's looking at me like I've grown a fucking tail. A wave of embarrassment crashes over me, and I zip into a vacated stall to escape scrutiny. My heart pounds in my ears. I'm burning up, and the world is tilting. I lean against a wall and close my eyes.

There's a knock on the door. "Jordan, you okay?" When I don't answer, Noémie says, "Let me in."

I don't want Noémie to see me like this—a mess. So why am I

unlatching the door? Why am I letting her inside when I just want to be alone?

She squeezes into the tight space, and we shut ourselves away from it all.

"Are you okay?" Her hands go to my face. She strokes my cheeks with her thumbs. I know she is trying to comfort me, trying to be helpful, but her nearness is not making things better.

Her proximity is a catalyst. It's like everything I was feeling moments ago gets whited out. Noémie's mere presence rewrites everything. All I feel now is pure, raw lust. I want to force her up against the wall, push up her dress, and yank down her panties. I want to bite down on her neck and mark her as mine. I want to …

I have to look away from her. I can't meet her eyes.

"Jordan, please talk to me. You're worrying me," she says softly. Still, her hands caress my face. Her touch makes me shudder.

Against my better judgment, I look at her. Our eyes lock for a moment, and then I'm staring down at her mouth. Her glossy lips are slightly parted. She licks them. I lick mine. Our eyes meet again.

Noémie's hands drop from my face. A flush of red colours her chest and neck. She's breathing heavier.

My gaze goes to her breasts. They're pushed up and on display. Just looking at them makes me ache.

"Jordan …" Noémie says my name and inches closer before hesitating, like she is teetering at the edge of an invisible boundary—one that she's not quite sure how to cross. Or maybe doesn't want to cross.

All I can think about is how good it will feel to kiss her. I forget about Hailey. I forget about Kristen. I have tunnel vision—Noémie is all I see.

I bridge the gap between us, pressing my body into hers. Noémie sucks in a breath as her back flattens against the wall.

Fuck, she feels so good. Her body is so soft and warm. I run my hands over her hips. I cup her ass. I rock against her, making her gasp. Noémie shivers, and I take it as a good sign. I bend my head. Our lips are a breath apart when someone bangs so forcefully on the washroom stall that the door rattles.

Noémie and I spring apart.

The person on the other side of the door keeps banging. "Get the fuck out. People out here have to piss!"

Noémie moves first, scrambling for the lock. When the door opens, she bolts.

I take off after her. "Noémie!"

She doesn't break her stride, heels clacking loudly on the cement. She pushes past a group of women and hurries up the steps.

I take the stairs two at a time, trying to catch up to her. Back on the dance floor, I grab her wrist. Noémie yanks back her hand. When she looks at me, her gaze is pure ice and I freeze.

Fuck—did I read the situation in the bathroom all wrong? Did I force myself on Noémie? Fuck-fuck-fuck-fuck!

My stomach rolls over, a wave of sickness punching me in the gut. I hug my stomach. Of all people, I should know better. I should be better.

I know what it's like to be touched without consenting. The darkest chapter of my life happened over the summer when I was fourteen.

I'd been at the rec centre and just exited the pool. Jamal, a boy of eighteen at the time, followed after me and then dragged me by my arm into a stairwell. Because he was tall, dark, and handsome, I don't think

Jamal had ever experienced being told no before. It had been inconceivable to him that I didn't want him.

"Quit acting like you don't want this," he'd snapped, right before …

I squeeze my eyes shut and push the memory away. Shaking my head, I tell myself that I'm nothing like Jamal. If Noémie gave me any indication that she wasn't interested, I would have stopped.

Opening my eyes, I stare up at her. "Noémie, I'm—"

"There you two are," Wayne exclaims, rushing over to us. "We need to go. There's an emergency."

Chapter 27

The emergency is Kristen. Apparently, she and Hailey got into a screaming match on the dance floor and the bouncers kicked both of them out. And now Kristen is crying into a pint of vanilla bean Häagen-Dazs on Noémie's couch. Corie and Wayne flank her shoulders. I'm kneeling in front of her, telling her that it's okay to be upset, that she's better off without Hailey. Noémie sits on the far end of the couch. Her expression is blank as she absentmindedly pets Céline.

In five minutes, it will be the New Year. We're off to a great start.

Corie kisses Kristen's temple. "Hailey sucked. Good riddance, I'd say. She wasn't even hot." Kristen bawls harder.

Noémie rises from her seat. "I … I'm going to sleep. You guys are all welcome to stay the night. I have guest rooms, but if you prefer the couch, there are some throws in the chest." Noémie cocks her head towards the wooden storage crate near the window.

"Thanks so much, Noémie." Wayne smiles sadly at her.

Noémie returns his smile for a second, and then she turns to leave the main room. She doesn't even look at me.

I know I should stay with Kristen, but I owe Noémie an apology.

And while I hate to have hard conversations, I can't sweep what I did under the rug. Noémie is my friend, and what I did to her was wrong on so many levels. I would understand if she never wanted to talk to me again. I would understand if she asked me to move out. I have to own up to what I did and beg for her forgiveness.

Hopefully, she forgives me. I don't want to imagine a life without her—without her friendship.

"I'll be back in a sec," I say, standing up.

Wayne's giving me a look that says, *Girl, where the fuck are you going?* But he doesn't say anything aloud.

I catch up with Noémie just as she's reaching to open the door to her bedroom.

"Hey, Noémie, can we talk?"

Noémie makes a sound. It's the kind of noise someone makes when they're annoyed—a cross between a groan and a grunt. She turns and looks at me. Her grey eyes seem vacant—tired. "What do you want, Jordan?"

"I … about what happened—"

"I can't talk about this right now, but Happy New Year," she says, opening her bedroom door. She steps inside and closes it behind her.

I stare at the door for way too long before making my way back downstairs to console my friend.

Kristen falls asleep minutes before one, and Corie decides to sleep beside her on the couch. Wayne announces that he will be sleeping in the same guest room he used when he housesat over the holidays.

As Wayne and I head up the stairs, he asks, "What happened between you and Noémie? What did you do?"

I don't respond. I go to my room.

Wayne follows me and tugs on my arms. "Seriously, spill the tea. Something is off. What happened?"

I shrug out of his grasp and throw myself down on my bed. Usually, I change out of any clothes I wear outside before going anywhere near my bed, but I'm too drained to care. Staring up at the ceiling, I wonder if Noémie is still awake. If she is up, is she reanalyzing all of our past interactions, looking for further evidence of my predation? Is she reconsidering our friendship?

"I fucked up," I say, rubbing my eyes.

The bed dips beside me. Wayne's face hovers over mine. Concern wrinkles his forehead. "What happened?"

I tell him what happened, but downplay what I felt in the moment.

"I told you not to make any moves on Noémie. I've begged you not to," Wayne says, sighing loudly. "But … maybe if you tell her how you feel that will make everything better."

"Tell her how I feel?"

"You care for her, right? Like, more than just a friend?"

I don't answer him. Telling Noémie that I have feelings for her would not help the situation. It would only make things worse.

"I made a mistake, and I won't do it again," I say.

Wayne groans and shoots up to his feet. "Whatever, I tried." He leaves my room, shutting the door behind him.

The next few days, I barely see Noémie. Actually, it's worse than that. Noémie switches her day shifts for nights, so we really don't see each other except in passing. When Noémie is home, she hides out in her bedroom, only leaving to work out in the basement or grab a delivery from the front door.

I've tried talking to her, but each time I manage to get her alone, she finds an excuse to escape. I worry that she's scared of me. I worry that I've ruined everything. I start to expect the worst—that Noémie will ask me to move out. And I can't blame her. She's got every right to not want to be around me. I would understand.

By Saturday afternoon, I decide that I can't anymore—I need to talk to Noémie. The coldness is killing me.

Heart racing, I ascend to the top floor and knock on her bedroom door. Noémie tells me to come in. I'm taken aback by her tone, it's upbeat—happy.

I step inside and scan the room. It's the first time I'm seeing it. The walls are a muted beige. Exposed wooden beams section the ceiling, giving the room cozy cottage vibes. The drapes and the large area rug are a soft grey colour like Noémie's eyes. Most of the wood furnishings are bleached. To be expected, there are pops of orange everywhere—the bedding, the cushions, and the artwork. The portrait I gifted Noémie with on Christmas is mounted on the wall next to a slim bookshelf and an armchair.

"Hey, what's up?" Noémie asks.

Blinking, I turn my gaze on her. For a moment, my mind goes blank, and I forget how to breathe.

Noémie's dressed in a dark-blue romper with a gold chain belted across her waist. She's sporting a full face of makeup. Smoky eyeshadow makes her eyes pop—they look more silver than grey. Her lips and nails are painted in her signature colour. Her long auburn hair is pulled into a sleek ponytail.

There's a pair of teardrop earrings with stones the colour of a sunset laid out on the dresser. Noémie reaches for them. "Jordan, I have somewhere to be, so—"

"Do you want me to move out?" I blurt. Fuck, I hadn't meant to start with that question—the plan was to apologize first.

"What?" Noémie almost drops her earring. She frowns at me. "Why are you asking me this? Do you want to move out?"

Okay, so this is definitely not how I saw this conversation going. But I'm so confused, isn't Noémie mad at me?

"You've been ignoring me," I say, swallowing and scratching the back of my neck. "I figured you were mad and avoiding me because of what happened on New Year's Eve. I … I don't know what I was thinking, and I'm so sorry, Noémie. What I did was not okay, and I …" My voice cracks. There's a lump in my throat, and I'm not sure I can speak past it. I look down at my socked feet.

"Jordan, it's okay," she says. "We were both a little tipsy. It's really not that big of a deal."

"It really is though." My stinging eyes snap up to hers. "I know what it feels like to …" Her eyes widen with understanding, and I can't finish my sentence. It's too hard. This is not something I talk about. I can feel the tears gathering to drop. I turn to leave, but a hand around my wrist stops me.

"Jordan," Noémie says, her voice is more tender than I've ever heard it before. When she twists me around to face her, I fall into her arms and cry.

It's so pathetic—I'm pathetic. But I can't stop.

Noémie wraps her arms around me tightly. "Jordan, you didn't do anything wrong," she repeats. "And I'm sorry that I've been avoiding you, but I guess I was kind of freaking out and embarrassed. Like, you're one of my closest friends, and I just—I don't know. Things got kind of weird, and I panicked a bit. But I should have talked to you.

I'm sorry too."

I'm glad she's not asking about what I revealed to her. I think she knows I don't want to talk about it. It's hard to pretend something didn't happen if I speak about it.

Sniffling, I step out of her arms and wipe my eyes. The shoulder of her romper is wet from my tears.

"Yeah, communicating would've been good," I say, clearing my throat. "But I'd rather walk into traffic than have a tough conversation sometimes."

"I guess we are the same in that sense," Noémie agrees. "Moving forward, let's make a promise to always be honest with each other. Maybe we can both try to communicate better instead of running away."

I nod. "Okay."

Noémie looks at me expectantly, as if she's waiting for me to expand and say more. But there's nothing more that I can actually say. I can't be completely honest with Noémie. I'm head over heels in love with the woman, and she will only ever see me as a friend.

Then again, could the reason for Noémie's panic be that she'd wanted me in that moment too? Thinking back, I remember how she'd inched towards me and said my name, almost pleading. I remember how she licked her lips. I remember how she gasped and shivered. If I kissed her, would she have kissed me back? Would we have stopped at just one kiss or would Noémie have let me go further?

Was Noémie freaking out because she's questioning her sexuality? Could it be that she possibly wants me too? Kristen said Noémie looks at me like I hang the moon. If I told Noémie the truth ... If I was completely honest with her, what would be the outcome?

I think about Noémie telling me to go for what I want on the night I met François. More than anything, I want her. I want to be with her in every way, but I'm so scared of opening myself up to heartbreak again. But I'm choking on my feelings for her. I'm already hurting so much right now, and we aren't even together. So maybe I should just take the risk and be honest.

"Noémie, I—"

The doorbell rings.

Céline hops off the bed where she'd been sleeping and begins to bark. She paws at the door, her tiny nails scratching the wood.

Noémie's gaze drops to the shoulder of her romper. It's still wet from my tears. "I'm going to have to change," she says. "Jordan, can you please let Felix in?"

Felix? The douchebag from the Christmas market? What's he doing here?

All my muscles tense. "Yeah, sure," I say, trying my best to sound nonchalant. "You guys going out?"

"Yeah, for drinks," Noémie replies, disappearing into her walk-in closet.

"Like a date?" I ask, knowing that I really don't want to hear the answer.

"Yeah," Noémie says. "Like a date."

Chapter 28

January bleeds into February, and Noémie and Felix are now a thing. Whenever I see them together, I seethe. I'm not succeeding at acting blasé. Wayne consistently lets me know that I'm being a bigger ass wipe than normal.

If Noémie notices that I'm saltier than usual, she doesn't comment. For the most part, when Noémie isn't out with Felix, we are carrying on as usual—we go to work, we go home, she makes dinner, and then we crash on the couch to watch Netflix.

Our routine changes around early February when Felix starts coming over. At first, Noémie tries to get me to join them for dinner, but I'd rather cut my tits off. More often than not, I'm eating dinner in my bedroom now, and I stop drawing in the living room. It gets to the point where even when Felix isn't around, I'm holed up and alone.

There is a highlight—I'm more productive than ever. I'm almost finished drafting the fourth volume of my graphic novel series. Also, I somehow grew a fucking backbone and connected with François.

To my shock, he is genuinely delighted when I reach out. We don't even talk about my project during our first chats. We talk about everything else—like the industry, the gossip, and the comics we're currently reading. It's easy to talk to François. We're alike in a lot of ways. For a really successful artist, he's super humble.

François thinks that my series has the potential to make it big, and we're developing a plan to gain me some traction online before I launch a Kickstarter.

It's all very new to me, and I'm kind of excited about it. For the first time in a long time, I'm allowing myself to dream.

Following François's advice, I open a few social media accounts for my brand and to promote myself. I begin to post daily voiceover videos of me drawing. Frankly, the videos are cringe. But I'm getting a little better at editing and more confident on camera with every post. My follower count is dismal, but François says, if I keep at it, I'll find success. I actually kind of believe him.

The first and only time Felix stays the night, it's the last Friday in February. The sound of their lovemaking assaults my ears and hollows out my soul. Needing an escape from the racket, I go out for a walk despite it being negative one thousand outside.

Canadian winters suck. I can't fucking wait for spring.

While I try to think about anything else, all I see in my mind's eye is Noémie and Felix going at it. On repeat, I conjure the images of them together—missionary, doggy style, reverse cowgirl … It turns my stomach. I go a little crazy.

Fifteen minutes into my walk, I shoot Audrina a message. I get no response.

My feet carry me to a drag bar in the Village. There, I down five beers and snort lines in the washroom with a hot Korean woman named Kim. We hit it off and have a super sloppy make-out session by the fire exit. Kim takes me back to her place. I know we have sex, but when I wake up, I can't remember if it was good or not.

Disentangling my limbs from Kim's, I struggle to stand and put on my clothes. I'm dizzy and nauseous as I trek back home on the TTC.

Céline barks in greeting when I walk through the front door. The sound scrapes against my brain.

Needing water very badly, I shuffle to the kitchen. When I see Felix sitting at the island, scrolling through his phone, I groan. He swivels his stool to look at me. Noémie stares up from a waffle iron that she just ladled batter on. The air smells like waffles, and I don't find it the least bit appetizing.

"Long night?" Felix asks with a grin.

Fuck him! I don't answer as I walk over to a cabinet. I open it and remove a glass. My hand shakes as I flip on the tap and fill the glass with water. I gulp it all down and then fill the glass back up with more.

"Do you want waffles?" Noémie asks.

Just the thought of food makes me wince. "No, no food," I reply. "There's some Gravol in my room that's calling to me."

Felix chuckles at my comment. Noémie doesn't. She looks a mix of concern and pissed off. "Do you need help getting upstairs?"

I shake my head. "Nope." Glass of water in hand, I retreat to my room where I strip out of my bar clothes and collapse under my sheets. The world goes blank the moment my head hits the pillow.

The sky is dark when my phone rings, rousing me. I reach for it. The caller I.D. displays Sarah's name.

I swipe the screen to answer. "Hey, what are you saying?" I answer, my voice all raspy.

"I wake you?"

"Yup. Long night."

"Do I even want to know?" Sarah asks.

"Probably not." I sit up in bed, repositioning my pillow behind my back. "What's up?"

"So … I'm moving back to Toronto."

I sit up a little straighter. "What?"

"I'm sick of Vancouver's sad weather," Sarah says. "Also, Veronica and I broke up."

"I'm so sorry, bud. I know you really wanted things to work out with her." I'm not surprised things with Veronica didn't pan out.

"It is what it is." Sarah sighs over the receiver. "Anything new with you, besides prepping for your Kickstarter? By the way, you're doing great. Your last reel is doing amazing."

I blink. "It is?" I tap on the Instagram app to check. "Holy shit! There's, like, ten thousand views."

"And counting," Sarah says. "Look at you, getting out of your comfort zone and putting yourself out there. I'm so proud of you, Jay."

We talk some more. Mainly, we complain about how the cost of renting in Toronto has become even more ridiculous. A few times, Sarah asks me about Noémie. I deflect any questions about her.

When our call ends, I rise out of bed, take a shower, and pull on some sweatpants and a hoodie.

I know I should probably work on recording another video to ride on my last video's success, but I'm not in the mood. My muscles feel like Jackie Chan beat the crap out of me. At least the Gravol worked—it's my hangover hack. I'm no longer nauseous. I'm hungry.

Exiting my room, I go down to the kitchen. Thankfully, Felix is not there. I hope he's left. His presence in this home is bad juju for my sense of peace.

I set the kettle on the stove to boil some water and grab a package of Indomie from the pantry. Leaning against the counter, I watch the kettle, which is a dumb thing to do. Everyone knows that water takes longer to boil if you watch it.

There's a slap of slippers on the floor. Looking over my shoulder, I see Noémie enter the main room. She's dressed down in a pair of yoga pants and an oversized white tee—no bra underneath. I avert my gaze.

The kettle whistles, and I turn towards the stove to pull it off the fire. I get to work and start preparing my noodles.

"You're always eating those," Noémie says, coming to stop beside me. "I can't remember the last time I had instant ramen. Want to make me some?"

Her nearness makes my pulse race. I consider correcting her, telling her that it's not ramen. "Yeah, sure," I say instead, walking over to the pantry and grabbing a second packet.

If the noodles were just for me, I would flip them out on a dish and have at it, but because Noémie will be having some too, I decide to get a little fancy. By fancy, I mean chopping up some fresh green onions to sprinkle on top.

I set our two steaming plates down at the dining table. Noémie takes her seat first, and then I take mine.

"It feels like we haven't sat down to eat together in forever," Noémie says. "I've missed you. Like, I mean … you're here, but it feels like I never see you anymore."

"Yeah, kind of feels that way," I agree, scooping up some noodles with my fork and popping them in my mouth. I chew.

"I guess it's for the best. All the work you're doing is paying off," she says with a half-smile. "Your last videos were very good."

They were not very good. They were better. I still have a lot to improve on. "Yeah, thanks."

Noémie frowns and puts down her fork. "Do you even want to talk to me? Everything out of your mouth is yeah this or yeah that."

"Sorry," I say. "I'm hungover."

Noémie drums her fingers on the table. "I didn't know you were going out last night." Her tone comes out harsh.

"Do I have to tell you when I'm going out?"

She blinks. Her face reddens. "No, but you usually tell me."

I don't know what to say to that, so I don't say anything. I continue eating. I'm almost done my food.

Noémie, I notice, isn't touching the noodles I made for her.

"Why don't you like Felix?" she asks.

The unexpectedness of her question almost makes me choke on a mouthful of noodles. I cough. "Who said I don't like Felix?"

"Whenever he's around, you get really quiet and disappear in your room for hours." Noémie sits back in her seat and folds her arms over her chest. "You're also so curt when you speak to him. It's like you become a whole different, colder person."

"I like Felix, He's … great," I lie. "And I'm sorry if I seem whack lately, I'm just running on empty. I barely have any brain space left now that I'm looking to launch my graphic novel."

"Do you need help?" she asks. "I told you already that I'd be more than happy to help you with recording and editing."

I shake my head. "I think I need to do it myself."

"Okay." Noémie bites her lip.

Done eating, I stand, grab my empty dish, and leave the table.

Noémie sighs loudly, and slumps down in her seat. She toys with her fork, and I'm a little irritated. Why'd she ask me to make her noodles if she wasn't planning on eating them?

Chapter 29

Living in Toronto, you can never be sure when winter is over. It's nearing the end of March, and last week was in the negative and snowing almost everyday. This week, the sun's out and shining. All the snow has melted, and today it's ten degrees Celsius. I'm itching to put on my new helmet and take my bike out from hibernation.

The mechanized garage door whirs open and I go to my Ninja, removing the thick black protective cover. The motorcycle wobbles precariously as I struggle to lower the rear tire from its stand—it's important to keep motorcycles lifted during long stretches of inactivity to prevent tire flat spots.

In the past, Sarah always helped me with lowering my bike, but she's not here, and I don't want to ask Noémie for help. We haven't really been talking lately. It's more me than Noémie. She's actively been trying to stir up conversation, but I just can't be around her right now—not while she parades her relationship with Felix in my face.

The two love birds are both flying out to Honolulu today at 10:00 p.m. Noémie's bags are packed and in the foyer. She's even taking Céline on the trip—leaving me completely alone.

Clenching my teeth, I make a second attempt to remove the stands. Thankfully, I'm successful.

Stepping away from the bike, I exhale a breath of relief and wheel it out onto the driveway where I wash the dust from its body, buff the paint until it gleams, check the tire pressure, and clean and lube the chain.

In the time it takes me to complete maintenance, the sky goes from sunny to overcast, threatening rain. Eyeing the clouds, I decide to take the risk. It's not like I'll be going far—I'll just be doing a tour of the neighbourhood. And I really, really want to feel the whip of the wind on my skin and the growl of the machine beneath me. It's been too long.

I straddle my motorcycle and slide on my shiny new Shoei helmet. All these months later, I'm still not sure how Noémie could afford it. She's still spending money like she isn't living on a barista's salary. Just last week, she randomly bought a PS5 after I mentioned to Wayne that I wanted to play *Elden Ring*. When the console arrived, along with the game, I questioned where she got the money for it, and it was a whole thing. Noémie called me difficult, and I accused her of always dodging my questions.

Turning the key, the engine hiccups and then grumbles to life. I knock back the kickstand, reverse onto the street and take off.

Even with all the stopping and going, the short ride around the city is enjoyable. If it weren't for the looming dark clouds, I would consider jumping onto the Queen Elizabeth Way and speeding down to the Niagara Region. I often make the trek out there in the summer. I like to stare at the Falls and conjure tableaus for my graphic novels in my head.

The scent of rain is heavy in the air when I zip into the garage, park beside Noémie's Tesla, and cut the engine. Pulling off my helmet, I run up the short staircase and open the front door.

To my surprise, shouting greets my ears. Noémie is screaming at someone, and my lips curve into a grin. Maybe this is when she finally breaks up with that tool, Felix. Maybe she won't go to Hawaii. Maybe things can go back to how they once were between us.

Céline rushes towards me. Before she can bark, I scoop her up into my arms and tiptoe towards the main area. I probably shouldn't eavesdrop, but I'm human. I'm curious. Sue me.

"Merde, I told you that I never wanted to see you again! Decriss! Leave—maintenant!"

"Nomi, let me explain." It's a woman's voice—not Felix. Great.

"I know I fucked up, but I miss you," she says. "It was a mistake, and I knew it instantly. I'll give it back. I'll give it all back."

"J'en ai rien à foutre! Leave!"

I stop at the entryway and go unnoticed. I can see both women. Everything about Noémie is red—her face, her neck, her arms. She wears a fiery expression. I don't think I've ever seen her this angry before. I don't know the second woman by name, but I recognize her face. She's Noémie's hot blond friend—the one featured in so many of Noémie's old Tiktok videos.

Céline is trying to climb up my chest to lick my cheeks. I won't let her lick my face, so she whines at me. In tandem, Noémie and the blond woman turn their heads in my direction. All the colour drains from Noémie's face. Her mouth drops open.

The blond woman scowls. "What the fuck is Hot Barista doing here?"

Hot Barista? I frown and put the dog down. Céline begins to chirp.

"She's my roommate, but that doesn't matter," Noémie says, her voice pure ice. "You need to go, Cara. Now!"

Cara doesn't budge. Instead, her eyes flit from Noémie to me and back to Noémie. "Thought you were trying out men again—"

"Cara, shut up. I swear … if you don't get the fuck out of my house!"

"Trying out men again?" I repeat and stare at Noémie. She won't meet my eyes.

Cara cackles. "Why does Hot Barista seem so confused, like she doesn't know you're—"

"Cara, you need to go."

"What is she talking about?" I ask.

Cara cocks her head to the side. "Nomi, don't tell me you followed your dad's orders and fell back into the closet," she says before fixing her eyes on me. "I'm going to assume she never mentioned me to you. I'm Caralyn, Noémie's ex."

I glare at Noémie. She winces like she's expecting me to lash out with my words. But I don't have anything to say. At least, I can't land on anything to say. There are too many questions. Too many thoughts buzzing in my head. I'm dizzy with confusion.

I end up doing the one thing I'm good at—I run away. Okay, not run. More like, slowly step back and head for the front door.

I push the button on my keys to lift the garage door. I'm back on my bike and fiddling with my helmet when Noémie rushes up to me.

"Jordan, wait … let's talk," she says.

I shut the visor on my helmet and turn the key in the ignition.

Noémie reaches for me. I bat her hand away. I don't want to talk. I need time to think and sort out my feelings.

I roll the motorcycle backwards out of the garage, down the driveway, and onto the street. I look at Noémie, and I can't put a name to the emotions that claw my heart. This whole time, Noémie lied to me. She let me go on thinking she was straight. She never once corrected me. I thought we were friends.

I twist the throttle and speed away. Before I know it, I'm merging onto the expressway. I shift from gear to gear, darting between the lanes. I'm trying to get lost in the feeling of the wind pushing against me. But I can't shake the questions that tumble around in my mind. What about our promise to be honest with each other? Why would Noémie purposefully keep this from me?

So preoccupied by my thoughts, I don't pay attention to the dark clouds above me until there's a crack of lightning and a boom of thunder. All at once, the sky breaks open and a torrent of rain pelts down on me, obscuring my visibility. I snap my visor up to see better, but I don't do it fast enough. The car in front of me breaks hard, its lights flashing red.

In an automatic response, I squeeze my front brake and realize too late that I should have applied both my front and rear brakes. My front tire locks up and my rear tire lifts. For a second, the world slows. And then I crash.

Chapter 30

I hear my mother before I see her. Paulette and Grandma Janet rush towards my hospital bed, their eyes wide with relief.

"God is good!" my mother says. She stares up at the ceiling, raising both her hands.

Grandma Janet nods her agreement. "Praise Him."

My mother crosses the tight space. Her fruity perfume overtakes the smell of antiseptic that's prevalent in the hospital. She grabs my face and turns it over in her hands to get a good look at me.

"My head's fine," I say, waving her off with my good hand—the one not in a cast.

"We were so worried when we got the call that you were in an accident," my mother says. "Why you ever decided to start riding that death trap, I'll never understand."

Grandma Janet sits down on the empty chair by the bedside. "God spared your life child," she states. "You must give him thanks."

I almost roll my eyes, but I'm not trying to get into a theological debate with them right now. The two of them have been trying to indoctrinate me into their church since I popped into the world. In their minds, it's only a matter of time before I stop sinning, trade in my pants for frocks, and marry a man. But it will take more than a near-death experience for me to make that kind of change.

"You didn't need to come all this way," I say. "I'm quite all right." I was admitted to St. Joseph's Hospital. For them to get here, on public transit, it would have taken more than an hour and a half.

They both tsk at me at the same time.

"Of course, we came," Paulette says.

"But you didn't have to. As you can see, I'm fine."

My mother frowns. "You are not fine. You crashed. Your hand is broken."

"They told me it was a clean break," I reply, waving my casted left hand for effect. "They're even releasing me soon. I'm just waiting on the prescription. I appreciate you coming, I really do, but I hate the thought of you both taking two buses and a train to get here. If you called me, I would have told you not to come."

"We did call. You didn't pick up." Grandma Janet says. "But you needn't worry, we got a ride."

"Uncle Weston dropped you off? Is he here?" I ask, hating that I inconvenienced yet another family member. Or maybe they took an Uber. If they used the ride-share app, I can pay them back. It's the least I could do.

"No, your roommate, Noémie, gave us a lift," my mother says.

As if her name being called summons her, Noémie suddenly comes into my line of view. She saunters towards the curtained off enclosure where I'm laid up. Seeing her makes my heart do a stupid little flip. I'm mad at her. She's the last person I want to see right now. But I'm also glad to see her.

Noémie's dressed like a celebrity trying to go incognito. She is wearing a pair of cargo shorts and an oversized Nike t-shirt. Her auburn hair is scooped under a Blue Jays baseball cap, and her face is scrubbed clean of makeup.

Coming to a halt at the foot of the bed, Noémie forces a nervous smile. "Hey, Jordan."

"Shouldn't you be flying to Honolulu right now?" I ask coldly.

Noémie's smile falters. I look away from her.

This whole situation is awkward. I want to escape it, but I'm trapped. I can't go anywhere. I have to wait for the doctor to come back and discharge me.

Minutes tick by. I stay silent.

My mother leaves to find the washroom, and my grandmother nods off in the chair. I feel Noémie's eyes on me, beseeching me to look at her. I don't.

Thankfully, the doctor doesn't keep me waiting long. He's a tall, balding man with bags the size of quarters under his eyes. He doesn't really acknowledge me as he examines the chart in his hands and prattles about the types of pain medication I'll be getting. He mentions something about me needing to get more X-rays in the future and something else about physiotherapy.

I should probably be paying more attention to what he is saying, but all I can think about is that Noémie is here. She isn't at the airport. She didn't go to Hawaii. Even as I want to hold on to it, the wick of my anger towards her is fizzling out.

I get discharged, and we all head for the exit. It's still raining outside. Reaching Noémie's Tesla, I opt to sit in the back with Grandma Janet. Noémie drives us all to Yorkville. My mother and grandmother fawn over Noémie's home for a hot minute before remembering why they are here. Despite being a grown-ass adult, they insist on tucking me in and praying over me. It's ridiculous, and I hate it. But I guess it's kind of heartwarming. I guess I'm kind of glad they're here with me.

Noémie offers to take them back to Scarborough. They accept her offer, and suddenly I'm alone. Well, maybe not entirely alone.

Céline paws open the door, slipping through the crack. Now she's curled up on the rug at the foot of the bed. Her beady eyes are relaxed but ascertaining, as if she can sense that I'm hurting more on the inside than the outside.

My arm throbs, so I pop a couple pain pills as per my prescription. I begin mindlessly scrolling through Instagram. Not long into it, my eyelids grow heavy and I fall asleep.

Chapter 31

I wake from my nap to see Noémie watching over me. She's wearing the black hoodie I wore the other day and discarded on the back of my desk chair. I get a rush from seeing her in my clothes. Heat flocks to my chest and spreads like wings. She sits on the cushioned bench beneath the window, hugging her knees. Her auburn hair falls loose over her face, looking dark brown in the dim lighting.

I sit up in bed and wipe my mouth and eyes.

We stare at each other, and I wonder who's going to break the silence first. Noémie does. "I'm glad you're okay," she says softly.

I lift my left arm. "If you can call breaking my arm okay—sure."

"It could have been worse. You're lucky it wasn't worse. You shouldn't have been riding in that storm. What were you thinking?"

My nostrils flare at the reprimand. Truth is, I hadn't been thinking. I had suffered a sort of cognitive vacancy after meeting Cara—Noémie's ex, who is a woman.

I decide to speak about the elephant in the room—something tells me that Noémie might not bring it up if I don't. "This whole time … you lied to me," I say. "You let me and Wayne and everyone think you were straight. Why? I thought we were being honest with each other. You could've told me. I'm not your family, I would never judge you for—"

"It's my choice if I want to disclose my sexuality. It's my choice to come out when I'm ready," Noémie snaps, her grey eyes glittering. Blowing out a puff of air, she rubs her forehead and turns to gaze out the window.

I stare at her side profile and don't know what to make of her outburst. In a way, she's right. She doesn't have to disclose her sexuality to anyone, but it hurts to know that she kept this part of herself hidden from me. I thought we were friends who told each other things. At least, I've shared things with Noémie that I never speak about.

Noémie sighs and runs a hand through her hair. "I'm sorry if that came out harsh, but …" She swivels on the bench and sets her feet down. Hunching over her legs, she anchors her elbows on her knees and looks down at the floor.

I count ten beats of silence, but it feels longer.

"I guess I should have told you, but I didn't say anything the day you hired me, and then it just got harder and harder to tell you. There never seemed to be a good time." She sighs and looks up at me with a sad, dejected expression that lances me through my gut. "There's so much that I need to tell you, but I … I don't want you to hate me."

"I could never hate you, Noémie."

She snorts. "You say that now."

Another curtain of silence falls between us, and I want to go to her. Even though I don't think I'm entirely wrong for my reaction to learning about Cara, I want to put my arms around her and hold on forever. I want to tell her that maybe I overreacted. I want to make it clear that it isn't her fault that I got into an accident. I've always been a bit rash and childish—it's my nature to run when a situation gets difficult. If I stuck around long enough to have an adult conversation with her, we wouldn't be here. I wouldn't have crashed, and Noémie wouldn't look like she's on the verge of breaking down.

Coming out as queer is never easy, and Noémie's father is one of Canada's biggest bigots. It makes sense that she would want to keep her cards close.

"The night my sister died was the night she came out to our parents," Noémie whispers. "I've never seen my father so angry. He yelled and cursed and threw things. Antoinette ran away in tears, and my father just let her go …"

Her words crush me. "Noémie …"

"The next morning we got the news that she got hit by a car," she continues, hugging her arms around her stomach. "It's been hard for me—talking about my sexuality."

My heart shatters for her. I leave my spot on the bed and sit next to her on the bench. I squeeze her knee, trying to express that I'm here for her.

Noémie chews on a fingernail. "Cara outed me to my brother," she says, her voice cracking. "Then Claude outed me to my parents and …"

"Your father cut you off?" I finish for her. It's no wonder she hadn't wanted to talk about it.

Noémie nods. "And he paid Cara to … to break up with me. And she took … took the money," she stammers. Her lower lip quivers.

I put my good arm around Noémie, pulling her close. She buries her face in my chest. Tremors rock her body as she sobs. The front of my shirt gets wet from her tears. I hold her tight to me, rubbing her back and wishing there was something I could say to ease her pain. I hate Hugo St. Pierre with every fibre of my being. I hate Claude. I hate Cara.

"None of them deserve you," I say. "You deserve the world. I would give it to you if I could."

Noémie peels away from me and sniffles. Her tears have stopped, but her grey eyes are puffy, red, and still full of emotion. She drops her gaze to my mouth and then meets my eyes. She licks her lips, and I go still. I stop breathing.

There's no mistaking what Noémie's thinking about. I've imagined this moment so many times. It feels unreal that it's happening. My heart jackhammers. More than anything, I want to erase the gap between us, but I know I shouldn't—not like this. Noémie's in a vulnerable state right now. She isn't thinking clearly. I don't want her having any regrets.

It's the hardest thing in the world to put some distance between us, but I do it. Or at least, I try to. Noémie doesn't let me, she grabs my thigh and leans into me. She kisses me, and my nerves fire up like I've touched a live wire. Her mouth on mine is electric and hungry, and I feel it all over my body. I kiss her back like my life depends on it—like her lips feed me the oxygen I need to function.

Heat pools in my core, but even as I ache for her, I break away with a groan. "Noémie … we can't—"

She hushes me with a finger to my lips and crawls into my lap. "I need this. I need you."

Her words make me shiver. The smell of her perfume—a blend of citrus and fabric softener—is intoxicating. "You don't know what you're saying—you're upset."

She brushes her lips against my ear. Her hot breath on my skin undoes me. If she keeps this up, I won't be able to control myself. "You don't know the first thing about what I want," she says.

That might be true, but she's hurting and I'm just an outlet she can lose herself in. But what will happen after, when she gains back her senses? We are roommates. We work together. She has a boyfriend.

The thought of Felix is sobering, but not enough to force her off me. Not enough to stop me from slipping my right hand under the hoodie and caressing the smooth skin of her stomach.

Noémie shudders and wraps her arms around my neck, bringing us closer. Our breasts push together. She moves against me and runs her tongue down the length of my neck before nipping my earlobe.

"Fuck," I gasp. "If you keep this up, I won't be able to control myself."

"I have no plans of stopping," she says, pulling back to look at me. I see no more traces of pain reflected in her eyes. All I see is desire. "Unless you want to stop. Tell me you don't want this."

I open my mouth to say as much, but I forget how to speak.

Noémie shifts forward in my lap and we're back to kissing.

"I can't stop thinking about the party," she murmurs against my lips. "I wanted you to rip down my thong, push your fingers inside me, and fuck me in the washroom stall."

Noémie's admission makes me wetter. She's saying everything I've fantasized about. "You did?"

"Yes," she says, digging her fingers in my hair and scraping her nails against my scalp. "You're such a distraction. It's annoying."

"You're the distraction," I shoot back, squeezing her ass and drawing her even closer.

She sucks in a breath and flips her hair over a shoulder. "I want you on the bed," she says.

I chuckle. "Is that an order?"

"If you're into that, then yes, it's an order."

I don't know if I'm into that. It's not something I've tried. With every partner I've been with, my role has been the same—top. I've never been interested in being touched. I've never submitted to anyone or let a lover call the shots. Samira loved how dominant I am—until she didn't.

I consider telling Noémie this. Maybe it will be the cold water to the face that will put out the fire burning between us. If I confess to her, telling her how rigid and set in my ways I am, maybe she'll want nothing to do with me. Maybe it's better to put a pin in things now, because I want so much more from Noémie than a casual hookup, and I know my hangups in the bedroom can be a dealbreaker. If given the chance, I would risk opening myself up to heartbreak to be with her. This revelation both scares and excites me.

Noémie slips off my lap and tugs off my hoodie and then the baggy Nike shirt she's wearing beneath. Her bra is orange lace. Her rosy nipples peak through the sheer material.

My mouth goes dry.

"Like what you see?" she asks, cupping her tits and then running her hands down the canvas of her toned body.

I swallow and nod.

Next, she unbuttons her cargo shorts and shimmies them down her legs in a slow and sensual motion. Her panties match her bra—of course they do.

"I thought I told you that I wanted you on the bed," she says, fixing me with a serious look.

"Noémie, I—"

"Why are you talking? Did I say you can talk?" She smiles sweetly at me, but her grey eyes sparkle with intensity.

I do as I'm told and get on the bed. I think I'm into it—Noémie's bossiness. But if we're going to do this, we need to lay some ground rules. We need to have the tough conversation that might ruin everything.

"Noémie, I don't like to be touched," I say.

"Okay." She doesn't bat an eye, like it isn't a big deal. "Do you not like to be touched everywhere or just …" She stares at my crotch.

"Just there," I say.

"Thanks for telling me."

I frown at her. "You're okay with that?"

She frowns right back at me. "Why wouldn't I be okay with it?"

"Because it's weird."

"No, it isn't," she says, sounding offended. "And I hope no one ever made you feel like it is."

"It's why Samira and I broke up," I confess.

"She's an idiot, and she knows it. She regrets letting you go. Her eyes give her away—the way she looks at you," Noémie says. She rolls her eyes. "But if we're done talking about your ex, I assume you have a strap. Where is it?"

I think about pinching myself. This can't be real. Noémie isn't in my bedroom asking for my strap. Those must have been some very strong pills the doctor gave me. But even if this is a fever dream, I'm dying to see how it plays out.

I clear my throat. "Top dresser drawer—in the closet."

Noémie disappears for a moment and returns toting my harness and my biggest toy. It's eight inches and an unnatural hue of purple.

She climbs onto the mattress and prowls towards me like a panther. "Lie on your back," she tells me.

I don't hesitate to do what she asks. Whenever I imagined us together, I never took into account her confidence and assertiveness. I don't think I've ever been with a woman so forward. She's the type of woman who knows what she wants and goes for it. I admire that about her, and maybe I wish I was more like her.

Noémie helps me out of my basketball shorts. Her fingers skim the thick band of my Calvin Klein boxers. "Je veux tellement que tu me baises," she whispers in my ear.

"Hmmm?" I don't know what she's saying, but it sounds hot. I like it when she talks French.

"I said, I want you to fuck me." She yanks my shirt off. Her hands roam over my shoulders and down my sides, filling me with sensation. She makes me feel so much.

"How do I say, I want you to come on my tongue in French?" I ask, raising up on my good arm.

She pushes me back down on the mattress, staring at me like I'm her favourite meal and she hasn't eaten for days. "Je veux que tu viennes sur ma langue."

I try to repeat her words, but it sounds all wrong. Noémie doesn't seem to care that my French skills are deplorable. Her pupils are blown. "Is that what you want?" she asks, her voice husky and warm. "Do you want me to come on your face?"

"Fuck yes," I rasp.

She moves forward carefully, so as not to knock my cast, and straddles my face, bracing against the headboard to support her hover.

The crotch of her panties is soaked. I groan. I can't believe this is happening. Can't believe how wet Noémie is for me.

I adjust the pillow behind me to get a better angle and then put my mouth on her skin. Though I'm ravenous for her, I take my time with her, kissing and nuzzling her thighs. I lick and nip the sensitive area above her clit. My good hand squeezes her ass.

Noémie gets tired of my teasing. "I need your mouth on my clit."

I decide to reward her, running my tongue down the length of her through her panties.

"Fuck!" Her body spasms. Her hips buck.

I slip her panties down to get better access. She's soaking beneath them, and I can't hold back any longer. I glide my tongue over her pussy over and over, sucking on her clit in intervals. She tastes so good, like salt and honey.

Noémie becomes frenzied. Her hips piston against my face as I eat her out—faster and faster. She convulses and cries out too quickly. I'm nowhere near sated, but she's too sensitive and pushes my face away.

She crashes down on the bed beside me, closing her eyes. Her breaths are rapid and her skin is flushed all over. She's fucking perfect.

I need to touch myself and get off too. I slip my hand down the waistband of my boxers.

Noémie's eyes flutter open, and her gaze dips to my moving hand. "Can I watch?" She asks.

I nod and slide down my boxers.

I hear her sudden intake of breath. "You're so fucking hot," she says, bringing her fingers to her centre and rubbing in quick circles. Just when I thought I couldn't get more turned on, Noémie does something to make me even wilder.

How could anyone choose money over Noémie? She's irreplaceable. She's everything I could ever want and will never deserve. I've never experienced anything like this before—this kind of chemistry. I love her so much …

"I want to watch you fuck yourself with your fingers," I say, amping the speed of my strokes. There's no delay, Noémie slips two fingers inside herself.

I groan, and she moans.

We lock eyes as we fuck ourselves, inching closer and closer to that place of euphoria. I find it first, my back arching off the mattress. "Fuck!"

Noémie, I notice, doesn't come. She removes her fingers from herself and watches me plummet back to earth.

When I catch my breath, I eye her suspiciously. "You didn't come."

"I thought I was clear earlier. I want you to fuck me." Her eyes dart to the strap that lies on the mattress a foot away from me.

I reach for it. She stops me with a hand on my shoulder.

"Not yet." She snuggles up to me and rests her head on my chest. "How's your arm feeling?" Her fingers graze my cast.

"I guess it hurts a bit." I shrug. "It's bearable."

"When I got the call that you were in an accident, I … I just about lost my mind," she whispers. "It was like reliving my worst memory."

"Your sister?"

She nods, and when she looks back up at me, her grey eyes are glittering.

"Hey, I'm okay."

"I know. I'm being dumb." Noémie sighs. "Sorry."

I hug her to me. "Don't ever apologize for your feelings. They're valid," I say, brushing my lips against her forehead and wiping her tears away with my thumb. I lift her chin and kiss her slow and deliberately—the way I've dreamt about. Her skin is warm against mine—the softest I've ever felt.

I unclasp her bra, and her breasts spill out. She whimpers when I dip my head and swirl my tongue over her nipples. I want to brand her with my mouth and make her mine. I want to fuck her so good that she forgets Felix ever existed. I might not have a real cock, but I know how to use the one I do have.

Pulling away from her, I reach for the strap. "Do you want it now?"

She nods and licks her lips.

Because of the cast, I fumble a bit with the harness, but Noémie doesn't seem to mind. She watches me through hooded eyes.

When it's on, she gets on her knees and comes to me. The dildo presses into her stomach.

"Want me to get the lube?" I ask.

"I don't think I need it," she says, wrapping her fist around the cock and stroking it. "I'm so wet for you."

Noémie lowers her mouth on the toy and puts on a show for me, licking the shaft and taking half of it down her throat. She moves her hair out of the way so I can get a better view and stares up at me as she works it in and out of her mouth.

I don't think I've ever been so turned on before. My clit throbs. "Fuck, Noémie …"

"Do you like it when I suck you off?" she asks, pulling back a bit. The shaft glistens from her spit.

"Yes."

"I wish I could take all of you in my mouth, but you're so big," she says.

I wince as a bolt of pleasure rushes through me. "Fuck, your dirty talk is going to be the end of me."

"Good, that's my goal," she says, easing onto her back and spreading her legs for me. She hadn't lied, she's dripping for me.

My mouth waters looking at her. I'm dying to have another taste, but that's not what she wants from me. She wants me to fuck her, so that's what I'll do.

I climb on top of her and kiss her. She whines and jerks when I slip the tip inside her. "Too much?" I ask.

She shakes her head. "No, it just feels so good. I need all of you. Please."

I try to give her more, but she's so tight, and I don't want to hurt her. Taking my time, I slide out and back in, repeatedly sinking a little deeper each time. Beneath me, Noémie writhes and moans. Her fingers dig into and scrape against my back. She's crying out things in French that I don't understand.

When I push the toy all the way inside her, she makes a guttural sound that makes me feral. I pick up the tempo, thrusting hard and deep. She meets my rhythm, arching her hips to meet every stroke.

I slip up but catch myself with my casted hand. Pain washes over me, and I grit my teeth. I push through the discomfort. I can't stop fucking her—not until she comes for me. She's so close. I can tell. There's more and more resistance as I pump into her.

"Fuck, Jordan!" Noémie's back arches above the mattress. Her legs wrap around me. "You feel so good."

Leaning forward, I capture her lips. Our tongues meet. And I keep going. I keep fucking her, fighting through the pain.

Noémie's head slams back. Her body spasms as she cries out. I've never heard a more beautiful sound.

I slide the toy carefully out of her and roll onto my back. Breathing hard, I stare up at the ceiling. I try to ignore the throbbing in my arm. Beside me, Noémie's breaths are just as ragged. When she recovers enough, she curls herself next to me and rests her head on my shoulder. We're both hot and coated in sweat.

I turn my head, and we lock gazes. She cups my face and strokes my cheek with her thumb. "I love you, Jordan," she says.

My heart flutters too fast in my chest; it's a wonder it doesn't burst out. Her words make me feel euphoric, but I question their validity. Women say things they don't mean during and after sex. The words I love you sit heavy on my tongue. I want to say them, but I can't. I need to be sure of Noémie's feelings for me first.

Blinking, Noémie drops her hand from my face and sits up. She frowns and clears her throat. "I have to use the washroom." She slips off the bed and goes to the ensuite. The door clicks shut behind her.

Yawning, my eyelids grow heavy. I drift to sleep.

Chapter 32

When I wake up the next morning, my broken arm is aching like a bad cavity. But the pain can't weigh me down. I'm in the greatest of moods. Noémie is into women. Noémie and I hooked up. Noémie doesn't seem to care that I'm a touch-me-not. There is a chance that we can be together. And the cherry to top everything off is that Sarah flies back into Toronto tonight.

Noémie isn't in the bed with me, which saddens me, but she's always been an early riser and it's almost eleven.

I get out of bed, stretching my good arm over my head, and reach for the painkillers. I take the recommended dose and go to the bathroom to wash my face and brush my teeth. Then, I pull on my discarded ball shorts and black hoodie. I love that it smells like her.

With a hop in my step, I hurry downstairs—my heart pounds in my ears. It's stupid that I'm so excited to see Noémie, but I can't help it. I can't stop grinning like an idiot. I walk into the main room. Noémie isn't there. Céline also isn't curled up in her favourite spot on the couch. It's likely Noémie took the dog out for a walk.

I go to the espresso machine to make myself a latte. Not the easiest thing to do with a cast. As I go through the motions, I recall the first time Noémie made me a drink on the La Marzocco machine. It had been perfection. Since that time, she's made me several amazing coffee drinks. She spoils me so much. God, I love her.

Sipping on my drink, I take a seat at the kitchen island and open the email app on my phone. There's an email from François, sending me suggestions for fonts for my graphic novel cover. We're just about ready to launch the Kickstarter, and I'm super anxious about it. But it's a good kind of anxiousness. François has been a godsend; he really makes me feel like my dreams are achievable. And now, thinking back on how upset I'd been about Noémie making the connection with him, I realize how foolish I'd been.

I finish my latte and start to get a little antsy. My leg bounces as I scroll through Instagram. The waiting is killing me. I want to see Noémie. I want to know when she'll be back home. I decide to call her.

On the third ring, Noémie picks up. "What do you want, Jordan?" Her curtness throws me off. On her end of the line, it sounds like she's somewhere busy, like a mall.

"Just woke up," I say, crashing down on the living-room couch. "Where are you at?"

For several moments, she's silent. Then, she replies, "I'm at Pearson—just about to board my flight."

My heart shatters like glass, splintering into a million little pieces. My dumb ass should have expected this. I should have known things were too good to be true. Noémie doesn't love me. Of course, she chose Felix over me. He's handsome. He's got money. He's someone Hugo would approve of. Me, I'm a step above a barista. I have no money. I'm a woman. All I have to offer her is my heart.

My eyes sting. I clear my throat to loosen the ball that's lodged there. "Cool, cool," I say.

"Did you want something, Jordan?" She sounds irritated.

"Nah," I say, trying my best to sound unfazed. At least, I hope she can't hear me dying inside. "Have a safe flight."

Tapping the large red button, I end the call. My phone slips from my finger and clatters on the floor. I don't bother trying to pick it back up.

When Samira called things off, I thought I knew what heartbreak felt like. Now I know that breakup was only a ripple compared to this wave of emotion crashing over me. I drown in it. Or maybe it's my tears that are choking me, making it hard to breathe.

The entire day, I don't do anything. I call in sick on Monday, Tuesday, and Wednesday. My excuse is the motorcycle accident. Those three days at home are spent wasting away in my dark room. Sarah calls me a million times—I let everything go to voicemail. I'm probably the worst best friend in the world, but I can't friend right now.

On Thursday, I force myself to shower and get ready for work. With limited sick time available to me, if I don't want my cheque to be impacted, I need to go into work.

Wayne knows something is off the moment he sees me. "You look like shit," he says. "But I'm glad to see you're in one piece after the accident. I was really worried."

I don't answer him as I open the coffee shop's front door.

We go through the motions of setting up the store, and then we're open. It's busy, and we're making mistakes, and my cast is making me slow. We're in the weeds, and I'm blown.

I can't do this.

Storming off the floor, I retreat to the back office. I yank off my apron and toss it on the floor. My head pounds. I start pacing back and forth.

"Jordan, what the actual f—" Spotting my tears, Wayne snaps his mouth shut. He gently closes the door and rushes over to me. "Oh my God, what's wrong, honey?"

I shake my head and collapse into the desk chair, holding my head in my hands.

Wayne comes to my side and kneels. "Jordan, you're starting to scare me," he whispers, rubbing my back.

I don't immediately answer him. I consider not telling him anything, but then I think that maybe the first step to getting over this is talking about it.

Meeting his eyes, I sniffle. "I'm in love with Noémie," I say.

He doesn't seem shocked by my disclosure. "Okay, so you're in love with Noémie. Why is that a problem?"

My eyes narrow on him as I realize something. "You knew she's into women." I say it as a statement, not a question.

Standing, Wayne takes a step back and crosses his arms. "So what if I did?"

"And you didn't think to tell me?"

"It's not my place to out people," Wayne says curtly.

"Since when?" I ask. "You're, like, the biggest gossip I know."

He pouts and ignores my question. "I'm still not understanding the need for these theatrics," he says, gesturing at me with a flourish. "And we've got a line out the door, Jay. We're swamped. You're needed on the espresso machine."

I sigh and rake my fingers through my hair. "I know. I just need a minute."

"Why is loving Noémie so terrible?" he asks. "Last time I checked, she's fucking gorgeous and you two are already living together, which saves you the cost of a U-Haul."

I glare at him. "She's with Felix in Hawaii."

Wayne rolls his eyes dramatically. "Okay, so tell her how you feel when she gets back." He doesn't get it. How does he not get it?

I grit my teeth. "Noémie and I hooked up Saturday night, and on Sunday morning she left me to be with her boyfriend in Honolulu."

"You did what? She did what?" Wayne's mouth drops open.

I chuckle coldly. "It's not that surprising. I should have expected it, but … I don't know." I shake my head and stare down at the floor.

"How about you call her? You can clear the air, tell her how you feel."

I exhale a deep breath and rub my temples. "No, there's no point."

"How do you know that if you don't at least try to talk to her?"

"She left me to be with Felix," I snap at him.

"No, she didn't," Wayne states. He throws up his hands in defeat. "I can't do this anymore. I told her to drop it, but does anyone listen to me? No."

"What are you even talking about?"

"Noémie is gay. Felix is gay. He's not her boyfriend. She's like a sister to him," Wayne says.

What? I frown. Wayne's got it wrong. I shake my head and almost laugh at the absurdity of Wayne's claim. Noémie and Felix are together. "They kissed at the Christmas market. I heard them hooking up," I say.

"Whatever you heard, I can assure you they weren't having sex." He sounds so convinced of what he's saying, I want to believe him.

"I swear, Jordan, you can be so obtuse sometimes," Wayne continues.

I glare at him. "What are you trying to say?"

Wayne glares back at me. "There's a reason Noémie came to our shop every weekday morning, and it wasn't because she loved our coffee. There's a reason she jumped at the chance to work here even though she's stupid rich. You know, when she graduated, she got access to a trust fund with more money than we can hope to make in a lifetime. She chooses to work," he snaps. "Anyways, that girl has been simping for you since forever, and you refused to acknowledge or even see it."

So, Noémie lied about being broke. Seems like she lied about a lot. It's a good thing I didn't say I love you back.

"If what you're saying is true that doesn't explain why she's with Felix right now in Hawaii," I say. "If what you're saying is true, why didn't you tell me?"

Wayne goes very still. He starts to fidget. "Before I tell you, I need you to promise you won't hate me."

The fuck? "I can't make any promises," I say, recalling all the whispered conversations between him and Noémie. I recall how they used to run off to the stockroom to have private discussions. I see red. "Spill it, Wayne. What have you and Noémie been keeping from me?"

"We sorta had a bet."

"A bet?" I repeat.

Wayne rubs his eyes and sighs. "Yes, we had a bet. Noémie was so convinced that she could wife you up, and I told her you'd steamroll her cold heart," he explains. "The deal was that if you guys slept together before you confessed to loving her, I'd get anything I wanted from her closet. And if she won, she'd get bragging rights…and I'd have to train for and run a marathon. Can you imagine me in a gym?

Sheeshh—what a relief it is to hear that Noémie finally caved. Frankly, I'm surprised the girl held out so long. Anyhow, Felix is just a chess piece Noémie's been using to make you jealous."

Speechless, I stare at my friend.

Can I even call him a friend? How could he betray me like this? Knowing the truth is somehow worse than thinking Noémie chose Felix over me. Like, I always knew Noémie was a bitch, but…I thought I knew her. Now I'm realizing that I never really did. Everything between us was a lie.

Chapter 33

Wayne's been begging me to call Noémie. He can go fuck himself. Noémie can go fuck herself. I'm done.

"Are you sure about this?" Sarah asks.

I thrust a cardboard box into my best friend's arms. "Yup."

"She'll be back in a day, why don't you talk to her first? I'm not trying to make any excuses for her—she did you dirty, but …"

"If you don't want to live with me, just say so."

"It's not that." Sarah adjusts her grip on the box. "But are you really telling me that you want to give up these sweet digs? It's so close to the coffee shop, and I know you still have feelings for her. Why not try to work things out?"

I drill Sarah with a dirty look. "I don't want to talk to her. I don't want to see her. She doesn't exist. She is Voldemort."

Sarah chuckles. "Wow, I seriously never thought I'd see you get so butt hurt over a chick. She's got you twisted."

I grit my teeth. "I'm not twisted."

Sarah snorts. "She's got you twisted tighter than a pretzel, fam."

"I'm not twisted," I insist.

"Sure you aren't."

I roll my eyes and wave Sarah away. "My uncle Weston needs his truck back in three hours. We can't waste time. Drop the topic of Noémie."

"Okay … for now," Sarah says. "I kind of agree with Wayne on this one. You should talk to her before moving out. You're taking the nuclear option, you know that right?"

I don't respond. Of course, I'm taking the nuclear option. That's the point. The best way to end something is to starve it. If I talk to Noémie, I'll just be feeding my emotions for her when what I want to do is pour gasoline over my feelings and light a match.

When all my things are loaded in the truck, I drop my key into an envelope and lick the seal. It's not until I slide the envelope through the mail slot that it hits me—I'm moving out. There will be no more over-the-top dinners paired with wine. There will be no more cuddling up on the couch next to Noémie to watch Netflix. There will be no more carving pumpkins and dressing up in ridiculous costumes. There will be no more barking every time the doorbell rings. There will be no more of a lot of things. Good.

Sure, it sucks that I'll still have to put up with Noémie at work, but she will be bumped to the evening shift. I wonder if there are any HR implications with doing that … Will I have to speak to the owners, disclosing a watered-down version of what happened between me and Noémie? Fuck, this is so messy.

I stare at the beautiful semi-detached Victorian, with its forest green shutters and red brick facade. My chest aches.

Blowing out a deep breath, I walk to the truck and get in. Eyes burning and throat tight, I start up the truck and reverse it out of the driveway. The radio station blasts "WAP" of all things. I shut the music off and blink back tears. These days, I'm such a crybaby—I hate it.

"You sure you want to do this?" Sarah asks. "It isn't too late to go back. You don't have a lot of things; we'd be able to unload and get your uncle the truck in time."

Even if I wanted to change my mind, which I don't, I don't have the key. It's in the mailbox, and I'm not about to try and fish the envelope out.

I can't live with Noémie. Not after what she did. She treated me and my feelings like a game. I need to make it clear to her that she lost.

Chapter 34

The air at the party is thick with sweat, alcohol, and bad decisions. I've been absorbed into the tight mob of revellers. There's got to be hundreds of hot bodies packed on the tiny dance floor, jumping, raving, and losing themselves to the EDM beats. I bop to the music, feeling the weight of loneliness and the bass vibrating through the soles of my sneakers.

A mix of painkillers, alcohol, and cannabis are my companions tonight. They're helping, but not numbing me to the degree I need. It lingers at the back of my mind that my father was an addict, and I've been spiralling down a dark path of indulgence over the last few days. I don't want to be like him, but in a lot of ways, I'm exactly like him. Sometimes, it scares me. I don't want to die alone in my apartment and be found a week later, stinking and bloated.

There are times when I think, if only I had called my father more. If only I spent more time with him. If only I had made the time. Maybe he would still be here.

I drive a cute woman with a bright smile and dimples up against a wall. I kiss her. She kisses me back, and I feel nothing. There's no desire. There's no wanting. Nothing.

I don't want to be like my dad, but I think I need another drink to feel something. I need to fill the emptiness.

I stumble back from Dimples and lace my fingers through hers. I navigate us through the crowd towards the bar located at the front of the venue. There's a slow-moving queue to put an order in with the bartender. Me and Dimples take our spot at the tail of it.

Dimples wraps her arms around my waist and begins mopping my neck with her sloppy tongue. I'm not into it, but Dimples is cute and I don't want to be alone tonight. So I allow it.

I don't know what makes me choose that moment to look towards the front doors, but I do. When I see her, I freeze. What the fuck is she doing here? Who told her where to find me? It had to be Sarah—the traitor.

Noémie struts into the bar like she owns it. She walks up to the front table to pay her cover.

I feel nauseous all of a sudden. The four beers I downed earlier aren't playing nice with my stomach.

Noémie slides out of her jacket—an oatmeal trench coat with an oversized collar—and hands it over to the woman working coat check. Tonight, she's wearing a scant dress that hugs her body sinfully. More than ever, she looks like heartbreak packaged in an orange wrapper.

Seeing her rips me to pieces. Seeing her makes me want. Seeing her makes me feel.

Noémie turns, and our eyes meet. My breath catches.

Her grey eyes dart to Dimples whose mouth is latched onto my neck like a lamprey. The colour drains from her face, the confidence she strode into the bar with leaks out of her as her shoulders drop.

Noémie's eyes glitter in the dim lighting. Her lips thin. She balls her hands at her sides.

If those are indicators of jealousy, good. Fuck her. My feelings aren't a game. I don't owe her jack shit. I don't owe her money, since I paid her last month's rent when I moved in. I don't owe her a reason for moving out. I don't owe her my heart. She doesn't deserve it.

I grab Dimples by her hair and pull her in hard, kissing her long and deeply. The woman moans into my mouth and melts against me. I'm very unstirred by the kiss, but knowing Noémie is watching gives me a sick thrill. I want her to hurt like I hurt.

A throat clears. "Line's moving," someone behind us says frustratingly.

I pull apart from Dimples. She smiles stupidly and tucks a lock of her black hair behind an ear. We shuffle forward.

Looking over my shoulder, I don't see Noémie. She's moved away. Gone somewhere else. I force myself not to look for her.

Dimples orders two beers and slaps a twenty on the bar top. The bartender cracks two bottles open and slides them down on the counter.

I pick up my Heineken and stare down the perspiring green neck. I take a very long swig. It doesn't go down easy. My stomach is in knots, and the room is tilting a bit. Perhaps I should have heeded the warning on the prescription where it clearly states that the painkillers should not be taken with alcohol.

"I need to get some fresh air," I say to Dimples. "Can you watch my drink?"

"Yeah, sure, I'll wait here," she says with an eager nod.

"Thanks." I hand her my drink and kiss her on the cheek.

Outside, I gulp in the fresh air because I need it. Then, I pull out a pack of cigarettes. I smack one out of the carton and light up.

I suck hard on the filter, filling my lungs with smoke. The nicotine buzzes in my head.

A group of mostly dolled up femmes stand in a circle smoking. One of them catches my eye and smiles. She's a platinum blond with a tan. She's prettier than Dimples but obviously taken. A short king in a powder-blue suit wraps a possessive arm around her waist.

I sag against a wall and stare up at the night sky. I think I must be very high, because I stare so long that my cigarette burns all the way down to the filter.

"Jordan!"

Blinking, I turn my head and see Noémie stalking towards me. She looks pissed. Good.

Looking away from her, I smack another cigarette out of its carton and pop it between my lips.

Noémie stops when she's a couple of feet away from me. "Jordan," she says again.

I light my cigarette and blow out a cloud of smoke. If I ignore her, will she go away?

As I told Wayne and Sarah countless times, I do not want to talk to her. I don't care if I'm being childish. Noémie can go fuck herself.

"Jordan, can you look at me? I'm trying to talk to you."

I stare at the glowing end of my cigarette. "What's there to talk about?"

She doesn't say anything for a few beats, and then she whispers, "Us."

That makes me look at her. "There is no us," I sneer.

Noémie winces and steps towards me. "Don't say that, Jordan.

Don't be like this."

"Be like what?" I snap, tossing my cigarette on the ground and stomping it out with my foot. "I'm not a game. My feelings aren't a game."

She bites her lip. "You're not a game. You've never been a game to me—"

"You bet Wayne that you could tie me down. You paraded Felix around me to make me jealous. Sounds like all I ever was to you was a game," I say, pushing off the wall. I shake my head. The world spins. I reach out to support myself. Bad move, I put too much pressure on my bad hand. "Shit," I say, cradling my casted hand.

Noémie rushes over to me. I stop her with a harsh look.

I close my eyes momentarily, trying to ground myself. But it doesn't really help. Even seeing only darkness, everything moves. "Fuck, I need to sit down," I mumble, stumbling forward.

Noémie catches me. "Look, I'm parked across the street. We can sit in my car while we talk. Is that okay?"

I nod, not because I want to be alone in a car with her, but because it's the only gesture I can make. My vision squishes together like my eyes are stress balls in a bodybuilder's firm grip. I feel so sick.

I lean on Noémie as she escorts me across the street. The next thing I know, she's helping me into the passenger seat. My body feels limp, like a soggy noodle. An elephant sits on my chest, making it hard to breathe. Closing my eyes, I rest my head on the window. The cool glass feels good on my face.

A second later, a woman is coaxing me awake and urging me to stand up. We walk for what feels like a hundred miles. A tiny wolf howls at me. It claws up my legs. I'm scared. Then there's so much light, it hurts my eyes. I'm told to lie down, so I do.

Finally, everything goes dark again.

The headache I wake up with is one of the worst I've ever had, which is saying something.

Groaning, I sit up and immediately notice where I am. I'm at home—no, not home. Noémie's place. I'm on the couch in the main room, and Noémie's sitting at the other end watching me.

She doesn't look like she's gotten any sleep. Dark circles are painted under her eyes. She's wearing a pair of plaid pyjama pants and an oversized white shirt. Her hair is tied up in a messy bun.

Noémie bolts to her feet and reaches for a glass of water sitting on the coffee table. She hands it to me. "Here, have some water."

Parched, I don't bother arguing. I take the offering, chugging it down and wiping my mouth afterwards. She takes the empty glass from me and sets it back down on the coffee table.

I rub my eyes. "Why am I here?"

"You passed out," she says. "I'm assuming you were drinking while on your painkillers, which is never a good idea. Don't ask me how I know."

I look down at my lap. "Thanks for taking care of me."

She kneels in front of me and squeezes my thigh. "Of course, I would never leave you like that."

Remembering that I hate her, I snort.

"Jordan, we need to talk."

"I don't want to," I say. "Talking won't change things. It won't change what you did."

"What I did was wrong. I should never have made that bet with Wayne. It was stupid and inconsiderate, and I'm so sorry." She's looks up at me with wide, imploring eyes.

Turning my head, I stare out the window. "Why did you do it? I know why Wayne thinks you did it, but I want you to tell me."

She sighs. For many moments, she's silent. Then, she says, "Because I'm a horrible person. Because it was a challenge. Because I was trying to find a way to rebuild my pride after what happened with Cara." The last reason, she whispers. "Because I wanted you."

I stare at her. "Everything between us was a lie. You lied about everything. I thought we were friends. I told you things I never talk about. I trusted you." My voice breaks, and I clear my throat before continuing, "And for what—a place in my bed? I've been told that I fuck everyone. If you wanted me to fuck you, all you had to do was ask."

Noémie's face burns like I slapped her. She shoots to her feet with clenched hands. "I didn't want you to fuck me. I wanted to get to know you. I wanted to be in your life. I didn't want to be another name added to the long list of women you fuck and ghost," she snaps.

I want to say that I wouldn't have fucked and ghosted her, but that wouldn't be true. "And you think that justifies you seducing me—"

"Seducing you?" Noémie rolls her eyes and throws up her hands. "Merde, I was not trying to seduce you. If I was trying to seduce you, I would have walked around the house in lingerie."

"I'm not buying that all those elaborate dinners weren't part of your greater scheme to lock me down," I say. Our fight is making my headache worse. I rub my temples.

Noémie grits her teeth. "Maybe at first," she admits. She drops down on the couch beside me and exhales a loud breath. "But then, I just did it because I liked cooking for you. I liked getting you to try new things. I just liked being with you."

Our legs are touching, and I consider moving over.

"You know, I started falling for you around Halloween," I confess, deciding to put everything on the table. Better to leave no stone unturned before ending things between us for good. Trust is the foundation of any healthy relationship, and I can never trust Noémie. She's a liar. "But I thought you were straight, and I valued our friendship. I loved you so much it hurts."

"Loved," she repeats. Her eyes go glassy. "You don't love me anymore?"

I do love her—even after everything. But love isn't enough.

"I need to go," I say. Shaking my head, I stand up—a little too quickly. The world spins. I wince.

"Really, you're not going to answer my question? You're just going to go? You're going to run away because of some stupid bet that I wasn't even taking all that seriously," she says.

I begin walking towards the front door.

Noémie follows after me. "I love you, Jordan. I want to be with you, and I know you want to be with me too," she says. "Let's try to work this out. Please."

Turning, I glare at her. "We can't be together."

"Why not?" Tears well in her grey eyes. She blinks, and they spill down her cheeks.

A ball forms in my throat. My heart weighs a million pounds in my chest. "Because I can't trust you, and I don't think I ever can."

Noémie stares up at me with wide, disbelieving eyes, and then she's crying into her hands. Each of her sobs is a spike hammered through heart.

The lure to go to her and take back my words is stronger than any drug I've ever taken. I want to enfold her in my arms and get high on her scent. I want to get drunk off kissing her tears away. And that's why I need to leave. I can't be around her and not succumb to the pressure of doing what my foolish heart wants.

I grab my jacket from the coat closet. Céline whines and then yawns as I exit through the front door.

I make it a block before throwing up.

Chapter 35

It's the middle of June when I get the wedding invitation in the mail. Claude and Amelia have invited me to their wedding. The paper stock is thick, with embossed gold lettering. Orange and purple flowers frame cursive writing. Guests are encouraged to dress in shades of tangerine or lilac. The wedding is set to take place in a week at Casa Loma—fancy.

I've only visited the historic castle once. Sarah sponsored my ticket to participate in one of their escape rooms. It was really fun, even if our group hadn't made it out on time.

I'm not sure why I've received an invitation. They must know that Noémie and I aren't friends anymore; we haven't spoken in months. She quit working at the coffee shop right after our fight with no notice, and without messaging me. I got the news from Wayne.

I'm receiving the invitation on such short notice too, which is also weird. Not that it matters. I'm not going to go. Tossing the invitation in the garbage, I grab my backpack, wave goodbye to Sarah, who's gaming on the couch, and exit our apartment.

François is in town, and we're meeting up for lunch. I'm super stoked to catch up in person after speaking to him almost every day virtually. With his help, I've sold over two thousand units on my Kickstarter, and I'm staring down a payday that's half my annual salary. I can't quite believe it. People are actually paying for my graphic novel. People want to read a story about a dyke assassin.

When I walk into the Irish Pub, François's already there and seated at a booth. Upon seeing me, he gets up and we exchange a quick hug. He kisses me on both cheeks. We sit down at opposite ends of the booth. He orders fish and chips, and I order a burger. We dive into conversation. François tells me about a new idea for a story he has—a sci-fi revenge story that features mechas. I dig it—I would read it.

Our food arrives, and I'm so happy that I can finally hold a burger properly—with both hands. I would never recommend breaking an arm to anyone. As a right-handed person, I never realized how much I relied on my left hand.

Halfway through our meal, François's phone buzzes. "Is it okay if I take this? It's Claude, and with the wedding only a week away …"

"Of course," I say.

François gives me an apologetic smile and accepts the call. "Salut, Claude, quoi de neuf?"

I can't follow his conversation, it's all in French, but at one moment, François gives me an odd look that makes me think I'm being talked about. The phone call lasts only a minute or two. François puts away his phone, and then drums his fingers on the table. "So, Claude will be joining us," he says.

I nearly spit out my Pepsi. "What?"

"He wants to talk to you. I'm not sure what about. But I hope it's all right."

It's not all right. The last time Claude and I were in close proximity to each other, he tried to pay me off to never see his sister again, and I threw liquor in his face.

I'm about to tell him that I'm not interested in seeing Claude when François's face lights up.

"Ahhh ... there he is," he says, waving to someone behind me.

Ten seconds later, I feel Claude's overbearing presence behind my back. François rises to greet his best friend. I stay seated.

"Salut, Jordan," Claude says, smiling down at me. "It's good to see you."

I eye him coldly and murmur, "I wish I could say the same."

François's eyes dart from me to Claude. I can tell he's trying to discern why I'm being so bitter all of a sudden.

"Would you mind giving us a moment?" Claude asks his friend.

François looks at me for permission.

"Yes, it's fine," I say, even if it isn't. But I'd be lying if I said that I'm not interested in why Claude is here, why he wants to speak to me.

François leaves us to go lean against the bar, and Claude takes the vacated seat across from me.

Not hungry anymore, I push my plate to the side. I cross my arms and stare Noémie's brother down. "What do you want?"

"Did you get the invitation?" he asks, unfazed by the bite in my tone.

"Yes."

"Will you be coming?"

"No," I say. "Noémie and I are no longer on talking terms. I'm sure that makes you happy."

He clucks his tongue, sets his elbows on the table, and leans forward. "You are wrong, I am not happy about your falling out. You were a good companion for my sister."

"Bullshit." I snort. "You tried to bribe me to never speak to her again."

"Don't make a devil out of me for trying to protect Noémie," he says. "I assume you know about Cara. I never want anything like that to happen to her again. As you said to me in my study, Noémie is priceless. I only want to see her with someone who knows that."

"So it was some sort of stupid test." I grit my teeth. "I see that playing games runs in the family."

"If it makes it better, I'm sorry for what I did. You had every right to throw your drink in my face. I deserved it. It's my hope that you can forgive me," he says. "It's my hope that you can forgive Noémie."

This whole conversation is unbalancing and unexpected. Not to mention that it's been weeks since I've talked openly about Noémie. Bringing up her name stirs emotions inside me that I want to keep settled.

Wayne's been on my ass, telling me that I should forgive Noémie because I forgave him, but it's not that simple. My relationship with Wayne is different. He's a colleague and a friend, and it's in his nature to betray me for a designer handbag. Also, after grilling him, I uncovered that he'd been actively trying to get Noémie to be honest with me. Apparently, that's what they'd been fighting about at the Christmas market.

"Do you know what she did?" I ask.

"The bet? Yes, I know all about the bet," Claude says.

"So you understand why I can't forgive her."

"Forgiveness is a choice."

"Maybe I don't want to forgive her."

"And why is that?" he asks, arching a brow.

I know the answer, but I'm not going to tell Noémie's brother that I'm terrified of opening up my heart to another assault. Every relationship I've ever had has taught me a hard lesson. It's clear—now, more than ever—that I am not cut out for love. I think Noémie can break me as a person. If we did get serious and things exploded, I'm sure I'd blow up too. And for the first time in a long time, I'm moving towards something good. I don't feel stuck.

I don't want love to destroy everything I've been working on personally and professionally.

It's been almost a month since my last smoke, and I'm drinking and partying less. My videos are getting more and more views—I'm gaining about fifty new followers a day. My Kickstarter exceeded my expectations. My new apartment with Sarah is above ground, and there's no faux-wood panelling or ants to be seen. Yes, all's good—except for the crater named Noémie that hollows me out.

"Noémie hasn't being doing well," Claude says, snapping me from my thoughts.

I give him a look, asking him to expand.

Claude leans back, and sighs. "Something broke in Noémie when Antoinette died. You know about our sister?"

I nod my confirmation.

He bites his lip in the same way Noémie does when she's anxious. Their resemblance really is uncanny. "There was a period of time where I really thought she might hurt herself. But then she started going to therapy and taking medication, and it was like I had her back. She finished her program at culinary school and got a position at a very prestigious restaurant in the city. Our father was in talks with her to open her own restaurant if she completed an MBA program. Everything was going so well for her … until the incident with Cara."

"I didn't know she was in therapy," I say.

"I would have been surprised if she'd told you. Noémie hates being on antidepressants," he says. "She wouldn't be happy about me telling you now."

"So why are you telling me?"

"Because I'm desperate. She's refusing to take her medication, and I fear that once she doesn't have the wedding planning to preoccupy her, she will spiral into her hole and not bother trying to crawl out of it," he says, exhaling a deep breath. "Back last year, things got really bad after Cara took the money and our father freezed her out. Noémie quit the job she loved and refused to get out of bed. I was sick with worry and tried my best to get her to leave the house.

"But then she met you, started working at the coffee shop, fell into a routine, and her spark came back. You make my sister very happy—happier than I've ever seen her. And I know she makes you happy too. I know that you love her—I saw it in the way you looked at her on Christmas."

"It doesn't matter if I love her. I can't trust her," I say.

"Merde." Claude spears me with a look. "Don't forsake Noémie for making a mistake—she's so young. Are you telling me that you've never made a mistake before?"

I don't say anything. I don't know what to say that I haven't already said. But I'm also still digesting everything Claude revealed. I hate that Noémie's not good. I can't imagine a version of her that isn't sassy and vibrant.

Claude stands and removes his wallet from the interior pocket of his blazer jacket. He pulls a card and flicks it on the table. It lands a couple inches away from the edge. "If you change your mind about attending the wedding, please visit my tailor. There's a strict dress code, and I'd wager you don't have an orange or purple suit lying around. You can tell Lionel to charge me the cost."

Claude exits the booth, but before leaving, he claps me on the shoulder. "I really hope you come. Noémie would love to see you, and so would I."

François slips back into the booth. I try to carrying on our discussion, but my mind is pre-occupied. I keep replaying the conversation with Claude in my head.

When I get back home, Sarah catches me rummaging through the garbage.

"What the hell are you doing, Jay?"

I pull the wedding invitation from the bin and give it a cursory look. There's no disgusting food juice on it.

"What's that?" Sarah asks.

"An invitation to Claude's wedding."

She frowns. "Noémie's brother?"

I nod. "Yeah."

"Odd … he's gotta know you and his sister aren't on talking terms," she says.

"He does know, but he wants that to change."

"Wait, wait, wait. So you're telling me that the guy who tried to pay you off to unfriend his sister now wants you to get back together with his sister?" Sarah says. "The math isn't mathing."

I sigh and go over my conversation with Claude. Sarah leans back against the kitchen counter, listening with interest. When I reach the end, she asks, "So what are you going to do?"

I stare down at the invitation in my hands. "I don't know."

"Do you still love her?"

Groaning, I sag against a wall and stare up at the ceiling. "What does it matter if I still love her?"

"It matters, Jay," Sarah says. "Look, I'm not team Noémie. She did you dirty, and I don't think I can ever fully forgive her for hurting you. But I don't think you're actually all that mad at her for the bet and—"

"What?" Of course, I'm mad at Noémie for the bet. She lied to me about everything. She toyed with my emotions. She faked a relationship to make me jealous.

Sarah holds up her hands. "Can I finish my thought?"

I grit my teeth. "Fine, whatever."

"I think you're clinging onto your anger about the bet because you're looking for a reason to not make things work with Noémie," she says.

"You have no idea what you're talking about."

Sarah shakes her head. "I know exactly what I'm talking about, Jay. You never want to put in the hard work for anything unless you're a hundred percent sure there's an upside," she says. "But that's not realistic, and it's not a way to live."

I want to say that Sarah's got it all wrong, but she's right. If François hadn't expressed interest in my graphic novel, I never would have taken the steps to get my work published. And the first time Noémie told me that she loved me, I couldn't say the words back because I needed assurance that she hadn't misspoken. And there are probably a thousand more examples I can pull from in my life.

I think back on the night I slept with Noémie. I think about how she held my face and looked at me with eyes brimming with hope and love. She must've been so hurt when I stayed silent. Maybe that's why she immediately ran off to the bathroom. I hope she hadn't been crying in there. I hate the thought of her crying over me. I hate the thought of her being depressed. I hate that I might never get to see her smile again.

Chapter 36

Even in the morning light, the gothic castle looms ominously, with its ornate stone masonry and soaring turrets. I park my bike on a residential street between a van and a Mini Cooper and remove my helmet. My Kawasaki Ninja is ridable, but evidence of my collision mars the lime-green paint. There's a long, jagged scrape along the gas tank. The exhaust is a bit dented too.

My mother screamed at me when she found out that I hadn't gotten rid of it, but I love riding. I love to feel the whip and resistance of the wind around me. Yes, I might get hurt again, but the risk is worth it. And I love Noémie—risking my heart by giving her another chance might be worth it too. I'm scared shitless. I really don't want to be hurt again.

As I advance towards the Toronto landmark, I chew fast on my nicotine gum. My climbing anxiety feels like a thousand bats are flying around and wreaking havoc in the cave of my stomach. It's a million degrees outside, but the sweat that trickles down my spine is cold. I spit my gum into a garbage can near a potted plant.

A sign just outside the entrance advises that Casa Loma is closed to the public for a private event. There's a gruff looking security guard standing just outside the large front doors. He waves in a group of guests after inspecting their invitations and referencing a list on a clipboard.

Next in line, I walk up and present my invitation.

"Name," he barks.

"Jordan Alexander."

He inspects the list for what feels like forever. Just as I start worrying that I'm not on it, he gestures that I'm good to proceed.

Shuffling through the entrance, I head for the conservatory where the wedding ceremony is scheduled to start in fifteen minutes. In accordance with the dress code, all guests wear tastefully understated hues of orange and lavender. While they are complementary colours, the combination could easily look tacky and cheap, but everything about the flower arrangements and decor shouts elegance and luxury.

Usually, I would stick out in a crowd like this. Most of the guests are older and white. The men flash expensive timepieces on their wrists, and the women sparkle in diamonds or other precious jewels. Despite not owning a watch and only sporting a pair of stainless-steel studs in my ears, I look like a million bucks. Lionel, Claude's tailor, really hooked me up.

After I decided to attend the wedding, I struggled with the decision to take Noémie's brother up on his offer to pay for my suit. But he'd been right though, I didn't own anything remotely acceptable for the event—almost every article of clothing I own is black. And while my Kickstarter is funded, it'll be a few more weeks before I see a dime of that money. Ultimately, I decided to swallow my pride.

Now, I'm happy I made the decision to visit Lionel because no one is giving me an odd look as I navigate my way to a seat in one of the far back corners. In the expensive single-breasted suit, I look like I belong. Tailored to fit me like a glove, it's a light shade of lavender with white pinstripes and four large gold buttons on the front. The white collared shirt that I'm wearing beneath is crisper than a fresh twenty-dollar bill. I'm not happy about buttoning the shirt all the way up or the cream tie that chokes me, but as they say, beauty is pain.

The conservatory buzzes with conversation as more people walk into the room and search for a seat. I see Hugo St. Pierre, the Poutine Heaven King, in the flesh, waltzing towards the front row with his walking cane and his wife, and I feel a slight panic. I start to question whether my attendance is actually okay. The last thing I want to do is create a scene. I figure that I can try to get a word in with Noémie privately, and I can leave right after if she wants. Or I can play the role of a friend. Or I can even pretend I don't know her. Whatever she wants.

A few minutes pass, and then there's a hush. Guests start rising from their seats, turning their bodies to face the aisle. I do too.

My breath hitches when I see Noémie enter, walking towards the altar with the rest of the wedding party. If it is even possible, she looks more beautiful than I remember. Like the bridesmaids, Noémie wears a Grecian-style dress with an asymmetrical neckline. It's orange, which tells me that Noémie probably played a bigger role in the design choices for the wedding than the bride.

Overall, the wedding is a beautiful affair. It surprises me to see Claude tearing up as Amelia is led down the aisle by her father. The vows are sweet, and when the newlyweds kiss, I feel a tug of happiness for them on my heartstrings.

Ceremony over, Claude and Amelia parade down the aisle, followed by the wedding party. Everyone is directed to go to the garden for the reception, and people start filtering out of the conservatory.

I make my exit and freeze just outside the doors. Noémie stands about ten metres down. She pointedly stares in my direction and doesn't look happy to see me. Her heels clack against the floors as she barrels my way. "What are you doing here, Jordan?" she says, glowering at me.

I scratch the back of my ear. "Claude invited me."

She looks nervously over her shoulder and then grabs my hand, jerking me hard towards the stairs. My heart hammers in my chest as I stumble behind her, following her up two flights of stairs and down a hall. Noémie tugs us into a dark stairwell and drops my hand. She puts distance between us, leaning her back against a wall and crossing her arms.

"What are you doing here?" she asks again, this time there's more force behind the question.

"I missed you," I say, answering honestly.

Noémie rolls her eyes. "And it took you months to realize this?"

"Yes. I mean, no." I frown. My pulse is beating so loudly I can hear it.

Noémie stares at me expectantly, like she's waiting for an explanation.

Why did I think this conversation would be easy? Why did I think that Noémie would fall into my arms and we could just pick things back up where we left them? I should've planned for resistance and drafted a speech. I feel very unprepared.

Sighing, I slouch against the wall opposite her and contemplate my words. I decide to start from the beginning. I decide to tell her everything. "I've always missed you. Even when you were just an aggravating customer. When you stopped coming into the shop, I felt your absence like an ache, and I wondered about you. Noémie, for such a long time, you've preoccupied my mind. And after living with you, and getting to know you, and falling for you …" I stare down at my shoes. They're shiny brown oxfords Lionel picked out for me.

Clearing my throat, I continue rambling, hoping I can melt the wall of ice between us. "I'm not good at this. The only thing I'm good at is running when things get hard or challenging, but I'm trying to change. I'm working on going after what I want, and I know that what I want is you. I'm not sure words exist to express just … just how much I miss you."

My words leave Noémie quite unstirred. She blows out an exasperated breath. "Okay, but you missing me doesn't change anything. You made it very clear that you don't trust me, that you might never be able to."

Pushing off the wall, I take a step forward. "Trust can be rebuilt," I say.

"Maybe, but I thought about it. We aren't good for each other, Jordan. We hurt each other. We don't communicate well." She bites her lip.

"Let's just be honest with each other from now on." I take another step towards her.

"Didn't we already try and fail at that?"

"I don't think we actually tried," I say.

"You deserve to be with a good person, Jordan," she says, shaking her head. "I'm not a good person. There's a reason Cara took the money from my father—she was sick of my shit. You've no idea how vindictive I can be. You know I flirted with your cousin because I didn't like seeing you with your ex. You know I only brought Felix around so much because I knew it bothered you. You know I left for Hawaii because I knew you'd be pissed."

I grit my teeth. "I guessed as much, but …"

"But what? There's nothing you can say that can defend my behaviour," she says. "Want to know something else? I was ecstatic when Wayne told me you had a tantrum at work because you thought I chose Felix over you. Knowing all this, you still want to be with me?"

"I do." It surprises me how quickly I say it. "Because you're telling me. We are talking about it."

She frowns and diverts her gaze. I don't think she was expecting me to say that. "I've heard you tell Wayne before that you hated how jealous and possessive Audrina was. I'm worse than her," she says. "Putain de merde. I wanted to kill that girl you brought over. I want to curse any woman that looks at you. On New Year's Eve, I just about lost my goddamn mind when you were dancing with Audrina."

She's right, I don't usually like jealousy in women, but it kind of tickles me to know that Noémie cares that much. "I didn't know you saw me with Audrina," I say.

"I wouldn't have let you know, Jordan," Noémie says, snapping her eyes to mine. "And that's my point. I lie. I lie a lot, especially when it comes to talking about my feelings."

Crossing the last bit of gap between us, I take her hands in mine. "You're doing a good job of talking about your feelings now," I say.

She snorts. "That's because none of this matters."

"Don't say that." I give her hands a gentle squeeze.

Noémie closes her eyes and shakes her head. "We aren't good for each other Jordan."

"You don't know that. You can't know that. We haven't even tried." I cup her cheek and brush my lips against hers. "You might be all those things, but you're also kind and thoughtful. When I got into my accident, you dropped everything and drove all the way to Scarborough to pick up my family. You asked your brother to introduce me to François. You pushed me to go after my dream."

She shivers and pushes weakly against my chest. "Jordan—no, we can't do this."

I should probably listen to her. I should probably give her the space she's asking for, but I'm desperate. I need her to change her mind about us. I need her to stop making excuses for why we can't be together.

I kiss her neck, and she groans. As I continue to gently suck and nip at her skin, the hands that push against my chest drift lower and bunch my shirt. "I love you so much, Noémie," I whisper in her ear before pulling away so I can look her in the eyes.

Noémie's pupils are dilated. Her expression is intense, but not angry. She looks more turned on than anything. Her lips are slightly parted. They look so goddamn kissable.

Bending my head, I kiss her and moan when she kisses me back. I feel her kiss everywhere. Warmth spreads through my entire body. We grope hungrily at each other.

Noémie fists my tie and yanks us closer. "I don't share," she murmurs against my lips. "If we do this, you're mine. Only mine."

I grab her by the hips and press into her. Needing friction, I rock into her. Nothing has ever felt so good. "I wouldn't want it any other way."

"Mon dieu, you look so sexy. I think purple's your colour."

Noémie's hands glide up my torso, fanning out over my chest. "I need you to touch me."

Hesitating, I briefly look over my shoulder. "Here?"

She nods. "Problem?"

"No," I say, hiking up her dress and kissing her. I dip my tongue in her mouth to taste her and palm her breasts.

Noémie grabs my hand and shoves it between her legs where she needs it. I rub her over her panties and she gasps. "You make me feel so much." She rolls her hips, grinding into my touch.

The crotch of her panties is soaked through. Knowing how much she wants me makes me ache all over. "I love how wet you get for me," I say, nudging the fabric aside and teasing her entrance.

"Stop playing with me and fuck me."

I chuckle. "You're always so bossy."

"I'm needed at the reception. We don't have—" Her words cut off when I push two fingers inside her. Her eyes squeeze shut. Her head knocks back against the wall. "Fuck," she whines.

I cover her moans with my mouth and curl my fingers inside her. She's so hot and tight and perfect. Mindful that it's only a matter of time before someone comes looking for her, I fuck her faster than I'd like to, pumping in and out of her. Noémie doesn't mind that I go from zero to maximum speed. Her nails bite into my back as she rides my fingers.

It's not long before I know she's on the edge of coming. Noémie cries out as she convulses, and I clamp a hand on her mouth to muffle the sound.

When she comes back down from her orgasm, she presses her forehand to mine. I hold on to her tight. Only her ragged breaths fill the space.

Noémie smiles at me, and I smile right back. "I love you," I say.

She kisses me lightly. "I love you too."

We disentangle. Noémie rights her dress and suddenly seems self-conscious. "How do I look?" she asks.

"Perfect."

She rolls her eyes. "I'm being serious. How's my makeup. I don't have my purse on me, and my compact mirror is in it."

I give her a once over. She really does look perfect. Asides from her skin being a little flushed, no one would ever guess what she'd just been up to. "Your makeup is fine. Not even your lipstick is smudged."

"Thank God for transfer-proof lipstick," she says, holding out her hand. "Let's go. I'm worried that someone's looking for me."

"You want me to come?"

She frowns slightly. "Yes, you're my date."

"What about Hugo? I don't want to create a scene."

Noémie sighs. "If my brother invited you, I think he's likely banking on us creating a scene. I think I told you that he tries to hurt my father any chance he gets."

"But what about you? I have no problem leaving if it makes things easier."

"Fuck easier. If my father has a problem, we can leave together," she says. "I'm done shoving who I am in a box just so he can sleep better."

I take her hand, and we go.

Chapter 37

The reception is held in the glass pavilion. Large centrepieces holding a tasteful arrangement of orange, purple, and cream flowers are positioned at the centre of white linen-covered tables. Chandeliers dazzle above our heads.

Chatter fills the room. The newlyweds have their own table at the front of the space up on a dais. Claude and Amelia look so happy and are laughing about something.

I clock François anxiously reading a crumpled paper—likely his best man speech. He mentioned being nervous about having to deliver it, explaining that while he has no problem talking to a camera, talking to an in-person crowd scares the shit out of him. I want to go to my friend and tell him that he'll knock it out of the park, but I can't leave Noémie's side.

Directly in front of Claude and Amelia, at a table just below the platform, sit Hugo and Hélène St. Pierre. A knot forms in my stomach as Noémie navigates us towards them. Her grip on my hand tightens a little more the closer we get.

"I can always just go," I whisper to her. "You don't have to do this."

Noémie shuts me down with a look and continues forward.

When we reach the table, Claude is the first to notice us. He beams at me. "Salut, Jordan, I'm so glad you made it," he says.

Interested to know who their son is welcoming, both of Noémie's parents turn their heads. Their scowls are immediate when they notice my fingers laced through their daughter's.

Hugo's chair scrapes against the floor as he bolts to his feet. "Noémie, what is the meaning of this?"

If it weren't for Noémie's death grip on my hand, I'd never guess at her inner turmoil. On the outside, she is completely calm. "Jordan's my date," Noémie answers cooly.

I'd never thought clutching pearls was a thing, but Hélène does it as her mouth drops open.

"Your date?" Hugo shouts, his face turning beet red.

"Not sure why you both seem so surprised. Didn't we go over this already? I'm a lesbian. I date women."

"Tabarnak, you do not! You are not." Hugo's teeth mash together. The veins on his forehead protrude, threatening to burst.

"Pourquoi joues-tu avec nous?" her mother says. The woman is almost a carbon copy of Noémie, but thinner and with lighter hair. She has an unmovable expression, likely due to Botox. I'm not sure how old she is, but she doesn't look a day over forty.

"I'm not playing games, Maman," Noémie says.

"Whether this is a trick or not, she has to go," Hugo spits out, pointing a stubby finger at me. "And perhaps you should leave as well, Noémie."

"No one is going anywhere," Claude says, approaching the table.

"I invited Jordan, and if you have a problem with her being here then the two of you can go."

"You have some nerve, boy." Hugo's eyes narrow on his son. "I paid for this wedding. And I—"

"And I'll pay you back, if that's what you want," Claude says. "But what you won't do is tell me who I can and cannot have at my wedding. You have no right."

From there, I lose track of the conversation as they all start screaming at each other in French. There's a noticeable dip in the conversation of the tables around us. Sparing a quick look to the side, I see that many guests are focusing on us. It makes me uneasy. I kind of wish Noémie had just let me go. I hate that I'm the cause for this argument.

"I have every right!" Hugo snaps in English, and I think it's because he wants me to understand. "I am your father. It's my job to steer you two on the right path."

"No, you cannot tell us what to do or who we can love," Claude shouts back. "Your bigotry is disgusting, Father. The only path you are steering Noémie down is away. Is that what you want? Do you really want to lose a second daughter because of your hate?"

At the mention of Antoinette, both Hugo and Hélène flinch. Seconds pass with them looking dazed, and then Hugo scowls and shakes his head. "Hélène, we are leaving," he announces, reaching for his walking stick. Then, to Claude, he says with a sneer, "I will have my secretary invoice you for the cost of the wedding."

There's a noticeable tightness to Claude's jaw. "I will pay it the moment it arrives."

Noémie's mother rises from her seat, looping her arm through her husband's. Then, without another word spared to their children, they leave. A few other guests follow suit, likely a show to demonstrate their fealty to the Poutine King.

I look at Noémie. "Are you okay?"

"No," she admits, offering me a shaky smile.

I pull her into my arms and kiss her forehead. "Anything I can do?"

"You're here. That's all I need."

Claude is staring at us with a wide grin. Despite the explosion with his parents, he looks rather pleased.

Amelia comes to stand at his side looking quite unbothered—like she couldn't care less that my presence ruined her special day. She threads her fingers through her husband's. "It's good to see you again, Jordan. I know Claude was worried you wouldn't be able to make it."

"I'm so sorry about everything," I say.

Amelia waves away my apology. "There's nothing to apologize for," she says, smiling like she means it. "But please sit. I fear we need to get the speeches started soon before François gives himself an aneurism. Poor man, I don't think he even noticed what just happened."

My eyes search for my friend. I spot him sweating in a back corner.

Claude chuckles. "I really don't get what he's so worried about."

The married couple return to their table, and Noémie and I take our seats.

François is called up to take the microphone a minute later. He's sweating profusely, and I feel so bad for him. Tapping on the mic, he clears his throat and looks down at the paper in his hands. "Bonjour—hello, everyone. I'm François, the best man, and I've known Claude for a very, very, very long time …"

I don't mean to tune out François, but Noémie takes up all of my attention. I stare at her long eyelashes, the bow of her lips, the glint of her hair—but what I settle on is the emptiness in her eyes and the faint signs of sadness. Noémie laughs when expected. She plays the part of the happy sister to perfection, and when she takes the microphone from François, she captivates the room with her words. She shares stories of Claude in his youth, and he turns several shades pink when his rakish partying days are brought up. There's a round of applause when she closes her speech with a toast.

Throughout the meal, Noémie is mainly silent while François talks my ear off. I'd think he'd have questions about me and Noémie being together, but he doesn't. He excitedly prattles about the launch of my graphic novel. And while I'm excited too, my heart just isn't in the conversation. I can feel Noémie's melancholy like it's a tangible object pushing against me.

When Noémie gets up to go to the washroom, I fall into step behind her.

"Do you need to use the washroom too?" she asks.

"No."

"Then I don't need you coming with me."

"Okay." I stop in my tracks. We're inside the castle, a few steps away from the staircase that leads to the restrooms.

"If that came out too harsh, I'm sorry." Noémie sighs and presses a palm to her forehead. "I've just been through a lot today, and it's taking a lot out of me to pretend to care about everything. I need a minute to myself to regulate. This is not me pushing you away, okay?"

Remembering what Claude told me about Noémie's depression, I wonder if she's still off her medication. Now isn't the right time to ask her though.

"Understandable." I birth a smile and pray it looks legitimate.

I guess it does, because Noémie brightens a bit and kisses me lightly on the cheek. "Thanks for understanding," she says. And then she disappears down the stairs.

The sun is starting to set, and guests are starting to ditch their tables for the dance floor. Charting music plays, and while I'm all for Sabrina Carpenter's "Espresso," it's not the kind of song I'd bop too.

I don't see François anywhere, so I don't bother heading back to our table. Instead, after ordering a rum and Coke, I stand off to the side and entertain myself watching the mostly middle-aged guests on the dance floor. Some have moves. Most don't.

"Lionel really outdid himself with that suit. Noémie's jaw must've dropped when she saw you in a colour other than black," Claude says. "You won't believe how often I had to hear her complain about your wardrobe choices."

"What?" I shake my head, finding it hard to imagine them having such a conversation. It implies a level of closeness between Claude and Noémie that I've yet to witness. Every time I've seen them together, they are arguing or shooting daggers at each other with their eyes.

"Oh yes," Claude confirms. "You know, even knowing that it would piss off our parents, it was always her intention to bring you as her plus one, even if you came only as her friend. She was super excited to have an excuse to play dress-up with you. I guess you should thank me for saving you from that nightmare."

This information is news to me. Noémie never mentioned wanting to bring me to Claude and Amelia's wedding. "I don't think it would have been a nightmare," I say, sipping my drink.

"Oh, really?"

I shrug. "If it makes Noémie happy, what do I care?"

Claude shakes his head. "Have you ever been to a shopping mall with my sister?"

I have to think about it. "No," I say.

"If you care anything for your sanity, maybe keep it that way," he says.

"I'll try to remember that." I chuckle. "I see Amelia really let Noémie have her way with the decor."

Claude arches a questioning brow. "Why do you say that?"

"Orange. Kind of a bold choice for a wedding."

He clucks his tongue. "You do know that Noémie's favourite colour is blue."

I blink. It's news to me.

"Orange was Antoinette's favourite colour," he clarifies. "I think Noémie adopted the colour into her wardrobe to always remember her, but I was the one who insisted on the colour being part of the wedding palette. I guess I wanted our sister to be a part of this special day too."

"Oh ... good to know."

"Is it? Anyhow, I need to get a drink for courage. My wife will be out any moment in her evening gown and I will be forced to dance." Claude makes a face.

"Don't like to dance, huh?"

"No. I don't have the coordination for it."

I smile and can't quite believe how much I'm warming to Noémie's brother.

"What are you two talking about?" Noémie pins her brother with a threatening look.

"Your brother was telling me that he fears dancing."

"I said nothing about fear." Claude rolls his eyes. "But I'm off."

When he leaves, I'm suddenly the focus of Noémie's intense gaze. "What were you guys really talking about?"

"Claude told me that you hate my clothes and you want to play dress-up with me."

Noémie laughs, and it's a real laugh that reaches her grey eyes, making them sparkle. The sound makes my chest grow warm and fuzzy. "I want to play a lot of things with you. But I don't hate your clothes. I just think it's a shame that you languish in black when you're obviously a soft summer."

"Soft summer?" I repeat, not understanding the reference.

"That's just a guess. We'd have to get your colour analysis done first to know for sure what season you fall under," she says, sounding a lot more like herself.

"Is that something you want me to get done—a colour analysis?"

"I think it'd be fun."

"Then let's do it," I say, smiling. "Maybe I need a little more colour in my closet."

Noémie beams at me and takes my hand. Leaning over, she kisses my cheek. "Je t'aime," she whispers.

The words are French, but for once I'm not confused. I know their meaning.

"I love you too."

Thank You From The Author

Thanks so much for reading French Pressed Love. Your support means the world! Every review helps, so please leave a review if you can.

Sign up for my newsletter if you want a bonus chapter.

M.C. Hutson

M.C. Hutson is a booktoker, author and host of A Very Sapphic Podcast. She was born and raised in Toronto, Canada.

When M.C. isn't reading, reviewing, writing or talking about gay shit on her podcast, you can find her in the kitchen replicating recipes she finds on YouTube or trying to get her morkshire terrier to behave. Before M.C. was domesticated, she lived to party and lived for lesbian drama.

Follow M.C.. On Social Media

@mchutsonauthor

@mchutsonwrites

M.C. Hutson